BIRTH OF A BRIDGE

ALSO BY MAYLIS DE KERANGAL

NOVELS
Je marche sous un ciel de traîne
La vie voyageuse
Ni fleurs ni couronnes
Dans les rapides
Corniche Kennedy
Tangente vers l'est
Réparer les vivants

FOR CHILDREN
Nina et les oreillers

Birth

of a

Bridge

Maylis **de Kerangal**

translated by Jessica **Moore**

TALONBOOKS

Talonbooks
278 East First Avenue, Vancouver, British Columbia, Canada v5T 1A6
www.talonbooks.com

First printing: 2014

Typeset in Arno
Printed and bound in Canada on 100% post-consumer recycled paper
Interior by Typesmith
Cover design by Chloë Filson
Cover image © Roger Ressmeyer / Corbis

Talonbooks gratefully acknowledges the financial support of the Canada
Council for the Arts, the Government of Canada through the Canada
Book Fund, and the Province of British Columbia through the British
Columbia Arts Council and the Book Publishing Tax Credit.

This work was originally published in French as *Naissance d'un pont* by
Éditions Gallimard, Paris, France, in 2010. This book has been supported
by the Centre national du livre, Paris, and the French Ministry of Foreign
Affairs, as part of the translation program. In addition, the translator
thanks the Collège international des traducteurs.

Liberté · Égalité · Fraternité
RÉPUBLIQUE FRANÇAISE
Centre national du livre

Library and Archives Canada Cataloguing in Publication

Kerangal, Maylis de
[Naissance d'un pont. English]
    Birth of a bridge : a novel / Maylis de Kerangal ; translated by
Jessica Moore.

Translation of: Naissance d'un pont.
Issued in print and electronic formats.
ISBN 978-0-88922-889-4 (PBK.).—ISBN 978-0-88922-890-0 (EPUB)

    I. Moore, Jessica, 1978–, translator II. Title. III. Title: Naissance
d'un pont. English.

PQ2711.E73N3513 2014   843'.92   C2014-903247-1
                                               C2014-903248-X

but, as the seas work in their secret ways
and the planet is porous, it may still be true
to claim all men have bathed in the Ganges

JORGES LUIS BORGES
Poem of the Fourth Element

IN THE BEGINNING, IT WAS HIM AND THE ground. Northern Yakutia, where he worked for three years – Mirny, a diamond mine to crack open beneath the glacial crust, grey, dirty, desperate tundra trashed with old wasted coal and refugee camps, deserted ground bathed in nights of chilblains, sheared eleven months of the year by a skull-splitting blizzard beneath which still sleep great beasts, scattered limbs and giant beautifully curving horns – furred rhinoceros, woolly belugas, and frozen caribou – he imagined them in the evenings while sitting at the hotel bar with a glass of strong translucent alcohol as the same surreptitious hooker lavished him with caresses, all the while pleading for a marriage in Europe, in exchange for loyal services, of course, but never did he touch her, couldn't, rather have nothing than fuck this woman who didn't really want him, he left it at that. So – the diamonds of Mirny. They had to dig to find them, break the permafrost with dynamite blasts, bore a Dantesque hole as big as the city itself – you could have tossed in headfirst the fifty-storey apartment buildings that already sprout up all around – and, equipped with headlamps, descend to the farthest depths of the orifice, pickaxe the walls, excavate the earth, branch the galleries into a subterranean arborescence lateralized to the furthest, hardest, darkest extent, reinforce the corridors and put down rails, electrify the mud, and then dig in the glebe, scratch the scree, and sift the guts, keep watch for the marvellous sparkle. Three years.

When his contract was up, he returned to France aboard a rather undemocratic Tupolev – his seat in economy was completely battered, a ball of wire drifting around beneath the fabric of the seatback, piercing it here and there and bruising his ribs – a few contracts later and we find him again as foreman of a site in Dubai with a luxury hotel to conjure from the sand, vertical as an obelisk but secular as a coconut tree, and of glass this time, glass and steel, with elevators like bubbles streaming up and down golden tubes, Carrara marble for the circular lobby where the fountain sounds its deluxe petrodollar *glug glug*, all this adorned with polished green plants, split-leather couches, and air conditioning. After that, he was on fire, he went everywhere. Football stadium in Chengdu, outbuilding for a gas port in Cumaná, mosque in Casablanca, pipeline in Baku – the men in this city walk fast in their dark gabardine coats that skim the hips, the knots of their ties like tight little fists under hard collars, black hats with three humps, sad eyes and thin moustaches, all of them look like that old crooner Charles Aznavour (he phones his mother to tell her) – water treatment plant north of Saigon, hotel complex for white employees in Djerba, film studios in Bombay, space centre in Baikonur, tunnel under the English Channel, dam in Lagos, shopping mall in Beirut, airport in Reykjavik, lakeside estate in the heart of the jungle.

TELEPORTED THUS from biotope to biotope, aboard long-haul flights that often end with a little prop plane, he never stays more than eighteen months on a site and never travels, disgusted by exoticism, by its triviality – absolute powers of whites against the vengeful colonization of amoebae, drugs and women docile for Western currency – and lives with very little, usually in an apartment near the site rented by the company – a place this radical is practically a joke, none of the tchotchkes people drag along with them, no photo tacked to the wall, just a few books, CDs, a huge TV with images in Classico colour, and finally a bike, a magnificent machine in carbon fibre, the expensive transporting of which from site to site becomes a contractual clause unique in the history of the company; he buys everything on-site – razor shampoo soap – eats his meals in greasy diners hazed with smoke, twice a week wolfs down an international steak in a hotel restaurant, if there is one; he gets up early, works regular hours, every day a short nap after lunch, and, on days of meteorological grace, mounts his bike for at least thirty miles, wind against his forehead, chest bent low, and pedals as hard as he can; at night he goes out into the streets, walks or sidles, temples cooled and brain alert, learns the local idioms in nightclubs, bordellos, gambling dens (the language of cards as a kind of pidgin English), and in bars. Because a dipsomaniac he is, everyone knows it, and has been for a long time.

TWENTY YEARS of this regimen would have had the hide of anyone, each new site requiring that he adapt himself – real conversions, climatic, dermatologic, dietary, phonologic, not to mention new patterns of daily life that bring about hitherto unknown acts – but his hide, on the contrary, reinvented itself, grew stronger, became expansionist; and some nights, going home alone after the last team had left, he would place himself in front of the map of the world pinned to his office wall, arms spread, skin and pupils equally dilated; and in a handsome lateral movement from Easter Island to Japan, his eyes would slowly inventory all his work sites on the surface of the globe. Each site to come jostled against the preceding ones like you jostle your hips in a fast salsa, and hybridized with them, thus activating the entirety of his experience, this experience contained within him that was sought after the world over. Yet, though his continually displaced body didn't get used up faster than a sedentary one (one defined by daily hour-long migrations), his mouth was a scene of upheaval: every language spoken on-site and easily picked up came to intimately shake up his French – a French that was already quite disturbed – so much so that he sometimes found himself at sixes and sevens in the short letters he wrote to his mother. All in all, twenty years of this regimen was nothing to him, didn't even count.

PEOPLE WANT to find out what he's made of, they ring him round. They describe him by turns as an engineer without a homeland, a mercenary of concrete and a patient clearer of tropical forests, an ex-convict, a gambler in rehab, a suicidal businessman who smokes opiates in the evenings beneath the frangipani trees or lets his gaze wander out over the Mongolian steppe, a chilled bottle between his knees; they call him the laconic cowboy, from nowhere, bent on his mission without a single wasted gesture and ready to do anything for the bonus – ah, there they were touching on something, a fragment of truth at least, a vague nuance, and they laughed at it – and likely he was all these men, simultaneously, successively; likely he was plural, drawing upon an assortment of variable dispositions, passing through life with a hook, crocheting it on all sides. They would have liked to find out that he was searching for himself, mysterious, passionate; they speculated on a gnawing secret estrangement that sent him running, pictured some regret, some abandonment, a betrayal, or better yet the ghost of a woman who had stayed behind in the city, with another man no doubt, who he had to flee – this woman exists, in fact, and is nothing like a ghost: she's alive and well, and lives with another man; he sees her sometimes when he's passing through France – they meet in Paris, she arrives on time, hair in her face eyes shining pockets full, and there they are, they're back, and wend their way through the city, bodies disjointed but hearts in tune, talk all night long in a bar somewhere, beer after beer making them slowly drunk so that they kiss at the moment when the sun rises, they're inside love, then, caressing each other's bodies, carried away, and then they separate, calm, king and queen, time doesn't exist, it's pure invention, and turn away from each other with such trust that the whole world murmurs thank you. People said being alone to such an extent, no one does that; they said it was a waste, unhealthy in the long run, a man like that, a force of nature; they imagined women deep within the consulates, beautiful women, innocent women, devoted women; they imagined young people, they imagined lice, an original sin, an origin at least, some intimate flaw from his childhood; they whispered that he was broken, at heart – though at the heart of what, no one knew. Plus he hardly ever went back to France (what about his mother? He must have a mother since he writes to her, doesn't he think of her, then?) – he flew over the country with a charged silence, kept only the nationality inscribed on his passport, a sagely padded bank account, a taste for conversation and for a certain amount of comfort, and he never missed watching the Tour de France. People would have liked to know that he was seized by an inward experience, isolated, vulnerable even – that would have been so simple, so much easier to believe – a man as solid and deep as he was, with such a brutal passion for alcohol, is always hiding something; they would have liked it if he didn't know how to love, if he were incapable of it, if he worked like a dog in order to forget. They would have liked it if he were melancholic.

BUT THOSE who had known him on the sites choked to hear this nonsense: fantasies of old ladies, cringe-worthy poems, sugary little clichés. They toppled this cardboard cut-out with a few shrugs and mocking glances, because they had actually seen him at work, had rubbed shoulders with the guy. They said: okay, it's true, time is nothing to him, that which passes, that which flies, all that is nothing to him, doesn't slip past or cause adherences or brackish fog – and is it precisely because we are alone in time, alone and losing at every turn, noses buried in our losses, in the sloshing bacillary liquids at the bottom of the bucket, in the tatters of sadness sewn to our fingertips like old bandages that must finally be torn off with our teeth? – he's not immune, true, but he doesn't think about it, isn't interested, hardly has the luxury to, and couldn't care less about origins, about history, has mixed his blood, thinks about death every day like everyone else and that's all there is to it. They said: his time is counted in snaps of the fingers – *uno! dos! tres! vámonos!* – and here, they joined the action to the word, miming a starting signal that was already headed for the finish line, the goal, delivery of a work whose deadline penned in scarlet ink at the bottom of the work order lays out days according to a careful plan, according to a duly calculated phasing, according to contracts and seasons – the rainy season especially, and the nesting season – that one is never in his favour, as we'll see. They said: his time is the present, it's now or never, do it right, deal with the situation at hand, that's his only moral and a lifetime's work, it's as simple as that. And also: he's a hands-on kind of fellow, a grassroots man, that's his element – he would even say so himself, eyes half-closed, cigarette dangling, mocking, would add without batting an eye that's where the adventure is, that's where the risks are, that's where my body is alive – and with these words, he would beat his chest with two closed fists like a gorilla in a tropical forest – but sometimes, all joking aside, he would lift his head and say stormily, the thing I abominate is a utopia, a tidy little system, the quixotic jewel floating above the earth *blah blah blah*, it's too closed, always too miniature, and so well oiled, it's bad shit, take it from me, there's nothing for me in that, there's nothing there that interests me, nothing that gets me hard. My name is Georges Diderot and what I like is working with the real, juggling the parameters, being on the ground, all up in the face of things, that's where I'm complete.

HE TAKES control of zones, excavates fields, occupies ground, raises up buildings, feeds himself with the multiple, the loquacious, the sonorous, with all the motley clutter and odours of skin, with the crowds in the megacities, with revolutionary unrest, with ovations in the stadiums, with the jubilation of carnivals, of processions, with the gentleness of wild animals watching the construction sites through forests of bamboo, with open-air cinemas at the edge of villages – the screen stretched into the night sky, those hours when spaces fit one inside the other and time plays within them – and with the barking of dogs at a bend in the road. Always outside, concentrating, empirical, disbelieving: the inner experience is never within, he says, laughing when those who are disappointed by his triviality badger him for more inwardness and more depth, it's not a folding inward, it's a tearing apart, and I like to tear it up.

WALKING
IN THE
VIOLET NIGHT

ON AUGUST 15, 2007, THE *NEW YORK TIMES* announced in its business section the construction of a bridge in Coca, a three-line newsflash in twelve-point lower case that slid by without attracting anything more than a few raised eyebrows – people thought: finally there will be some jobs; or: here we go, they're off again with a policy of major construction projects, nothing more. But the engineering firms that had taken a blow during the economic crisis began to ramp up: their teams set to work researching, securing contacts within the companies that had sealed the deal, planting moles within them, all so they might place themselves in the ranking, in a good position – to provide workers, machines, raw materials, services of all kinds. But it was already too late – the die had been cast and the agreements sealed. These agreements were the result of a complicated and delicate selection process that, although expedited, still took two years to materialize in the form of official signatures at the bottom of contracts at least a hundred and fifty pages long. A series of phases that resembled a hurdles race: September 2005, Coca's city council launches an international call for applications; February 2006, five companies make the shortlist and the call for bids is sent out; December 20, 2006, the bids are submitted; April 15, 2007, two companies are chosen as finalists; June 1, 2007, the name of the winner is announced by the president of the CNCB (Commission for the New Coca Bridge): Pontoverde – a consortium of companies from France (Héraclès Group), the United States (Blackoak Inc.), and India (Green Shiva Co.) – is the lucky winner.

The competition had involved an infernal number of hours and had placed hundreds of people around the world under immense pressure. There was excitement and there was damage. The engineers worked fifteen hours a day and the rest of the time had their BlackBerries or iPhones glued to their ears, shoved under the pillow at night, sound turned up when they were in the shower or sweating it out at squash or tennis, vibrate setting on high when they went to the movies, though very few of them went to the movies 'cause they couldn't think about anything but that fucking bridge, that fucking proposal, they grew obsessed, excepted themselves from daily life. The weeks slid past, the children grew distant, the houses got filthy, and soon they weren't touching any other bodies besides their own. There was overtime, depression, there were miscarriages and divorces, sexual encounters in workplace cubicles, but it wasn't fun, it wasn't playful, just opportunity making the thief, and the inability to resist the promise of pleasure when your neck seizes and your eyes are scorched after twelve hours in front of Excel spreadsheets, sudden fever transmuted into quick coitus, a little haphazard, and finally, even though they were excruciatingly disappointed by the announcement of the winner, the ones who lost were somewhat relieved: they had aged, they were exhausted, broken down, dead tired, not a drop of juice left except the tears of fatigue they let spill once alone in the car on the way home from work, when the radio played a rock song, something saturated with youth and the desire to let loose, "Go Your Own Way" by Fleetwood Mac or anything by the Beach Boys, and after nightfall when they were pulling into the garage, they didn't get out right away but stayed instead in the darkness, headlights off, hands on the wheel, and suddenly imagined letting everything go, selling the house, paying off the credit cards *hup*, let's go, everyone barefoot into the car, we're heading to California.

THE OTHERS – the ones who worked for Pontoverde – went home victorious that night, re-energized, they had a bridge to build, their healthy bodies personified progress, their own hands would place a stone, they relished this coup shaped like fate, sure of themselves now as main characters in the world play. They too lingered in their vehicles, engines off, eyes riveted to a dried laurel leaf on the windshield and arms crossed over their chests, seat leaned back, and they too sat silently thinking about their coming expatriation; weighing their careers that were suddenly accelerated because they knew how to nod at an opportunity; counting the points they would rack up before going back to head office to occupy a superior position, which would include overseeing the reorganization of whatever department they would now be in charge of; and also reflecting on a potential move with the family, or imagining themselves relocated and single, commuting during school vacations – they too were suddenly ready to go, but this wasn't a joyride, wasn't dropping out, not really a vacation; now they had to gear themselves up to talk to their wives, to tell them the news; and some wives would puff up their chests with happiness and pride, they were good companions, their husbands were successful, had stature, and they would daydream themselves into a near future where they were spoiled by the company, served by local maids, a villa with a pool, yes, at the very least, two cars, a gardener, and a full-time nanny who was also a devoted cook, brilliant! Already they were laughing and going to wake up the kids, ready for the sweet leap up the social ladder; others, dismayed, would tidy the kitchen nervously in silence, and finally turn an anguished face towards their husbands because, dear, what are we going to do about school for the older ones, about my sick parents, about the little one's speech therapist? These wives would need to be reassured, promised that they would have their say in all this, the whole thing had to be toned down, they had to be made to understand that their husbands were counting on them; while finally there was a handful of others, these ones the toughest by far, who would light up a smoke once the washing machine was on, and then, *whoosh*, they'd spin around to face their husband, butts pressed against the sink and faces lit strangely by the overhead light, unreal and yet marmoreal, like Marlene Dietrich, an ambiguous shading that made them enigmatic, abominably distant, and these ones would smile and conclude in a sardonic voice, I'm very happy for you, dear, but what's my place in all this? These ones would hold tight to their jobs, they would need to be convinced, pressured, until finally one night their foot consents once again to creep beneath the sheets and caress the foot of the man stretched out next to them; their husbands would have to use cunning until they made this little gesture, this caress of the skin, a subtle sign of agreement that would grant their husbands the world – and these latter could then silently triumph, lying on their backs perfectly still. Then, once the family's departure date was set, restlessness would set in. They would still need to cancel the lease, the phone, and the electricity, find storage – and then sort out this mess, the kids' messes and their own, broken toys, outgrown clothes, piles of old magazines, chipped vases, faded photographs, everything in the dross; go to the doctor, say goodbye to friends and family, and finally pack their bags and head to Coca. And this is exactly what they did late August, early September.

THEY WEREN'T the only ones to leave. All kinds of people set out in the violet night and converged in the city whose soda pop name jangled like thousands of corrosive little pins in their dry mouths. The want ads that popped up on the web called for cable riggers, ironworkers, welders, concrete form setters, asphalt paving crews, crane operators, scaffolding builders, heavy-lifting contractors, excavators – these skilled workers packed their bags in a single movement, synchronized, a tight manoeuvre, and set off by any means they could. A first wave stuffed themselves into cargo planes chartered by subcontractors who specialized in recruiting skilled labourers – these companies worked fast and with clichéd racism: preferring the strong Turk, the industrious Korean, the aesthetic Tunisian, the Finnish carpenter, the Austrian cabinet maker, and the Kenyan geometrician; avoiding the dancing Greek and the stormy Spaniard, the Japanese hypocrite and the impulsive Slav. The chosen ones, poor terrified guys dealing with their baptism by air, barfed up their guts at the back of the cabin. Others jumped on the backs of freight trains where they were immediately jounced about, asses bouncing on the floor as though on a tatami, and propped themselves up against their bags that knocked together, soon dizzy with noise and dust, heads between their knees because their eyes were tearing. And there were others still who boarded the buses that fill the night highway, those public dangers handled by drivers with bugged-out eyes – lack of sleep, coke – transport for the poor who don't have three hundred dollars to put down on a used car and so are picked up like stragglers by the street sweeper, that's why it stinks in here, the velour of the seats soaked with fatigue and cold sweat, a smell of tired feet – we all know that's the real smell of humanity; these ones wait in miserable little parking lots at the city limits and lift a gloomy arm so the driver will stop, the news of the site had spread like wildfire, and the city already shimmered in a corner of their brains; finally, there were some who arrived on foot, and it seemed that nothing could make them deviate from their path – they headed straight there, like dogs, as though they had followed the scent of a magic rag rubbed against their noses, while still others were simply vagrants, people for whom here or there was the same thing, who had a certain idea of their life and proudly believed that they had a right to adventure.

A thin-legged Chinese fellow with a profile like a cliff is among these last – his name is Mo Yun. Nine months earlier, a miner among millions of others – miner because his father and mother are miners, miner because he's nothing else and 'cause to descend to the bottom of the hole is simply to follow the greater movement – he suddenly turns his back on Datong, world capital of slag heaps, violent proletarian hot pot – a real survival instinct, since scampering off from the rut of childhood meant giving his youth a chance; after that, even if it was miserable, wandering has the taste of the potato chosen from among all the rest for its shape and colour, and the smallest radish smells like freedom. Mo crosses Mongolia huddled in the back of a four-by-four with a couple of Russian botanists, and once they're in the suburbs of Ulan Bator, hops to his feet and turns off to the right, heads straight to the sea, three months of travelling, who knows with what money and especially where he finds the strength, then boards a Dutch container ship and does Vladivostok–Vancouver in fifteen days, fifteen days of darkness at the end of which Mo emerges from his waterproof bulkhead compartment one icy night. The city looks deserted. He heads south at the back of a Greyhound bus, and once he reaches San Francisco, Chinatown, knocks on the door of a scuzzy joint on Grant Avenue, a greasy but profitable dive where one of his uncles exploits him sixteen to eighteen hours a day for four months. It's there, in the back kitchen, that he first hears talk of the bridge, and he calmly puts down teapots and rice boxes, unties his apron, passes through the restaurant by the central aisle, and pushes open the front door – the customers' door, the main door – he chooses this one and not another one, the inaugural door, see ya! His brown feet, at present, are thickened with corns, callused, and etched with the wrinkled trace of the world map, he's seventeen years old and he can see the lights of Coca.

Among those who come to the site are Duane Fisher and Buddy Loo, nineteen and twenty years old, red skin, black skin, mixed blood. For the moment they're squatting against the wall drinking cans of beer in the parking lot of the Coca bus station. They're out of breath, dazzled, just emerged from the opposite bank, rolled out of the forest after three months bushwhacking in a clandestine gold-panning station that was held up too often by police and ordinary crooks, three months sifting rivulets of a gold-bearing alluvium, necks devoured by parasites, nothing to eat but boiled beans and yucca in all its forms. They split from there and followed the ravines, feet bare inside their sneakers, mud up to their ankles, and sticky clay full of worms squelching between their toes *slurp slurp*, mosquitoes caught inside their jeans, ticks beneath their waistbands, but they have gold, yeah, a few ounces, a pinch, enough to buy themselves some tequila and a pork chop to cook over twigs snatched from the sickly weeds growing along the sidewalk on Colfax Avenue outside the city limits. In front of them, sitting on the hood of a Mercedes four-by-four, two men in steel-grey suits talk in low voices, put their heads together, then move towards them. They have recruitment forms in hand: a year of work, boys, a salary, health insurance, a pension, and the pride of participating in the creation of a historic landmark, a golden opportunity, the chance of a lifetime. The two boys hold the paper, don't read it 'cause they can't even read anymore, exchange a look, sign at the bottom, and receive a summons to appear on September 1st, and there it is, it's done – they're in, bridge men.

WOMEN ARE there too who had to elbow their way in to get a job on the site. There are only a few, but they are there, polish corroded on black nails, mascara swaddling their lashes, the elastic of their panties worn out around blurry waists. They've done the calculations and come: the pay is good, especially if you include in advance overtime and compensation of all kinds. Most of these women cleared out of their homes overnight, telling their colleagues at the very last moment, with enough time to offload a plant or a cat into their affable hands, then a quick hug and *whoosh*, steering clear of beers between gals on the last night, steering clear of promises. Once in Coca, they lobbied Pontoverde's local hiring office till they were hired, volunteered themselves for the hardest jobs, under-qualification requires it, and signed up for the shittiest hours – weekends, nights. Then they rented a room in one of the motels that abound on Colfax, their rival signs uncoiling thick fluorescent pink or golden-yellow ribbons into the night between the Kmarts, the Safeways, the Trader Joe's, the Walgreens, the parking lots full of used cars, outlet stores, and all the discount clothing warehouses in the world.

In one of these motels, the Black Rose, in one of these rooms with succinct furnishings and minimum comfort, one of these women, Katherine Thoreau, uncaps a Coors and smiles. She still has her parka on and a contract swells her breast pocket. None of the people watching TV – a man, two teenagers – looked up when she came in; we might even wonder if they heard her – well, I can confirm it: they heard her plain as day when she pushed open the door and then took a bottle from the fridge. She leans a shoulder against the wall, takes a mouthful straight from the bottle, and then, still smiling, says: I got it! The two boys leap up, *yes!* The younger one runs over to her, presses his cheek against her belly, and puts his arms around her waist. Katherine buries a hand in his mane, strokes him softly, thoughtful, then lifts her head – don't you think the TV's a bit loud? She meets the eyes, serious eyes, of the older one, and repeats, I got it, we're gonna get through this; the teen nods his head and turns back to the screen. You can't hear anything besides Larry King's swinging and brutal, professional voice, and Sarah Jessica Parker's laugh that displays her big teeth and pointed chin between golden curls, laughter and applause, the program's credits. Katherine says again, turn it down a little, it's too loud, it's gonna give you a headache. She slowly finishes the bottle, then lifts the younger one's head, still pressed against her, smooths her hand across his forehead and whispers, did you guys put Billie to bed? He gives a solemn nod. The man, disabled, immobile in his wheelchair, hasn't lifted his gaze from the set, hasn't once looked at his wife.

ANOTHER WORKER joins the group without being noticed – not a single one among us would have cast an eye on his angular, shifty form, tattooed with a safety pin, a mistreated cat that would take a beating and dream of giving one in return. Soren Cry arrived after six days hitching from Kentucky and the Eastern Coalfields – a ghostly rural zone, scrappy, dismal little hamlets scattered over an area hammered with misery; drugs and alcohol to eradicate the threatening spectres of Cheyenne warriors hidden in the Appalachians; youth who bury their noses in rags soaked with white-spirit or turpentine, hunt squirrels with rifles, organize car rodeos in the mud, empty out cartridges into bottles of beer downed one after the other, light fires in the carcasses of rusty pickups, all this just to get their rocks off a little once night falls; they listen to heavy metal loud enough to burst their eardrums, music like decibels spewed, like death rattles. A quagmire. Kicked out of the army six months earlier for acts of violence against a superior – the colonel was a thirty-three-year-old woman, a technocrat hayseed who had humiliated him in public, treated him like a hillbilly, and spluttered in his face, no doubt because she'd seen too many movies, and something in him had given way. He broke her teeth. Since then he's been living with his mother, taking one-off jobs, seasonal work, and the rest of the time, nothing, time off fiddling around, playing GameBoy in front of the TV in the condo he shares with this pious, poor, and depressive woman – who he has imagined stabbing to death or strangling countless times, but who he kisses tenderly each night on the temple – and probably he left so he wouldn't have to kill her.

SO IT'S a multitude that moves towards Coca, while another multitude escorts it, a thick and sonorous stream mixing chicken roasters, dentists, psychologists, hairdressers, pizzaiolos, pawnbrokers, prostitutes, laminators of official documents, television and multimedia device repairmen, public letter writers, T-shirt vendors, makers of laurel lotion to treat calluses and cream to kill lice, priests, and cellphone agents – all of these infiltrate the place, siphoned from the flood that such a site causes, betting on the economic spinoff of the thing and getting ready to collect this collateral manna like the first rain after a dry season, in stainless steel bowls.

AUGUST 30TH, NEARLY NOON. HEADING towards the Coca airport is a young man at the wheel of a deep-blue Chevrolet Impala – heavy, slow, a clunker. Sanche Alphonse Cameron had rolled down the window to smell the asphalt burning, the freeway is new, fluid, he's got a full tank of gas and seizes the day, knows that soon he'll be spending his hours a hundred and fifty feet in the air at the controls of an amazing cab crane and that all this horizontal propulsion will be over.

HE KNOWS the way: ten days earlier it was him landing at this airport where he was welcomed by his own name on a sign held by a large hand, a disproportionate hand, it had seemed to him at the time, with thick and slightly reddened digits, with manicured nails painted magenta, a hand extended from the robust body of Shakira Ourga – her husky voice rolled the *R* of her surname. Discovering her in entirety once she had extracted herself from the small waiting crowd, Sanche had to be careful not to let his gaze lose its head like an excited kid at the gates of the fairground, because the girl was tall, taller than him by a head, a bizarre body, thin and burly at once, a wide back and slender arms, prominent joints, narrow hips and round breasts held high without a bra beneath a thin camisole with spaghetti straps, long thighs moulded into a pair of jeans, tanned feet in heeled mules. She had picked up his suitcase while smiling at him, a smile as copious as the rest, and a stunned Sanche had followed her back pockets, flecked with glitter, to the metallic sedan that sparkled in the parking lot – the Russian's beefeater step required him to synchronize his own and he trotted along behind. Cellphone meowing in her bag, she had walked away slowly from the car to raise her voice, furious, rapid delivery, coming back with a red ear and forced smile, and finally, looking over the roof of the car at Sanche, she'd put on a pair of black, monogrammed sunglasses and shouted in a thundering voice, welcome to Coca, the brand new Coca, the most fabulous town of the moment!

SANCHE HEADS for the access ramps, double helixes of concrete that hover around the airport terminal, looks at his watch, he's perfectly on time, drives the Chevrolet to the parking lot – seventh level underground, the walls seep – and when he returns to the light of day lifts his eyes towards the sky, cobalt-blue surface at this hour, hard, absolutely clean, an immense doorway: he's come to pick up the man who, at this very moment, is flying above the territory of Coca in business class: Georges Diderot.

THE PLANE begins its descent, fifty miles away. Passengers roll their necks and look at their watches, they're hungry, the flight attendant walks slowly up the aisle, impeccable, banana chignon and flesh-coloured hose, casts quick lateral glances to verify seatbelts and the angle of seat backs, and sways her hips so gently that she calms the most aerophobic passengers, who always grow more tense during the landing. Georges Diderot crushes his profile against the double focal of the window, salivating, trembling: the theatre of operations. Here we are! he whispers into his burning hands cupped around his mouth. Two immense and Siamese regions are welded to each other via a serpentine seam below, and from this height it's a wildly powerful blueprint. Diderot squints his eyes, his heart beats stronger, he's touched to the core.

TWELVE THOUSAND feet. The earth's surface sharpens its binary partition: to the east, a clear stretch, chalky ceruse pulling at the pale yellow, dry stubble strewn with needles that converge in a metallic cluster; to the west, a dark mountain range, black moss with emerald highlights, dense, irregular. Ten thousand feet: the white zone vibrates, crackles, thousands of scattered splints sparkle while the black zone remains impenetrable, perfectly closed. Eight thousand feet. A frontline comes into view, organizing the two sides, against which they rub or slide like two tectonic plates along a fault line: the river. Diderot's smile is a smile of complicity. Five thousand feet. Track the course of the river now as it vertebrates space, articulates it, breathes into it, a movement that gives it life. Three thousand feet. Watch from this sovereign height the river's chromatic variations – red clayish brick all along the banks, dark and brown and then purplish blue at the midpoint of the bed, turquoise shadows at the edge of mangroves and white tongues in the hollows of the bends – an incision of colour in the middle of this space cleaved into black and white. Two thousand feet. Rapidly scan the ground that complexifies, there's a tug-of-war below, a battle, disjuncture: a topography of confrontation and tension in relief, you'll have to be careful. One thousand feet. Lean your head back and breathe widely, close your eyes, what is the job of the site? Bringing these two landscapes together – there, that's the site, that's the story: electric sintering, reconciliation, fluidizing of powers, elaboration of a relationship, this is what there is to do, this is the job, this is what's waiting for me. Oh Lord!

Later, at the very instant that the belly of the plane caressed the surface of the water before the asphalt of the runway, Diderot trembled violently, rapid spasms running under his skin, he shook his head. People cast worried or irritated glances his way. It was like seeing a large horse snorting at the back of its stall, digging in the straw with a hoof and demanding the outside, light and the prairie – but the truth is, it was just a shiver of joy and terror.

HERE HE is now crossing the concourse of the airport, Diderot, you can't miss him: he's not that tall but he's strong, dolichocephalic head and chest like a coffer, square wrists, long calm legs, tanned close-shaven face, rotted teeth, white hair swept back and crowned with tinted Ray-Bans, and always this air of having just arrived from very far away, from the confines of space with the wind of the plains at his back – Astana, Kazakhstan: the presidential palace unveiled three days earlier was a replica of the White House – Diderot had delivered the work on time to the local dictator and had gotten violently drunk the same evening with a young chess master just returned from Berlin. Sanche parts the crowd, heading to meet him, extended hand exaggeratedly firm, and takes it all in: the aviator jacket, the diver's watch, the white shirt with the collar turned up, the soft loafers, the clean jeans belted at the waist, and the folded newspaper under his arm, the red leather sports bag inside which a number of objects jostle in rhythm: laptop, high-power Maglite, tape measure, change of white shirt, underwear, a few packs of Lusitanias, thick wad of cash, and, protected inside a thick three-ringed binder, a half-size set of plans for the bridge to be built. Greetings, handshakes in the middle of the wave of travellers. Diderot, says Diderot, and Sanche responds, Sanche Alphonse Cameron – his full name, since Sanche Cameron smells too much of that little Spanish follower and Sanche is only five foot three – whereas Alphonse, standing right in the middle with the *A* in the shape of a mountain, this gives him a few more inches: Alphonse, a royal name in Spain, is his symbolic high heel.

RIGID SKY, stiffly shellacked, temperature so hot they can't bear to have the windows open; the Chevrolet limps along. Far off, the buildings of Coca rise up from the ground, Lego shapes of disparate heights. No radio in your ride, Sanche Alphonse? Diderot says Sanchalphonse with a click of his tongue and Sanche hears sarcasm, he kicks himself, he shouldn't have said his full name, shit, shit. No radio, sir, Sanche answers with his eyes glued to the Dodge pickup coming up alongside them on the left, no A/C, no suspension, no radio. Well then, no special treatment, eh. Diderot takes off his jacket and tosses it in the back seat, undoes the buttons of his cuffs carefully, lifting his wrists to vertical one after the other, pushes up his sleeves; he seems slimmer, more elegant, lights a Lusitania: are all the guys here? Sanche casts a quick glance in the rear-view mirror, all of them, now we're just waiting for the girl. The pickup pulls in front of them at that exact moment, then speeds ahead – it's the latest Viper V-10, five hundred horsepower, mounted on twenty-two-inch rims, a beast worth forty-five thousand dollars, Sanche knows it well. Diderot taps his cigar in the ashtray that rattles around above the gearshift. Ah. What's up with her? Sanche steps on the gas, nothing, she had some problem, personal troubles.

Silence. The plain is a broiled straw mattress with livestock and industrial warehouses clumped together here and there. Diderot watches Sanche's slim fingers tap the wheel, nervous, *taptaptap*, leans his head back, contemplates through his tinted glasses the quilted headliner of the Chevrolet and the crusty marks and oozing cracks in the vinyl. He knows what's going on beneath the surface of their conversation. The little guy said *personal troubles* and with that he just dealt a first dirty blow to this girl who he's never met – *personal troubles* – the words seep psychology, inner torment, they stink of women, *personal troubles*, what does that even mean? She has her period? – because he knows very well, the little worm, that on a three-billion dollar site (as they say at head office, chests puffed up and smiles to match as they crack open magnums of champagne) – yes, that on a three-billion dollar site, there's no room for personal troubles, ever.

WE LEAVE the freeway and enter Coca. Sanche drives at the same speed in the left lane, the silence weighs on him, he adds, her grandmother died or something like that and Diderot responds quietly, I don't give a shit about her grandmother, then rolls down the window with the manual handle, sticks an arm out, estimates the temperature of the air at thirty-seven or thirty-eight, dry heat, continental, nice. We approach the river south of the city and stop in front of a brown brick building in a quiet neighbourhood beside the water, Diderot grabs his bag and opens the door – before he gets out pivots his torso and plants his eyes in Sanche's own, tomorrow, seven o'clock, site meeting.

THE GIRL'S NAME IS SUMMER DIAMANTIS AND she's cavorting on the other side of the world, in the streets of Bécon-les-Bruyères, sidewalk sunny side pumps and bare legs, in a hurry to pack her bag, having just been informed via the very mouth of the head of the company – a large mouth, yet one of few words, the kind that only forms subject-verb-complement sentences and emphasizes them with a nod of the head – that she will be on the bridge team, so at the moment she's an ecstatic girl, chosen, named, hired as the manager of concrete production for the construction of the piers. In a hurry to pack her bag because she leaves tomorrow, no joke, tomorrow I leave for Coca, this is what she says to herself as she rushes towards the RER station, I'll be boarding the plane while my friends are sitting down in front of the TV to watch the finals of the Cup Winners' Cup, sitting shoulder to shoulder, chests leaning back, feet spread wide and falling onto their outer edges, can of beer balanced on their crotches, held with two fingers, the other hand smoking or cheering, and the Tiger among them will have the knowing silence of one who's been on the pitch. I'll take off five hours before my father turns off the TV and crunches a sleeping pill, and just a little after the Blondes, leggy, decorated like reliquaries and made up like crimes, late as always, will emerge on the rooftop of their building to wave to the Boeing 777 as it carries me away. Oh Coca!

This morning, the phone. She's not sleeping, has had her eyes open for a while now looking at the unfamiliar pair of sneakers near the bed. It's a call from the director's secretary: they want to see her, they have something for her. Naked and alert, Summer walks to the window. The dawn stirs, the acacias are turning brown. She answers tonelessly, yes, okay, I'm coming. Later, she pulls on a pair of panties, makes a coffee, and in her bed the Tiger stirs – one shoulder first – lifts an eyelid heavy with tobacco and images still spinning. He looks at her through his lashes, she whispers, the Coca thing, I think it's gonna happen, and he smiles. It's the first time he's come over, the first time that – 'cause that's how it is, everything always happens at once.

I'M LEAVING tomorrow. Summer Diamantis is standing in the train car, hanging on tight to the door handle, body swaying with the turns and heart compressed, I'm leaving for Coca, I'm going. The train ploughs under the Seine, the windows shake in a racket of underground rails, they're black and liquid and the Tiger's face is reflected there, blurred by speed; the profile of the Blondes like shadow puppets beneath the platinum of their manes of hair, the silhouette of her father. When they emerge from the tunnel, night has fallen. Port-Royal. Summer shivers. She pushes the strap of her bag up on her shoulder and gets ready to let go of the handle and step out onto the platform. Only a few people in the station, her heels resonate *clack clack clack* on the flagstones. A pharmacy that's open, that's what she needs. Stilnox for the plane, Dramamine for later, vaccines too, yes, she has to make sure she gets all this, and find a way to go and kiss the Tiger.

BECAUSE SHE'S leaving tomorrow, going far, far away, to the other side of the world. Because in exactly seventeen hours, we'll see her coming out of the Coca airport, getting into a lemon-yellow taxi, ponytail well elasticked, forehead and neck clear; she'll give the address to the driver who'll start the car without answering, heading into a labyrinth of express lanes that will suddenly propel them into the middle of a wide and empty plain where the sky will play an excessive part. Summer will grow dizzy when she sees the unbounded landscape, an immensity as uncontrollable as her breathing, she can't keep it steady any longer, bit by bit she'll suffocate, a faintness that will cause a bitter taste to rise up in her mouth, her head will ache, she'll ask the driver to stop so she can get some air, he'll park the vehicle on a shoulder without asking any questions, and once she's outside she'll breathe for a long time, bent over, hands on her knees, will spit on the ground a few times and then when she straightens up again will step over the guardrail to take a few steps into the pink, powdery plain, almost lunar in this razing light of dawn, a skin. She'll stand stock still for a brief moment to listen to the silence, perforated by the rare cars that speed past behind her; a mineral silence where each sound rings out distinctly and pollinates space – a stone rolls, a branch cracks, a scorpion scratches the ground; a real silence, like that of a wildcat, while the lever of the night will cause the day to rise, stretching out space as far as it can go, like a screen, and the horizon will suddenly be so close that Summer will reach out her hand to touch it, she too, touched in that moment, and suddenly hearing the sound of human steps behind her will jump, the driver will be there, you okay, miss? They'll head back to the car and Summer will roll down her window and lean back against the seat, shaken, they'll drive till they reach the suburbs of Coca, fragrances will rush into the car, garbage, plastic cups deformed from the heat, rotting meat, newspapers smeared with gas, wilted flowers, mouldy vegetables, dirty laundry, and lots of sweat over everything – here it is, the smell of Coca, Summer will think, as though the odour of a city was first and foremost that of its trash. Once she has arrived, she'll say goodbye to the driver and he'll look her in the eye and nod, good luck miss, and then, following the directions given to her by the company and learned by heart, she'll enter the code at the entrance to the building, a lobby, a hallway, an elevator, she'll reach the second floor, and when she's at the door will take out a little golden key, *click*, she'll unlock the door, push it open, holding her breath – will feel around in the darkness, walk to the window, a curtain, it will be six o'clock in the morning. She'll concentrate to remember what she has to do in the next few hours – first of all, plug in the laptop and wash her hair – then will take a quick inventory of the room where she'll be living from now on; there will be a bed, an empty set of shelves, an ordinary table and two chairs, a television, a telephone, an armchair, a sink, a hotplate, a refrigerator, a square of carpet, and in a bathroom with pale-green tiles, a bathtub, a sink, a cabinet. She won't stop to look at the papers tacked to the door – safety regulations, instruction manuals for the appliances, evacuation plan in case of fire – will open the window instead, a balcony, the street, and will see the building across the way, a young pregnant woman will be hanging laundry carefully and their eyes will meet, the young woman will smile over the line and Summer will give a brief wave without really knowing why, will go inside and sit on the edge of the bed, look at her watch, look around her, she should unpack, open the cupboards, fold her clothes, have a shower, and finally pull her laptop out of its case. She'll leap up, string her movements together rapidly, as though each pause, each silence, would be something come to weaken her.

AN HOUR later, she'll pass through the gates to the site, back straight, breathing shallow, and heart beating madly, hard hat in hand. The esplanade will be silent, parked vehicles, not a living soul, she'll continue on her course, her step growing more and more sure, her silhouette cut sharply against the immense open space. At the end of her path, a building, and in front of the open door a few men who turn towards her and hold out a hand, welcome, Diamantis, we were waiting only for you, Diamantis, did you have a good trip, Diamantis? Diderot will suddenly appear and greet her in a similar fashion and Summer will immediately be wary of the guy, would have preferred a more clean-cut character, a whiz at equations, gold-plated communicant's pen hooked in his breast pocket, brush cut, and a direct gaze – instead there's this guy, Diderot, the legend, who resembles a colossal and outdated Steve McQueen and looks her up and down like she's just a kid but also like she's a woman – she'll be disappointed. Sanche Cameron, for his part, will step back to get a better look at her while she introduces herself to the others, will scrutinize her without managing to form an opinion, will find her strange, a good-looking girl, but a heavy one who walks like a gorilla, short hands and square shoulders, wide hips, beautiful olive skin, thick blonde hair, but with a protruding chin, a nose like a dog, yes, that's it, and she will be hyperconscious of being the strange animal – she'll want to make a good impression and won't crack a smile, a girl in charge of concrete is not common currency.

ORCHESTRATING THE TRIAL AND ERROR

JOHN JOHNSON, A.K.A. THE BOA, IS A MAN of medium height, hairless body, weightlifter's torso and Asian complexion, strong neck, thick eyebrows above little slitted eyes, no lips, pointy teeth, grey tongue. He takes over Coca's city hall in January 2005. He's been elected; now he invests in his image. Puts away the black satiny shirts and fedoras, acquires a tailor on Savile Row, orders a dozen custom suits in anthracite grey. Goes on a diet, gets hair transplants, pays for a beautiful smile, takes up golfing. Far from seeing his new position as retirement with an unobstructed view of the leisurely pension of corruption, he is suddenly seized by grandeur. He remembers his campaign slogans – phrases concocted by professionals, powerful formulas that smack like flags in the stadiums and the town squares, twelve-foot-high watchwords that lend power to his voice, give him the chin of an orator – and speaks them softly into the golden night, standing on the balcony of city hall, which in his mind is a gangway revealing him to the world; he imagines an appropriate gesture and, galvanized by his own words, captivated by the marvellous promises he made to the crowds, the blood rises to his head, his heart beats wildly: he will become the man he said he was, he will – he's deciding it right now. From now on, he treats fortune like the useful gadget of respectability and doesn't think about anything except making his mark. He will impact his time – people will remember him.

A FEW WEEKS after his election he takes a trip to Dubai. It's his first journey off the continent and he's in a state. On the plane, he takes sleeping pills, drinks champagne, tries to smooth-talk the flight attendant, and falls asleep just before they land. He's ushered into a special lounge at the airport and then into a white limousine with tinted windows; another limo will follow with the bags and the people who make up his select cabinet. What he sees on the drive from the airport to the city fills him with a simultaneous sensation of euphoria and crushing defeat.

The cranes are the first things to gobsmack him: clustered together in the hundreds, they overpopulate the sky; their arms are fluorescent laser-sabres brighter than any Jedi warrior's, and their pale halo crowns the construction-site city with a cupola of white night. The Boa cranes his neck to count them all, and the man in the white dishdasha sitting next to him tells him that one-third of all the cranes in the world are requisitioned here: one in three, he repeats, one in three is here, in our city. His tiny mouth, accentuated by a thin line of moustache, says very quietly, we are building the city of the future, a Pharaonic undertaking. The Boa says nothing more. He salivates, bewitched. The proliferation of towers stuns him – so numerous you'd think they were multiplied by a fevered eye, so tall you have to rub your own eyes, afraid you might be hallucinating – their white windows like thousands of blinding little parallelograms, thousands of effervescent Vichy pastilles in the faded night: here people work 24-7, the workers are housed outside the city, the changes of shift happen via shuttles – the man whispers each piece of information, escorting the Boa's surprise with great delicacy. Farther on, he points with a waxy index finger to a building under construction, already a hundred storeys high, and says: This one will be 2,300 feet tall. The Boa nods his head, suddenly inquires about the height of the Empire State Building, the Hancock Center, and the towers in Shanghai,

Cape Town, and Moscow, he's euphoric and stupefied. Thus, in Dubai, the sky is solid, massive: ground to develop. The drive is long in the long car, the sea takes its time to arrive, the Boa waits for it: flat, unaffected, heavy black oilcloth whose edges are erased by the night, and he is startled to discover that it too is constructed, rendered solid, crusted over, and apt to become the base for an artificial archipelago, a reproduction of the world map (Great Britain selling for three million dollars) or a luxury housing complex in the shape of a palm tree: thus the sea too is ground to develop.

The Boa arrives at his hotel bowled over, cheeks red and eyes bugged out, he has a hard time falling asleep, the night is too bright, as though filtered through hot gauze, and he is far too excited – the Burj Al Arab is one of the tallest hotels in the world, an immense sail made of glass and Teflon, swelled before the Persian Gulf which is completely black at this hour, and closed as a chest that raggedy pirates armed with AK-47s might try to steal. When he wakes, the Boa is convinced he's found the inspiration that was missing for his mandate. A mastered space is what offers itself up to his gaze – a space, he thinks, where mastery combines with audacity – and that is the mark of power.

AT MID-MORNING, the man who had welcomed him the day before comes to pick him up and guides him around the city. His keffiyeh floats out calmly at his back like a mage's cape any time he quickens the pace – no one knows, except me, that he has sunk into a dire melancholy, that he shepherds officials around in order to flee the palace; no one knows that he plans to return to the desert to live with the oryx, the fennecs, and the scorpions; that, stretched out inside a tent lightly ventilated by the desert breeze, he will write poems and smoke a narghile; no one knows that he spits with rage into the mirror that reflects him – him and the wide hall of his villa that is just as empty and marbled, just as huge, inert and senseless as the rest. The Boa rushes along, his cardiac rhythm speeds up with pleasure and exhilaration. The city appears as a consumerist phantasmagoria, a gigantic ghetto for nomadic billionaires, the model of a virtual universe where you can lose your mind: strange combination of hotels with ostentatious pomp, shopping malls with unmatched opulence – the largest duty-free mall in the world, with miles of shop windows, brand names that assault, conjuring desire and striking an exclusive clientele of Arab princes, Anglo-Saxon rock stars, Russian oligarchs, and Chinese industry leaders – and extravagant theme parks – an indoor ski hill with a snowy summit, mechanized lifts and a polar bear, an Andalusian-style spa, a Nubian village, an underwater hotel, and a giga-zoo. The Boa loses himself in space-time. In the very near future, we will have attained the grand number of fifteen million visitors; the accompanier states these facts in such elegant English that the Boa has difficulty understanding, he's losing his grip, he succumbs, stammers in a continuous loop when I think that twenty years ago there was nothing here, nothing, just a little patch of desert, a sandy bit of Earth's crust, and not even any oil – and now what? Paradise.

He's driven to the palace a little before noon for a short audience with the emir Mohammed bin Rashid Al Maktoum – the man the Boa unwisely calls "my counterpart." He waits for three hours in the antechamber, using the time to imagine partnerships between Coca and Dubai; he mulls over ideas while behind the thick, padded door, sheik Mo nibbles pistachios with his minister of war, murmuring a few questions about the technical and military capacities of the Rafale jets showcased the day before on the tarmac at Bourget, in Paris. Finally the Boa is received, and here he is, perfumed little guy in a room paved with marble that reminds him all at once of Grand Central Station in New York. He is bursting with an idea, the horses, and his step is full of drive.

From a ways off the sheik looks massive and immaculate as authority itself, but his form becomes more and more human the closer he comes – the akal of his keffiyeh falls a little over one ear, making the monarch's head a bit lopsided. The Boa greets the prince according to protocol – above all, don't get too close to the sacred body of the sheik. Then the latter snaps his fingers, has a new bowl of pistachios brought to his guest, and here they are seated fifteen feet from each other. So, the horses. The Boa, instead of fawningly paying his respects, tells the prince about his wish to develop stud farms in his city, Coca. The sheik frowns, doesn't know where this energetic little being comes from, has never heard the name Coca, and nods his head, very calm. The Boa winds up, gaining momentum, the high plains to the east of the city are among the best pasturages in the world, the grass is marvellous and the water is pure. This is a subject that the sheik enjoys: he is a horseman, had his chance to shine in the competitions, and the royal family owns the largest stable of thoroughbreds in the world, magnificent animals bought for their weight in gold, most of them at the yearlings auction in Deauville. The conversation flows in this way for more than four minutes, a record, and finally the sheik agrees: a collaboration begins to take shape. The Boa cuts the inside of his mouth while violently crunching a pistachio.

IN COCA, what is now called the Dubai Trip creates a buzz. Its influence can be measured in the feverish urbanism that seizes the city. From then on the Boa is crystal clear about the single goal for his city council: put an end to three centuries of conservative prudence, once and for all get rid of the stranglehold of old money that reigns in the affluent downtown neighbourhoods, cut down the dynasties of the Cripplecrows and the Sandlesses that have been rubbing shoulders incestuously for the past two centuries, between satin sheets and plumes of cigar smoke – rather than being leaders of the city, they are masters over it. He wants to be done with their erudite conceit, their culture, their archives, too much Europe here, too much Europe, he repeats this time and again, heavy identity, sticky traditions: it stinks of death! He gets to work busting open the city centre, breaking its hard pit, its historical pit, pulverizing its meaning and scattering it to the periphery. The old buildings and bourgeois neighbourhoods, traces of the origins and symbol of the pioneers' values – physical courage, a spirit of conquest, work, piety, monogamy, and all other qualities that glorify rootedness – are removed to museums: dust is what suits them best, sneers the Boa, his action is oriented elsewhere, out of range of patrimony, far from all the old fictions that begat the city plan. I'm going to air out all that. I'm going to free the city and put it on the world map. An era of grand manoeuvres follows, in which manila envelopes circulate containing wads of new bills that crinkle like biscuits.

In less than three months, the Boa manages to have Coca declared a free-trade zone by the Senate and twinned with Dubai; obtains, from the state bank – now under control of his own investment company – a loan at a low fixed rate for a large-scale city planning venture, and grants the municipality a lease of fifty years for each main facility. His private collusions in municipal projects alarm his shrewdest and most servile collaborators alike, but not one of them says a word and everyone knows why: the Boa presides over a fortress built on insider influence and he controls all the entrances and all the elevators, he is strong, rich, and not too concerned about the price one has to pay in order to remain in the good graces of the city's respected institutions and organizations. Anywhere he can, he uses the tactics of the carnivorous reptiles he's hunted since he was a child, and deploys such discreet strategies that only those who have a darkness to match his own can detect the long-term predatory power – these rare few, rendered speechless and weak, run for their lives – and then, buoyed up as he is by microscopic advantages that accumulate and activate one another, with the icy brutality that is his trademark, the Boa shifts without warning into attack mode and strikes. Those who might have tried to stand in his way are publicly mocked, dried up, simple-minded, sad. They don't understand anything about the ways of the world. He's sorry, but he eliminates them – what else do you expect, really, what do you want me to do? The implacable machine that's running now at full throttle slowly suffocates them. After all, isn't the Boa acting for the good of the city? Doesn't he put himself entirely – himself, his companies, his screens, his men, his dogs – at the service of his fellow citizens? He has ideas for Coca – he was elected and he's a man who keeps his promises: he is John the benefactor.

FROM THEN on, he commands the territory by ukase, walking slowly around the huge maquette of the city he's had installed in the middle of his office – a general on a campaign planning strategies, that's what he makes you think of – chest leaning over his scaled-down model, hands crossed behind his back, examining a portion of cardboard and then suddenly grabbing a wand and ordering an internet city here, a media city there, a shopping centre here – a maze of malls paved with porphyry and adorned with fountains and cappuccino kiosks – a multi-purpose stadium here, a skating rink in the shape of a flying saucer there, an underground multiplex with fifty rooms, a cinder track on the roof of a row of low-rise buildings, a casino under a glass bell. He wants transparency, plastic and polypropylene, rubber and melamine, all things provisional, consumable, disposable: everything must be mobile, light, convertible, and flexible. Supercharged, he devotes himself to the manipulation of giant Meccano that he reconfigures daily, intoxicated by the infinite scope of new formal possibilities, by the hubs he draws, by the work sites he carves out, by the activity centres he defines and positions on the map. He has only one idea left in mind: to pull Coca out of the provincial anonymity where it has been sleeping peacefully and convert it to the global economy. He wants to build the city of the third millennium, polyphonic and omnivorous, doped up on novelty, shaped for satisfaction, for pleasure, for the experience of consumption.

AND YET there's something that wounds his pride: isolated as it is, Coca's energy is rationed and dependent upon the coastal cities. The investors have fled for this very reason – it's impossible to squeeze development out of a stingy little dump with a tight-assed population where spending is watched so closely. Moreover, the oil tankers that supply the city and its few industrial sites only come grudgingly up the river to the storage tanks downstream – the Boa sees condescension in this – isn't he paying them cash, for Christ's sake? He fulminates, mulls things over – alone at first, because he's convinced that his people are incapable of coming up with a single idea. One evening a documentary on biofuel is on TV. It's a revelation – he's hooked by the subject and proceeds to study it in depth. Corn grows abundantly in the valley, and Coca has thousands of acres of preserves – the high red plains and the forest, whose edges could be cleared out, plus the interior of the massif if the Natives "play the game" – just don't screw us over, that's all I ask of them – this is how the Boa talks to himself. At the end of a brisk council meeting held at the beginning of March, he decides to convert the city to ethanol. An independent port will be constructed upstream at the oxbow in the river, a terminal with the capacity to hold ships of all tonnages and the corollary refineries. Fuelled thus, the city will export the surplus of energy to the coast, reverse the trend and shine at the forefront of global eco strategies. Coca, the green city! The Boa rubs his hands together, delighted with his coup, he's done well. Now he just needs a bridge. A bridge by which they can enter the forest and reach the fertile valleys southeast of the mountain range, a bridge to connect the city to Ocean Bay.

The old Golden Bridge is in the crosshairs. The thing is narrow, it strangles traffic, causing irritation, middle fingers brandished through car windows, slowing the pace and putting business in peril. It doesn't suffice. The Boa can't even look at it anymore without flying into a rage. I want to be finished with the slow, the old, the broken down. I want it destroyed. I want it tossed in the trash, the rubbish; I want it to fall into decay, to be torn to shreds. Certain associations, however, are up in arms. Petitions circulate to save the bridge – it's the soul of our city, a piece of our identity, it holds our memories – deploring the homogenization of cities, all the fast-food joints and clothing-store signs identical from Quito to Vladivostok, specificities of identity caving under capitalist pressure, globalization contaminating the tiniest bit of sidewalk and harmonizing every storefront. The Boa is dumbstruck – he hears but doesn't understand, doesn't see the problem, appeals to the desires of youth and modernity: enough! What a drag! What's wrong with wanting to move forward? And anyway the old bridge is falling into ruin and the river beneath its piers is dark, putrid. Rust wreaks a toxic leprosy on the beams and girders, the wood of the deck is cracking, you can feel it move. The Natives ended up colonizing the little covered stalls lining the bridge deck, tiny little alcoves where they coagulate for entire days, heaped together smoking or half-heartedly selling all kinds of jewellery, charms, pipes, trinkets. Little pieces of crap for little budgets, thinks the Boa: I want it gone.

SO THE BOA wants his bridge. Not just any arch, not just any viaduct hastily dreamed up but a bridge in the image of the new Coca. He wants something large and functional, he wants at least six lanes – a freeway over the river. He wants a unique creation. Scans his debtors, his acquaintances, expresses his desire but no one sends back the interpretation he's waiting for. In secret, he grabs a piece of paper and a pen and does some sketches of his own, but no matter how fast he draws his lines, trying to capture a pure form – ridiculous at the moment, and touching: dishevelled, maladroit, and miming the gesture of the artist – he can't quite get it. One of his councillors cleverly suggests that he launch a contest. Such a subject requires expertise, prestige, an architect whose glorious career will carry the ambitions of the city as high and as far as possible. The Boa sees himself as a Medici, a princely patron in a velvet cape, likes himself even more, and far from taking offence, he accepts that a foreign glory could come to build upon his land, thereby raising his own glory higher.

WAS IT BETTER TO CLUTTER UP THE EARTH rather than the sky? Was it best to demonstrate strength, opt for a powerful creation, a combination of massive, heavy pieces like the bridge in Maracaibo? Was it best to choose a transparent, ethereal work, a construction that concentrated the material into only a few elements, an option with finesse, like the Millau Viaduct? Was it best to open a city up or weld two landscapes together, to defer to nature, use its lines, and incorporate the structure into it? The Boa can't decide, he wants everything. He wants innovation and reference, a flourishing enterprise, beauty, and the world record. A man arrives with the solution. His name is Ralph Waldo, he comes from São Paulo: an architect who is both famous and a mystery. He enters the room for the contest auditions, hands free and calm alongside his body, and describes the form that gathers the areas together: to illustrate the adventure of migration, the ocean, the estuary, the river, and the forest, the vined walkway above gorges and the span that plays above the void, he has chosen a highly technological hammock; to demonstrate suppleness and strength, flexibility and resistance to seismic shifts, he has chosen a nautical web of cables and massive concrete anchorings; to symbolize the ambitious city, he has chosen two steel towers planted in the riverbed, skyscrapers power emitters energy catchers; to evoke the myth, he has chosen red. That is, a suspension bridge of steel and concrete. The architect announces measurements comparable to those of the longest suspension bridges in the world, most of them estuary or ocean channel bridges. Length: 6,200 feet; centre suspension span: 4,100 feet; width: 100 feet; height of the deck above the water: 230 feet; height of the towers: 750 feet. A delusion of grandeur, like an enormous desire contained within a very small body. Just the presence of the bridge in the heart of Coca, Waldo assures them, will make the city seem bigger, more open, and more prosperous – a simple trick of proportions in relation to the harmonics of the space, the perception of a crossing greater than that of a bridge, an optical singularity.

GIVE ME THE PLANS AND I'LL BUILD YOU WHAT
you want, whatever it is, even a bridge to hell – Diderot's
smoking in his office on the twentieth floor of the Héraclès
tower, La Défense district, Paris, in front of the bay window,
a black mass backlit against the baby-blue pane, large-format
man overlooking a confetti capital electrified by Friday
night departures – give me the plans, goddammit, the plans,
that's all I need.

THE CHAIRMAN and CEO of Héraclès, interrupted in
his flummeries, stepped back and smiled, flinging a folder
onto the table, and at the blunt sound of cardboard against
the wood – a smack that echoed in the room like a starter's
gun – Diderot took an enormous breath, inflating his rib
cage exaggeratedly, and furtively lowered his eyelids: it
was happening, the site was his. He didn't turn around
right away towards the messenger, rather savoured the
good news: he wouldn't end on the construction of a new
wing in some famous private museum, the addition on
a nuclear power plant, or the digging of an umpteenth
ultramodern parking lot in a provincial city, no, the men
from Comex (the board of execs at Héraclès) were giving
him a bridge to close his career, a coronation, managerial
shenanigans – he would keep his mouth shut, contain his
disgust, would let them come congratulate him, pat him on
the shoulder, conclusive slaps that would make him want to
smash his fist into their hypocritical faces, but he wouldn't

do anything, would take what he could get, a bridge, would mime docile pride and, as for the rest, the crown and the cajoling, that would all be postmarked return to sender: all he cared about was the work to be done. Of course they would talk within the company, gossip about him getting the field marshal's baton, Héraclès owes you a lot, thank you my friend, and the young engineers who had rushed into the ranks at the announcement of the opening of the site would have no trouble grumbling in the hallways 'cause, shit, Georges Diderot may have been a legend, but he's old now, his management methods are frankly not clean cut and he's not from the inner circle – not a young jackal from the famous École Polytechnique (the X) with ants in his pants, not a showman from the prestigious engineering school les Mines or head of the class at the ParisTech, not a supersonic brain lubricated with force diagrams, functions with multiple variables, derivatives, strength-of-material analyses, Euclidean spaces, and Fourier series. Diderot's was a complex career, difficult to follow, more lateral than vertical, hybridized to the extreme with all kinds of skills, a mix of freelance star and in-house engineer come in through the back door and ended up reigning over Comex, a guy who smokes in the elevator, who calls janitors and CEOs alike by their first name.

WHEN DIDEROT finally turned around, the man who he ironically called the Grand Chief was in the doorway of his office, and with a raise of his eyebrows indicated the folder, you've got some reading to do. Inside the mundane cover were the results of the first surveys done by geotechnicians in Coca and the specifications for the work. Seated at his desk, Diderot flipped through the surveys – which were ordered in reverse.

On the first sheets, he recognized his language, he was at home. Measurements, tables, graphs – these results gave a precise illustration of data from probes recently placed on the ground in Coca, homing devices armed with little explosive charges whose deflagrations were analyzed – noise and propagation of shock waves – in order to understand the reality of the material, its internal morphology, the content of its constitution, its potential. For Diderot, these notes held something terribly moving: it was like reading what reverberates from the little taps of the white cane that the blind person makes against the ground simply in order to walk upon it – but here they had to construct their own white canes, so that they could be trusted – invent them and then manipulate them with care so that they hit the ground correctly, with clean, sharp little taps. This was the perceptible, tender description of a gigantic trial and error and it contained exactly what he loved – this resembled real life.

NIGHT HAD long since fallen and the tower emptied out when he finally took a look at the quantitatives, numbers that lined themselves up or lay themselves out in columns over several pages. Numbers that speak only of themselves, the young ones (formerly moles running through the corridors of graceless high schools) would have said; numbers that have to be coaxed to speak, Diderot would have retorted, rubbing his hands together. These measurements involved other things besides themselves, a certain temporality, an organization of the work. A million cubic yards of concrete. Eighty thousand tons of steel. Eighty thousand miles of cable. Diderot absorbed these figures without letting himself be impressed, whispered them to himself, and quickly translated and prolonged their meaning: planning the construction of an on-site concrete mixing plant and anticipating the delivery of its components – cement, gravel, water, sand – foreseeing the steel supplies, coordinating their transport to Coca, and above all, once they reached the Pontoverde platform, having them brought to the bridge site beside the river. There would be quarrels among the engineers – the partisans of the land route would argue for the construction of pathways – roads or rails – that would avoid lengthy and expensive load changes, since the metal would be loaded at its production sites in the steel factories of Blackoak Inc. in Maryland, New Jersey, and Pennsylvania and unloaded directly at the foot of the bridge piers; while those partisans of the marine route would argue for the smoothness and convenience of floating barges that would migrate along the river, and these latter, Diderot among them, would win out.

DIDEROT GOT up again and went to the window. A bridge man again. Good. He exulted in silence – building a bridge is still a source of elation, even in a stinking hole like Coca, a dump that no one's ever heard of. The ultimate job for an engineer. He paced in front of the bay window, then pressed his burning forehead to the pane that crackled with lights of the night like paper on fire, and already the thought of disconcerting his entourage amused him, they were so quick to compliment him; the thought of thwarting this childish admiration because, come on, the symbolism of the thing – the link, passage, movement *blah blah blah* – went straight over his head, he didn't give a rat's ass: what really excited him was the technical epic, putting individual competencies to work together within a collective project; what thrilled him was the sum of decisions contained within a construction, the succession of short events leading to the permanence of the work, its inscription in time. What filled him with joy was to operate the life-sized fulfillment of thousands of hours of calculations.

SITE MEETING – SOMETIME AFTER SEVEN
o'clock in the morning and Diderot is talking, standing
mountainous at the end of the oval table. Bare room, thin
partitions, thin carpet hastily placed, smell of glue, smell of
new, freeze-dried coffee, classroom chairs dragged in. These
accommodate some fifty individuals, among them Sanche
Cameron, the crane operator, and Summer Diamantis,
the girl in charge of concrete – Diderot watches these
two surreptitiously, the boy with the dazzled face, the girl
who takes notes without lifting her head. He directed the
comment at them when he said, fingers joined in a bouquet
over his chest, hey, rookies, call me Diderot.

HE CLEARS his throat and begins in a loud voice. Okay,
let's get started. Plan of action: one, dig the ground – he
lifts his thumb; two, dredge and clear the river – he lifts
his index; three, get started on the concrete – he lifts his
middle finger. Turns to pull down a wall-mounted screen,
starts up a laptop, turns back, slowly surveys the audience,
and then slams down the first words.

So, dig the ground. He turns to the geotechnical
map projected on the screen, takes a zapper from his back
pocket: two types of soil coexist here. One – a red point
of light lands on the map, perfectly synchronous: Coca
side. The limestone plateau of the high plain. Arid on
the surface, fractured farther down – hard, with a tender
heart, it's the trick of the cream filling, we know it well,

we're not crazy about it, but it's better than the opposite, right? The room agrees, laughter erupts, soft and complicit. The problem – Diderot whips around without a smile to look at the audience – we've got limestone rocks sitting on marly clay that could cause landslides. Be very careful. Two – same choreography: Edgefront side. Damp and inhabited ground, roots to tear out, we'll have to pierce the glebe and go deeper to get to the mineral in order to have a strong foothold for the foundation. So, two types of ground, which is where we get two types of material, but one single strategy: the Neolithic gesture! In other words, cleave the ground – and as ever he joins the action to the word, the blade of his hand slices the space in front of him, he brings the scene to life, he likes theatre. Finally, he recapitulates in a loud voice pointing two red spots one after the other on the map: we'll start by making two holes in order to anchor the bridge. Got it? Good. Moving on. Dredge the river – Diderot continues while the map changes on the screen: we'll proceed as usual, we'll send in the dredger, clean it out, remove the sludge, stow the biodegradable materials in clearings here, and here – two consecutive shots of the zapper in the forested area – and put the contaminated materials on a barge that will travel all the way back downriver and shove this shit four thousand feet down into the ocean. There you have it. We signed agreements with the municipality, it has to be done. And back there it's not over, we clear out the river, dig the channel again, enlarge it all the way up to the future port, and then we consolidate, we raise the embankments where the steel cables will be anchored, and we dig, we dig the river bottom to embed the towers.

Notes being taken in notebooks and spidery scrawl of the men in light short-sleeved shirts, it's hot, they open the portholes to let in some air, the room swells with the clamour of the outside – zooming on the freeways, hubbub of the stock market, panic of wild ducks, *putt putt putt* of motors on dinghies out on the river, barking of dogs, gunshots – and Diderot's voice coils with all this without drowning it out. Funny soundtrack, thinks Sanche Cameron who had closed his eyes for a moment, since he didn't close them at all last night, seized as he was beneath the sheets by the restlessness that had overtaken him, so happy that the site was starting up, that the grand life waiting for him there was finally beginning. He slants a glance sideways at Summer as she tries desperately to write everything down, tells himself it's just like a girl to be meticulous like that. Diderot has started speaking again.

And now, the concrete. Your domain, Diamantis! – he turns towards Summer, their eyes meet, the girl immediately sits up straight in her chair, Diderot spreads his arms and makes circles in the air, he adds flatly: you're responsible for feeding the site, Diamantis, you're in charge of perpetual motion. Then he retracts the screen with a sharp movement the way you'd pull on a blind, turns off his computer, and circulates copies of a handout detailing phase one of construction. Since no one has spoken any questions aloud, everyone leans over their documents, comments to one another about the technical data, and then the surveyor confirms the plan measurements, the steward presents the menus for the first two weeks, they ask about beer at lunchtime – one 473 ml can per worker – and Diderot cuts them off, forget it, white with rage. Get out, all of you. Meeting's over.

Summer Diamantis has only one idea in mind: to go see the mixing plant. Shuffling of papers, repositioning of chairs, she holds herself apart at the end of the table, dawdles, pretending to read over her notes, waits for the men to finish leaving the room, and now some of them turn towards her from the doorway, see you tomorrow, Diamantis! And ready to roll, eh, Diamantis!

IT'S ALMOST nine o'clock in the morning when she leaves the building and the heat takes her by surprise, the hot breath of it, and though nothing budges in the sky, a cushion of burning vapour grabs her by the nape, already she's mopping her forehead. She sets off across the site, a hundred yards on the diagonal, rocky ground the colour of plaster, crunch of her steps in the silence; she continues past the cranes and the parked vehicles that gleam, the bluish sheds; steps over pairs of rails and goes round the water tanks; the earth smokes in her wake and quickly coats her ankles in a fine flour, not a living soul on this side, nothing, it's crazy, she looks at her watch mechanically, thinks tomorrow at this time we will have started, continues on her way, throat tight, step growing firmer, silhouette precise against the backdrop of the tidy site, hand soon held as a visor at the level of her eyebrows; she speeds up, repeats Diderot's words to herself, maxillae strained by a smile that clogs her mouth since she doesn't open her lips (too restless, she too) – he'd said: the concrete, Diamantis, that's your domain – she'd nodded her head in all seriousness, yes – the plant, the towers, the bins, the drums, all that, that's you – his gesture was wide and his voice loud, he'd looked her deep in the eyes, he'd designated her place. All this, she sees it now that she's reached the plant, all this takes up about a hundred yards by sixty – in other words, a fair portion of territory, edged by a quay on the river. Summer immediately begins to familiarize herself with the internal organization. Her eyes move from the river to the quay, from the quay to the giant mounds placed in the centre of the space – cement, gravel, sand – following the line of the conveyor belts that link the materials cone to the blood-orange concrete towers, notes the mixing buildings, walks past the control room, inspects each of the twelve mixing trucks, drums aligned neatly and ready to go, lingers by the recycling pit, the basins for water treatment and reuse of aggregate and waste concrete.

Panoramic tracking shot, traffic plan, Summer takes in the validity of the organism: an open-air factory, a concrete factory. So all this is me?

IT'S UNDERSTANDABLE that she would have her doubts. Although the Coca bridge had selected her, Summer had not always been chosen. This contract redeemed in one fell swoop a particular event from her childhood, an event that was labelled a core trauma by a psychologist who coloured checkerboards on graph paper during their sessions: when her mother left, she took Summer's little brother with her, in her arms, and left Summer behind. Not enough time for two children, not enough money either, not enough space in the one-bedroom apartment in the chic suburb of Saint-Raphaël where she was going to start a new life. Rationality, then, pragmatism, you're big enough, you're seven now, my darling, my darling, she murmured, and also the little girl was so much like her father, didn't need anyone, so brave and other suspicious caresses on top of her head. Thus Summer stayed with the ex-husband who had asked for it – since he'd fallen into an admirably regimented and quite sincere polygamy. So you're stuck with me, then, he said to her the night they found themselves alone at the kitchen table before a Pyrex dish in which a shepherd's pie was getting cold. From then on, it was Saint-Raphaël during school holidays, her mother didn't ask much of her. Neither did her father, in his own way. The little girl was left in peace. At least we'd like to believe that. Would she have had to be born as a boy in order to be chosen by her mother? Would she then have had to replace, for her father, the pudgy little male carried off to the French Riviera? We can see that she brought herself up as a boy, or rather how she imagined a boy should be raised, which led her to consider optional and even random phases as mandatory. She equipped herself in such a way as to compensate for the lacking maternal touch:

soccer and video games, comic books and sci-fi novels, math, physics, and industrial design. Always dressed the same – jeans, a jacket, not many colours, hair in a ponytail – she learned to take apart a moped motor and then put it back together; during parties she took her place by the stereo and DJed rather than lining up against the wall at the first bars of a slow song, drank like a fish and smoked like a chimney – Marlboros, you guessed it – cowboy for cowboy, she's an expert on westerns, unbeatable on questions of all the Rios and all the Rivers, which will end up being very useful, as we'll see. Tough, concise, indefatigable, dry-eyed girl of steel – someone you could count on, in short, someone you didn't have to baby – how's it going, big girl? What are you thinking about? It was so obvious, so clumsy, that no one saw through her strongman poses, this outrageous sham – especially her father, caught up in a multiplex harem from which he struggled to extricate himself, and who congratulated himself each day for this child who asked so little of him, didn't make demands, wasn't into drama, never cried; a girl, finally, who was so little like a girl is what he thought, watching from the window as she left through the garden gate, a good little soldier, yes, how lucky he was. We can understand how Summer, encouraged in this way, began to see kids her age as lesser beings. She hastened to escape their obsession with love, their interminable confessions, their masochistic laments, the acidulous fragility they put on so willingly in order to seduce. In so doing deprived herself of their skin, their laughter, their nocturnal complicities, their solidarity – foolishly deprived herself of their sweetness. And decided for herself, at thirteen years old, one day when she let herself be felt up at the movies by a boy who she liked but who didn't care about her one bit, she knew it – he kneaded her breasts shamelessly, slid his hand up between her thighs, and scraped the roof of her mouth with a harsh tongue – decided that love, okay, fine, but let's not get carried away.

Not at any price. Thus deciding something for herself, to do it for the rest of her life without glutting herself on hogwash like the heart has its reasons *blah blah blah* – love allowing us to make all kinds of stupid moves, to lose our time, to surrender our skin, to clash and wound the better to devour each other immediately after, to scream in stairwells, to call each other at all hours of the night, to drive drunk through the hostile countryside, 'cause that's how it happens, that's the only way – yes, for a girl so young to judge love like this, coldly, clear-eyed, was certainly surprising. She zigzagged between boys. They found her hard, cold, proud, and all in all not very feminine. These were their reproaches. It's hard now to measure the incredible strength she needed to call upon in order to maintain her independence and the splendour of solitude, to choose that she would never again be placed heart pounding on the scale, or "stuck" in second place for lack of being chosen. At twenty, she looked affectivity up and down with a free smile – what does a free smile look like? What does it look like, Summer Diamantis's beautiful smile?

She liked school and sports, she liked competition. Had tried taking part in other selections where she excelled too often without winning: any time there were only two candidates left, a mute panic drilled into her solar plexus and paralyzed her momentum, and they picked the other one. A token finalist, rarely the champion, Summer got a label: it was confirmed that the choice of her mother, whose heart (and the square feet of plush carpet that went with it) she failed to win, had resulted in a failure complex: she often stayed slouched on the players' bench, even if she did so elegantly. Her father, immune to these analyses, suppressed such propositions with ever the same bored silence and rewarded his daughter every morning with a debauched British smile yawning vaguely no big deal. Then came the Blondes who don't take any bullshit and who beautifully inked out this jinx the way you'd push a lock of hair back from your forehead sharply, for more visibility, more presence, and more joy. They made Summer part of their club one July night while all three of them were spread out on the grass in the stadium, their bodies arranged in arrows in front of the end zone, after Summer had blocked their penalty shots with happy approximate dives. There was no question of second place: they needed a third to share the cost of a rental in Manchester in August. Summer had seen them before around the club, had envied their blondeness, their heads held high, and had admired their getups even though they had also irritated her with their hysterical giggles, the showy complicity of girls. James Diamantis must have watched the scene from the terrace of the lodge, radio glued to his ear, cigarillo under Panama hat, and when his daughter came back, he delicately inquired about what she would be doing in August, put a hand in his wallet, and gave her a nice pile of money.

A YEAR GOES by and Summer is admitted to the National School of Public Works. Her father takes her out that evening to celebrate her success – he had these conventional gestures that he dispensed with the ostentation of one who wants to appear as a man of principle, in spite of his debauched life. The scene takes place in a dance hall on rue de Malte: flattering chiaroscuro, champagne, "It Had to Be You," the passably decadent paraphernalia of an aging womanizer, this is what Summer thinks with her legs tangled under the chair. Before the floating islands arrive, James Diamantis places a construction hard hat on his daughter's plate, looks at her with a rare tenderness, says you'll have to start thinking about taking better care of yourself. Summer shakes her head, laughing, embarrassed, goes to the washroom, puts the hard hat on, looks at herself in the mirror, hands against the edge of the sink, thinks she looks awful, feels manipulated. And while the crooner slicks his hair back with brilliantine backstage before starting the second set, while her father listens to the messages on his cellphone, Summer, red, hurt, and feeling as though her brain has been slapped, grows drunk with rage and breaks the mirror with great swings of the hard hat.

IN HER LAST year of grad school, Summer chooses concrete as her specialty. People around her laugh, grimace, concrete, that's not attractive, not even a little bit sexy, what is she trying to prove? Are you sure, Summer? James asks her one day from his far-off planet and she, foolishly emboldened by the question, answers swiftly that, yes, quite sure, when she's specialized it will be easier to find work. You have such crazy ideas! James turns the pages of his paper, she's stuck there, furious, dries her lacrimal canals by sticking her index fingers in the corners of her eyes. More months pass and in the spring, the concrete gets its revenge. A dinner on the terrace, a candleholder, six place settings, wicker chairs, a short stool for James Diamantis in a new Panama hat – he's prepared the meal, let the wine breathe, cut a bouquet of wisteria, brushed his hat. The guests are their neighbours. Summer feels pretty, she talks, she drinks. This young lady is studying concrete, believe it or not; James serves the wine in unmatched glasses. A guy is there who Summer thinks is cute. He asks her what she does. Public works, I'm a concrete engineer. Oh. The guy lifts his head. His eyes screech over her and she knows now that they will spend the night together. He is amazed. That's exactly what I would have wanted to do, something strong, tangible, a job that's in direct contact with the real.

SUMMER WALKS away from the plant and reels towards the river, heart suddenly heavy, approaches a little stretch of green at the end of the quay, tufts of grass have cracked the asphalt, the water laps against the bank, she crouches down, pushes up her sleeves and redoes her ponytail, shakes her head, looks at the opposite bank, impenetrable, throws three stones in the water *hup hup hup*, a hummingbird manoeuvres close to the river, turquoise speck above the golden-brown liquid, I'm here now, I'm here now, she closes her eyes, I'm here, then stands up, dizziness, thinks hunger, jetlag, thinks tomorrow I have to be in good shape, knows finally where she is, black veil for a moment and then again the ecru sky.

AT THE OTHER END OF THE PONTOVERDE platform, Sanche Alphonse Cameron is also getting his bearings. His "office" is a windowed cabin, six feet square, set at the top of a tower crane, a translucent box more than a hundred and fifty feet above the ground. He reaches it via an elevator that slides up and down the mast, but some days, to be mischievous (read: to impress the crowd), he climbs two by two the bars of a hoop ladder without pausing on the landings. I'm staying in shape is what he claims when those on the ground are alarmed to see him rise, frail little guy, all the way up the structure. Once inside his cab Sanche sits at the console, back straight against the seat, and carries out the steps of taking his position – checks the control panel (headlights, joystick, walkie-talkies, function displays and graphic readouts, anemometer, push buttons); checks the brakes and the safety system; settles his hands on the controls and concentrates. He spots Summer crossing the esplanade, follows her determined silhouette with his eyes, watches her disappear behind the machines parked near the plant and then re-emerge at the water's edge, the blonde straw of her hair smooth in the sunlight, what's she up to?

He likes it in this technological enclave where his small size no longer causes him grief, since he is now a hundred and fifty-six feet four inches tall, since he is massive; he's comfortable in this paradoxical chamber that incorporates him into limitless space, while each movement is controlled to an eighth of an inch, in front of this dashboard that endows the tips of his fingers with an insane amount of power since each thrust of the joystick is a matter of precision, minutia, vigilance; he feels at home in this cramped room where, eight hours a day, the exemplary nature of Imperial units is proven, a system that calibrates space in relation to the human body, in relation to the foot, indeed, to his abdomen, to the jut of his nose like an eagle's beak, to his long slender feet and his baby giraffe's eyelashes. From up in the crane cab, Sanche casts a panopticon eye on the site and surroundings – this confers upon him a new sense of power from an ideal distance. He is the solitary epicentre of a landscape in motion, untouchable and cut off, he is the king of the world.

And yet, in the beginning, he lived on Earth like everyone else, and more precisely in Dunkirk – proletarian concrete, harbour industry, family tourism, cool cheeks and wind on your forehead, dunes and light beers – where he was born in the municipal hospital one Sunday in November 1978, the sole offspring in a late brood. It was a miracle: no one would have bet a cent on his mother, forty-two years old; she herself had long since stopped lighting candles to the Virgin, rubbing her belly with castor oil, or wearing red undergarments – she herself had stopped believing. The baby had barely uttered his primal cry and even though he presented a skinny little body accompanied by a disturbing face – flattened forehead, wrinkled yellowish skin, two black marbles that never blinked – he was already praised to the skies. He was the first and the last child, beauty itself and love personified. Amen, amen. But the father – what did he have to say? Nothing, precisely; he lay the stones of his dry silhouette against the counter of a seedy bar and kept quiet, dumbfounded by his paternity and even more flabbergasted by his wife – a girl from Alentejo who he met in a parish youth group and who had never had anything but conjugal attentions for him, an unvarying assortment of heavy meals, starched shirts, submissive nods of her head, and dominical sex – he remains prostrate, like the reckless driver caught by the patrol and stripped of a chunk of cash. He is no longer the master of his house: strengthened by her child, his wife has become a different woman, she radiates new strength. Rules the house, holds the purse strings, decides on the priorities, sings out loud. An end to the trembling hands and the little voice that begged for grocery money at the beginning of the week, an end to the sad evenings waiting for her old man, an end to shame and regrets. Life's course now hinges on a single axis: the child will be dressed like a prince, housed like a master, fed like a prelate: they'll bleed themselves dry. The father drives heavy loads between Dunkirk and Rotterdam or Paris, he's often absent, so the mother has free rein. Accumulates as many hours as she can to bulk up her wad: in the morning, housekeeping in the offices of the port, at noon the cafeteria of a private school downtown – she feeds her boy there before lunch is served, keeping aside the best pieces of meat for him, pinching the best fruit, doubling the portions – and in the evening takes care of the two little daughters of a bourgeois couple next door, children she observes with interest, and bases his education on them. She brushes Sanche's hair till it shines, drives him to the library, speaks to him in fine French. Enrols him in the same classical dance classes that the young neighbours go to – he is a little prince in white tights, held up as an example. Sanche is a frail, solitary, and precise child; clothed in ruffled wimples and royal-blue velvet knickers, he bounces around the living room. The father can't stand it, yells at his wife, you're making him into a little faggot, so he drags the child to the stadium on his Sundays off, Sanche is happy to please his father but catches a chill in the bleachers, a cold and an earache: the couple quarrels. At eleven years old, when people ask what he wants to do when he grows up, Sanche hesitates solemnly between a conductor and an archaeologist, ambitions that junior high erodes inescapably, that high school (private schools, his mother knows other housekeepers there) strives to tame: the boy is a good student, he needs a real job, why not the construction industry? With this direction, the boy keeps mum, the father is satisfied, the mother desolate. One morning she buttons up her black silk dress, belts her Alcantara coat with the rabbit-fur collar, and goes to deliver three determined knocks on the principal's door: her son is Portuguese, does that mean he has to become a mason? Well-argued protestation and cold anger shaded with the suspicion of racism: they're keeping us down. The two-faced principal reassures her, construction presents a Pleiades of occupations – positive impact of the word *Pleiades* on the mother who sees sparkling brilliance, and perhaps even a little bit of heaven – and finally, after obtaining a bachelor of technology, the crane reconciles everyone, tall and flamboyant, a centrepiece. Operating one requires superior qualifications, an eagle eye (a vision that resists glare and perceives relief), a fine ear (auditory acuity in a noisy environment is tested before getting a job), and the cold blood of a marksman. The becalmed mother accepts the crane, and sees in it an aristocratic position, one where you stay clean, sheltered, detached, with dry feet, high above the mass of workers who swarm below with their hands in the muck, sees it as a good position that could possibly come with middle-management status, while the father slips a word in Sanche's ear, you'll be cushy, free, no boss on your back, and adds as he puts an arm around his shoulders, complicit for the first time: like me in my truck.

Sanche suffers from neither vertigo nor the difficulty of working alone in a small space; he has a sense of balance and of responsibilities, a sense of safety – cranes are dangerous – and last but not least he's blessed with an incredible capacity for concentration: he's found his place. He learns to drive and operate cranes – lattice boom truck cranes, crawler cranes, telescopic cranes of all tonnages – he takes the related training courses for drillers, for equipment managers – he heads a team of thirty people on the site of a tunnel in Luxembourg – and goes overseas, Nouakchott, Mauritania, where he oversees loading and unloading operations between boats and the oil-rig drilling platform. It's here that he meets the man who introduces him to politics, and who he listens to at first simply in order to beat the boredom that comes when the breaks are long, when weariness takes over from fatigue. The man works on the rig, he's Portuguese like Sanche, took refuge in France during Salazar's wars. Over a couple of sleepless nights, while the warm and salty ocean air corrodes their skin just as it oxidizes the steel ladders, he introduces Sanche into a new immensity that echoes like a cathedral: the Revolution. His voice captivates the crane operator at first, black flow exploding everything in its passage – fuel like the oil they've come to extract off the coast of Africa. Words spin in the atmosphere, high-powered lassos able to capture the substance of thoughts, with a flick of the wrist capable of bringing to mind recalcitrant concepts that seem rather outmoded in this early twenty-first century. Sanche is drawn to the theory immediately, sees clarity in it, and power; he pronounces certain words for the first time, words like *peoples, dialectic, collective, alienation, emancipation,* words like *capital* and *oppression,* expressions like *historical materialism* or *enlightened avant-garde of the working class,* he turns them over on his tongue to feel their weight, their thickness, to appropriate them, as though these magical terms were the revelators of the world's logic, of its form, its mechanism, its flows, and its future. He takes all he can from this, it's a good warm-up, this is what he tells the man over their last handshake at dawn one morning in November, when the ardour of the all-night discussion has dried out both their mouths. After that, he returns to France, and his jobs are back to back without any time off; he becomes one of the best files in the temp agency that manages his career. And now: the bridge.

IT'S THE FIRST DAY OF THE BRIDGE, THE FIRST morning. Polaroid dawn. Blacks that lighten and whites that get darker, progressive pigmentation of all the greens – fluorescent, emerald, pistachio, olive, forest, lime, turquoise, Wrigley's Doublemint, spinach and malachite, chartreuse and mint cream – becoming fixed on the retina, and the river is there, supple, calm folds, long fluorescent grasses stretching out on the surface, thickets drift, as do cans and bottles: the water is milky and dirty.

Diderot has walked around the perimeter of the Pontoverde platform which is his domain from now on, a surface of two square miles, cleared out, asphalted, open to the river via a long empty quay and striated with rails that link hangars, workshops, maintenance and repair shops, team facilities, engineering offices, cafeterias, and locker rooms. And now he's smoking a Lusitania. In profile he really does have a big nose, a prominent chest; his Ray-Bans are pushed up on his forehead and his shirt is untucked, he's ready to go, he's exactly in his element, and at the bottom of his pocket his hand taps a secret tempo. It's the peak hour, the hour before all hands on deck, the hour of silence before battle, and the moment the skier stands poised at the top of a steep run – evaluate the slope before launching forward, visualize the route, go over the difficulties, the turns, the bumps, the hollows, the patch of black ice just after the twelfth gate, take note of possible acceleration zones, the exact flexion of the knees needed to jump and then glide on the last curve, the exact thrust of the chest, balance of the head, position of the arms – the hour of meteorological worry, and Diderot has his preferences, knows what he needs: continental climate, dry and rough winters, hot summers. For a man like him, there's nothing worse than rain, wind, and storms – nothing worse than mud.

ON THE OTHER side of the gates, the men are already waiting. The newcomers and the local workforce, silent types with hair in side parts, cigarettes dangling, clean hands, and lunch boxes tucked under their arms, guys in tracksuits, baseball caps front to back, visors at the neck or a hood hanging between the shoulder blades, young guys with cheap sneakers, a handful of women – but it's confirmed that there are no kids there, contrary to the rumour and the alerts from international organizations. Among them, in priority, are Natives aggregated in groups of three or four, solid, with closed faces, hired in large numbers since they're immune to vertigo and used to the climate, to parasites, familiar with the terrain because they're at home – the Boa had ordered their presence on-site, a neutralizing strategy. Of what awaits them, they know little. The unemployed Natives who had applied had asked about the qualifications to emphasize – which ones? And the hiring agent, the one who typed the names into the computer before handing over magnetic ID badges that allow them access to the site when swiped through the time clock, had pinched his biceps: qualifications, my darling, involve three things: muscle, muscle, and more muscle. No one had laughed, and everyone had showed up.

When the doors open, they move forward onto the site like a Roman tortoise. There are nearly eight hundred of them. Mo Yun is there, ready, a clean T-shirt over his hollow chest and miner's glasses around his neck, he looks all around him, trying to imitate those who surround him – only knows the words that ricochet off of kitchen sinks – and floats in the crowd like he floats in his blue-collar overalls nabbed at a thrift store for fifty cents, standing on tiptoe, head back so he can breathe more easily, so light that the human mass lifts him from the ground and moves him, so thin that he's carried along by the crowd, and among others by Duane Fisher and Buddy Loo, who force their way forward a few feet from him, don't want to let themselves be pushed around, outdistanced – the day before they had been able to sell part of their loot at a cruddy apartment in the Church district, a woman had weighed the gold on an electronic scale while a Doberman licked her feet, and once they'd pocketed the thin wad they immediately blew it all at the arcades, got all excited drinking warm beers at the consoles, laughing like kids with their hands on the joysticks, then went to catch the ferry to Edgefront when night had fallen, once their pockets were scraped down to the last quarter, and there, on the other bank, they had bummed around looking for some digs, some little squat where they could sleep, and without really knowing it, disoriented, they had walked towards the forest, that same forest that had held them like a fishing basket, the same one they had fled – and farther back, at the rear of the multitude, Katherine Thoreau moves forward, cellphone to her ear, tells her sons to buckle the little one well in her stroller if they go out along Colfax and reminds them to read, not to stay slumped in front of the TV all day, not to fight. And brushing past her without seeing her, Soren Cry, suspicious, hooded eyes, shady complexion, switchblade like a comb in the back pocket of his jeans.

All of them reach the workers' facilities after beeping their sesame at the front gate, and once they get to the locker room, take possession of the metal locker where they hang their clothes and grab their hard hats, mandatory since the construction of the Hoover Dam in Colorado and then the Golden Gate Bridge in San Francisco in the mid-1930s. They settle in and groups form instinctively: those who speak the same language, those who travelled here together, those who come from the same town – including the guys from Detroit, who were driven out of the city when the car factories closed down, twenty of them, young, a fearsome gang, it's as though a chain riveting their working strength to mechanized procedures had broken clean and liberated their gestures, so they take up space in the locker room, take big steps and windmill their arms, talk loud – and finally those who found themselves side by side in front of the gates and offered one another a light for their smokes. The Natives also gather together in a corner of the room, they're grey beneath the neon lights, slow, chests tattooed with foliage from shoulder blades to waists, they speak together in low voices. And then the siren sounds – now it's time to go.

IN THE MIDDLE OF THE HUGE WASTELAND THAT borders the river, a man shouts in a port voice, Anchorage One, Anchorage Two, and so on until Anchorage Six. Men jump from shuttle boats that have carried them along the river to here, move forward on the quay built roughly against the edge of the bank, and form small teams that walk towards the end of the work site where two enormous stationary machines sparkle in the sun.

ANCHORAGE. ANCHOR the bridge. Dig to ensure solid foundations for the structure: two holes in the riverbed to plant the piers that will hold up the towers, and another hole on each bank – thirty million cubic yards of concrete will be poured before the cables are placed.

Tackle the bridge from below, then, start from where it's darkest, dirtiest, most elementary, begin in reverse, advance by receding, start by subtracting, digging, emptying, smashing. Work like a dog. We are dogs, this is what Diderot thinks as he docks in the Zodiac and it hits him once again that in order to create a work, to erect it before the eyes of the world, to make it rise up from the ground, you have to first stick your head into the dirt and the depths of the ground. And Mo Yun, who's wiping his precious glasses on the fabric of his overalls, says exactly the same thing to himself, because he's one of those who thinks first about the hole before evaluating the structure. He remembers that there were not always mines in Datong, they didn't just appear one fine morning as though issued from a divine breath, chasms nearly seven hundred feet deep buttressed like cathedrals, complete with open-wire cages to carry men and mine-cart tracks down, no, these gigantic caverns had to be built, and one day, walking between his parents in the red mud that coated the city streets as soon as the first rains came, an idea had seized him, alarmed him, and with his feet sunk in the ground of the People's Square (transformed into a thick and viscous wading pool), he had asked his parents: what was here before? What was here, even before Datong shone as a first-class industrial city of the People's Republic? The man and woman, of the same height and wiry build, had frowned, and then remembered, as through a haze, emerging for a moment from the coma of labour – yes, they had known the city when it was still covered in green, the suburbs where miserable little troglodyte hovels had proliferated, the skinny fowl and the little grey pig, they had known the ground when it was intact, but were sincerely puzzled by their son's question, because that was a long, long time ago; it was another time, a time before the Revolution – in other words, before the light of Reason had shone across the country; that was the prehistory of humanity and they lowered their eyes chastely, surprised, it's true, they had been among those who had built the tool that rendered them useful, that had made them into agents of Progress, with their own hands they had made the iron cage that had thrown them below, they had dug the holes.

Mo looks at the field and looks at the men, fear sweeps the ground out from under him, his head spins, and he has to fight the urge to run away. Before him, the excavators warm up their motors and set themselves in motion, slowly, mechanical mastodons capable of digging a hole the size of a football field and eighty feet deep in a single day. His eyes widen and he stifles a cry, he thinks he recognizes them; they've travelled all the way from the open-pit mines, all the way from Datong, from the crucible of black mud that he'd left behind. They've found him here, crossed the ocean and come up the river at a high price, in dismantled pieces they've come to remind him. The men assembled are admiring them, ah, the heavy artillery of Pontoverde, while Mo is seized by a nightmare, stunned, no longer hearing the foreman who harangues them as though they're an army heading into combat – boys, we're attacking the anchorage phase, we've got a bridge to build, a bridge that will be the most beautiful bridge in the world – Mo panics, tucks his head down between his shoulders, and moves forward to dissolve into the Anchorage Five team.

A HUNDRED and fifty feet from Mo, Soren Cry's head also spins – crazy, all these guys in a daze – at the first shout of *anchorage*. But it's not the proclamation of the inaugural phase of construction that he hears, not these orders shouted as though they were performing a military manoeuvre, leaving the barracks, not this bombast meant to galvanize the workers: it's the call of a wolf that tears at him, and with it the shame of having been thrown out of paradise lost. In another life, Soren Cry had lived in Anchorage, Alaska – he would speak of it like this, he would say "in another life," because this past no longer belongs to him, he can't even tell the story, but oh he feels it like a burning brick in the back corner of his brain; he had liked his life there, felt no different from the other guys who passed through the place, men disinclined to conversation, seasonal workers whose focus was hardly distracted by bowling, beer, and sex. Soren works as a carpenter first, on a boat-building site. After three days, he calls his mother from a telephone booth at lunchtime – an extraordinary gesture for him, since he doesn't really speak anymore – clears his throat and says: I'm gonna stay here, this is the city for me, I think it's gonna work out. At the other end of the line, the woman with her hair in pale-green rollers and a housecoat the same colour nods her head without really knowing what to think, this enthusiasm is suspicious, doesn't sound like Soren – so incapable she is of seeing the possibility of such a conversion in him, she imagines at first that he's in the clutches of a sect, drugged, in danger. Meanwhile in Anchorage, Soren likes living far away from his mother, loves the blue light and the glassy cold. The darkness that bathes the streets eight months out of twelve saves him from his own ugly face. It gives him a second skin that protects, a camouflage that hides: he dissolves into the polar night with a newfound joy and quickly gets used to this place, this wild life where men live side by side with great furred mammals: bears make garbage out of houses, linger in the change rooms of stadiums, swagger on the shores; moose hang out in the parking lots of supermarkets; grizzlies venture right up to the doors of the McDonald's; and finally, above all, there are wolves. Death prowls, men are armed, all around are enormous and carnivorous animals, and Soren feels more alive here than he has anywhere else and makes his way among all of them. Once the construction is finished, he becomes a warehouseman in a fish factory, then a bus driver. In the end he knows the city like the back of his hand, the smallest street, the most unremarkable suburb. He drives his little yellow four-wheel-drive bus, picks up kids after school, helps the disabled, even waves to the old folks. Often after his shift, when night has fallen, he drives north, gets out of the car, and moves forward into hostile nature. At the foot of the first ice hills, he listens to the rustling of space, becomes part of it. Listens to the wolves. Calls to them. Then one night a woman is there, recording the pack, crouching in the dark. These human cries are wrecking her work, she shouts at him in the night. In the end they find each other in the darkness – she's a researcher in a zoology lab, he knows the place well. Soon she comes to live with him in his one-bedroom apartment where the electric heat dries out their hair and makes their eyes red. Soren cooks for her, they drink quietly and go out on farther and farther excursions into the wild. And then it all goes to shit. One morning, Soren flees the city, takes the first plane for Chicago, gets on a Greyhound, eyes glazing before the dreary, muggy countryside that comes back to him all at once, sticky as fate. He heads towards Kentucky. The next morning, seeing him come through the door of their house, his mother understands but says nothing. He sits down on the couch, takes off his shirt: his winter coat is spattered with brownish stains and so are the bottoms of his jeans. She doesn't ask any questions, just stuffs everything into the washing machine and turns it on, so happy he's home.

THE EXCAVATORS churn up the ground, the men dig, and they're off. The field seems to offer itself up without resistance, loose, cleared now of all human habitation, though the imprints of geometric shapes in the earth attest to the fact that, until just recently, this ground was occupied. Strips of thick grass border these bare surfaces, traces of tires brush them, some tracks layered so thickly they leave crevices in the earth; there are several stinking pits, hearths covered with fine-grained ash, and if you look closely, if you pay attention as you lean closer to the ground, you can still find lots of things here to fill a trash can.

Diderot trips over a deflated soccer ball and tucks it under his arm. He knows little about the expropriation campaign that preceded the start of the project. On this field, for example, the inhabitants had been reluctant to leave, complicating the task of the men from Pontoverde. The latter had protested at first – no one here possesses the least title of ownership, in fact these people are nothing but squatters who, after years, put their mobile homes up on concrete blocks, slapped a roof onto their sophisticated tents, weatherproofed their wood cabins – like the second little piggy's house – dwellings all rigged up with satellite antennae on the roofs. Nothing worse than squatters' rights, the Boa had cursed, scratching his head, we're screwed. Pontoverde had finally hurried in an armada of super-technical young lawyers armed with laughable repossession notices, but the people were dogged and quick, they knew their rights, the jurists didn't have a leg to stand on and the furious Boa demanded they be sent home: he would do the negotiating himself. New, functional lodgings in the suburbs of the city were offered to the inhabitants. Some of the women went to visit them, suspicious, haughty, inspecting the taps, testing the switches, flushing the toilets. They came back spitting no, rather die than leave their homes. Cameras were set up in the field and before long these families were given the chance to speak every evening. Their refusal to submit was praised, as were their contempt for modernity and their freedom. The sausages speared on sticks and cooked over a wood fire, barefoot kids growing like wild grass, the warmth of community against the anonymity of prefabricated houses, urban solitude, and individualist instincts. These images warbled of endless holidays, the coolness of poor-but-happy princes: the inhabitants of the field became heroes. According to the Boa, all this was a bluff, and the bids rose higher. He smiled: would they really prefer their potholed strip of grass on the river's edge to a new duplex, these tribes, these huge families, these marginal, long-haired characters? But soon, weary and fearing the negative effects of a police raid at dawn, billy clubs in hand, evacuating the dwellings and pushing screaming families into vans before work on the bridge even began, the Boa turned again to Pontoverde. The company would compensate the inhabitants, pay for the moving costs, and find housing for everyone downtown.

A MILE TO the south, Duane Fisher and Buddy Loo jumped onto the dredger, side by side – these two are joined at the hip, sleep under the same blanket at night, drink from the neck of the same bottle in the same tin shack hidden on the green bank – watched the movement of the group on the beach behind, and were soon spotted by the engineer Verlaine, who took down their names in a spiral notebook before leading them through increasingly narrow passageways into the machine room where the din was so loud no one spoke anymore. Duane and Buddy had never been in a boat of this size – the dredger is a hefty vessel, some hundred feet long, fifty wide, equipped with a hydraulic drilling machine capable of digging up to sixty feet deep, attached to which are vacuum tubes and discharge nozzles; these two only know dugouts propelled by motors borrowed from speedboats whose owners tanned dark in the Fifties, off the coast of Florida, water-skis bikinis fishing all with big jugs of rum coconut whisky lots of quick turns and vertical jets of water like celestial rain; they only know pistons unscrewed quickly, brokedown cars where you'd attach an axle and a propeller, and Verlaine's aware of this, the guys they send him are always the same – there isn't a single one who has a clue, he seethes; conversely, Verlaine himself (who's sometimes seen in the Gare du Havre when he goes home to visit his two sons) only knows service boats, dredgers, tugboats, the barge that never leaves port and hobbles along in the canal on one foot, lame, with a measured step. Duane and Buddy are appointed to control of outflow – they keep an eye on the regularity of flow in the pumps, make sure the motors don't overheat, it's a job that requires a good ear, and these boys have two each (so at least they aren't deaf); you have to hear when it shakes, when it drags, and when it gets tired, Verlaine explains all of this to them in rudimentary English, and at every chance he gets joins the action to the word.

THE DREDGER advances slowly in the river's current, heavy and stubborn; it clears out, scrapes, sucks, scours the riverbed of all the shit that's been thrown there, that's still thrown there, day after day; blasting the channel, it's hailed as the marvellous irreplaceable scullery maid, as its enormous drill with three heads – three times the strength and power of the best deep-water oil-drilling rig – digs into the rock to carve out a passage for the hulls of majestic ships, freighters, and state-of-the-art oil tankers. The two boys take a step back in front of the tanks where the riverbed is poured out, blackish sludge of sediment risen from the depths, ageless alluvium, no sparkle in there, nothing, still they watch for a section of a wreck, a piece of iron, some human debris, maybe a skull, yeah, a skull or a chest full of gemstones, a treasure, yeah, that would be awesome. They're getting excited, grinning, seeking nothing, hoping for nothing, not even luck, for the future has no form for those who live day to day, with no other weight on their shoulders than the weight of youth. They hold out their hands with vast palms and able fingers, always ready to take the next gamble, to make a little cash, always ready to take off on the next bullshit plan.

IN THE FOURTH week, the divers show up. There are fifty of them. Their aura precedes them, plume of anguished admiration, and when they get out of the black vans from the Deep Seawork Co., jumping out one after the other in agile bounds executed at regular intervals – Navy commandos when it comes to projects – everyone scrutinizes their faces the colour of Dove soap, their heroic faces. After which their reputation pushes its way through the crowd of assembled workers, the waters part, the divers advance in slow steps, relaxed, large sports bags slung over their shoulders. Among them, the deep-sea divers get the most attention: amphibious creatures twenty thousand leagues under the sea, they elbow dragonfish, moray eels, and lantern fish, graze stray jellyfish migrating towards the surface, caress the bellies of cetaceans, and tug on the moustaches of seals, are blinded by plankton suspended in the bars of light, marvel at the coral, collect strange algae; multiplane workers, they walk helmeted with heavy feet upon the earth's crust, a hookah giving them something to breathe from the surface; frogmen who dive with webbed feet, a reserve of oxygen attached ad hoc to their backs. These are mutant men, and the darkness of the abyss is their office, their factory, this is where they toil, repair, weld, smash, explode, dynamite the riverbed, pulverize the sedimentary layer, cut the banks anew, level the shallows; this is where they assist with the drilling operations launched by the engineers above water, activating a satellite system on the surface able to integrate the least variation in the earth's curve, they control the extraordinary precision of the work – they are as meticulous as box hedges planted in a French garden. Underwater, their lungs inflate, bit by bit hold the compressed air; their rib cages crack under the pressure, their hearts are heavy inside, but little by little they adapt and beat more slowly, and their malleable bodies hold up.

DIDEROT GREETS them personally, shakes the hand of the team leader for a long moment, a small man with a waxy pallor who he recognizes from projects in the Port of Busan, South Korea, where reinforced seawalls had required powder, he's very pleased they're here: internationally renowned divas, the boys from DSC are mostly old minesweeper divers cast aside by the army and who now transfer their experience from one site to another – and their participation comes at a pretty penny – Pontoverde must have stretched the cash, quality doesn't come cheap.

Their plan: prepare the riverbed for the foundations to come. Knock down the base rock, locate the flaws, then break the crust with explosives – dynamite will be tossed down from the surface in fat steel pilings. The divers will work blind, the waters are murky here, muddy, full of alluvium, they'll have to be prepared for strong currents, for strange centrifugal swirls and unpredictable draughts from gas escaping, from the resurgence of springs, or from climatic hazards that can swell the water's rate of flow and speed its course. Diderot warns them of all this in a low voice in the intimacy of the meeting room. Then, he continues, we'll hammer sheet piles into the bedrock and line them with concrete so that, once sealed and weather-proofed, they will form cofferdams, each of which can contain nine million gallons of water, then we'll pump out these giant pockets before pouring a hundred cubic yards of concrete into them and they'll become the indestructible sheaths for the towers to come. A herculean anchoring.

IT TAKES A FULL DAY'S DRIVE ALONG THE logging road and then a walk for several hours along the path to reach the Native village. A pathway furrowed by rains and full of potholes, obscured by huge toppled trees, disappearing at times beneath giant ferns or even the carcass of an animal. This route has its dangers – the risk of being attacked by a carnivorous mammal is high, and the risk of getting lost is even higher. Better to take a motorboat upstream from Coca, then switch over to a dugout and paddle the two days' journey to the village. To arrive at the end of the day, when the children are swimming in the river, splashing each other playfully, some diving in the waterfalls and others fishing with blowpipes; when the men are strolling and smoking, the women are talking, while the evening air settles with an incredible softness. This is also the time of day when Jacob makes the coffee, spooning grinds and pouring water into a large Italian coffee maker placed on the fire pit in front of his house, and he waits there, for the coffee to heat and for the villagers, his friends, to stop by and drink it with him in white tin mugs.

THIS PARTICULAR evening, hearing of the construction of a motorway bridge over the river, Jacob is seized by a tremendous fatigue. He swallows his coffee in small sips, his gaze running over the surface of the water, opaque now, and reflecting, through the green canopy, fragments of a spilled-milk sky. In the spring, it will have been twenty years that he's been coming here, for long stretches at a time; twenty years that he's been studying this small community besieged by history, and doing its utmost to ignore it. He's changed a lot, of course – the young intellectual, fresh from Santa Fe, armed with his belief in the power of ideas and determined to describe this precious alveolus of unchangingness with rational transparency, has little in common with the man who, this evening, thinks that a society cannot be deducted from a system, and for whom living here one semester out of two means investing in a different way in his own existence. The matching half of his year plays out in Berkeley. A few men from the community have arrived by now, and are drinking coffee with him, joking around; passing women greet them, their hair smoothed back from their foreheads and held with obsidian combs, their faces wide, cheekbones full, they laugh, hip to hip, one of them pregnant beneath a large white T-shirt emblazoned with the Los Angeles Lakers logo. Jacob lights a cigarette – never could bring himself to smoke anything but lights – he knows perfectly well how intrusive roads are, is aware of the probable degradation of the forest, the planned disappearance of the Natives, and has already been struggling for a long time against nostalgia: he won't be the herald of an academic ethnography, and he won't be a pitiful scholar; no, he'd rather die than that. And yet, in this moment – the coffee hour, peaceful hour when fullness is so complete it hurts, like a stone in the belly – when the heart feels squeezed inside the rib cage – he's thinking only of his life, his life here and now, and his greatest emotion is for this present, wearing thin. His fatigue comes from this. He places his mug down on the white wicker table and goes inside to lie down. He needs to sleep.

WE MIGHT ask how Jacob got wind of the story of a bridge in Coca – we could imagine the murmur of the construction site travelling all the way to him, slipped between the scales of a fugitive trout, hidden beneath the wings of a junco or perched on the petiole of a hardworking ant that made its way right to the heart of the massif via some network of underground tunnels. But really it was just men, always the same ones, who'd come upstream from Coca – people like you and me – bringing the news. These guys trade with the villages of the "interior," know how to reach them without danger, branching off into one arm of the river, then another narrower one, and another still, following a path that only they know in the aquatic labyrinth that webs the forest. It's they who, among other things, bring Jacob his bricks of coffee and his cartons of smokes. And this evening, like every other time, they docked their boat in front of the village houses, unloaded bundles of clothes and blankets, cases of canned goods, batteries, a television and two radios, then went like everyone else over to Jacob, who'd seen them coming and held out mugs to them, lifting a hand in the air – hey guys, come on over, come over here. There are three of them – two brawny guys and a teenager with an orange cap, and they come, shaking hands with "the professor" – that's what they call Jacob – then the two older ones give instructions for the transaction, quantities that Jacob translates using categories like *a little*, *a bit more*, and *a lot*, and the Natives start bringing out the baskets – baskets of a rare beauty, woven baskets whose round bellies depict the cosmos, very high-quality baskets. This is when the young one with the orange cap starts talking about the bridge in Coca – soon we won't be coming anymore, it won't be worth it, we'll load up a truck and all this will be done in a day's work, in two shakes of a lamb's tail! He has his hands in his pockets, concludes by saying that'll be faster, huh, we won't have to sleep outside anymore, and he smiles while kicking at the pine cones that carpet the ground; and Jacob, who has been watching the coffee maker, turns, looks him deep in the eyes and asks softly, controlling his surprise and feigning nonchalance, oh yeah, is that right, they're building a bridge in Coca? The boy takes the bait and goes on, yeah, an awesome thing, six lanes they say, it'll give us some breathing room, they've already started, they're planning it out, you've gotta see it! Jacob hands him a metal box while a few yards away the men load the baskets into the boat, careful to cover them with plastic tarps, sugar? He speaks so sharply that the boy jumps and takes his hat off quickly, his hair's ginger, as orange as the fabric of his hat, he splutters, yes, two cubes, and when Jacob hands him his cup, he takes it in one hand, holding it against his chest like a man, and squares his shoulders. The men have finished loading. One of them looks at his watch – a ridiculous gesture in these parts – and says, time to hit the road, let's go. They want to stop for the night in another village, shaking the professor's and the Natives' hands – the youngest doesn't dare look at Jacob, vaguely aware of having said too much, of having been the bird of ill omen – and hop into their boat that rocks gently. The kids see them off, shouting between branches or clinging onto the hull; the men in the boat don't pay them any attention, occupied with manoeuvring the boat out, and finally the kids wade back towards the banks, and it seems then that the trees bow down towards the river, that the long grasses draw in along the banks, supple as elastic, and once again it's the village that smokes, calm that hums in the forest gangue, this infinitely dilated realm at the heart of nature, this little pocket of time: the cleft of life that Jacob has chosen.

THE NIGHT is far along when Jacob leaves his house and walks the length of the river, getting farther and farther from the village. The blackness is thick, dense, saturated with matter and noise, and Jacob uses his ears to navigate. The starlight barely passes through the canopy – too many zigzags, too many ricochets to perform – but when it does penetrate, there are shinings soft as paraffin that touch a stone, a leaf, a point of water, providing shadows to Jacob's body, a third dimension; in other words, something with which to construct space, something to help him move forward. At the base of a tree, cold and damp, is a dugout. Jacob unties it, pulls it to the water, climbs in. He pushes off from the bank with the end of his paddle and soon he's floating through the wood. Though he knows the way, he's never left the forest at night, alone – a sensitive operation, similar to astronauts' excursions into space, when excitement and terror combine deep within the same gut.

SLOWLY, JACOB glides through the humid woods, alert, on his guard. Knows he should turn when the sound of the water rises – a sign he's coming close to a stronger, faster current. It would be a mistake to trust the regularity of his movements, the care he takes not to hit the surface of the water too violently, precisely to avoid a slap and the clamour that might prevent him from hearing – even for a second – the murmur of the massif; a mistake to trust the precision of his movements, his buttocks contracted inside the boat, his chest held straight, his face open, and his eyes that work to tear through the aniline night – it would be a mistake to trust all this because it's a fever that makes him do it. A black fever, sprung from anger, a suffocation of bile.

THOUGH HE never managed to find sleep that night, he had at first stretched out on his back in bed, completely still, eyes closed – then turned on his side, changing tactics, but the face of the red-headed kid, announcing the construction of the bridge, kept coming back to him wide and vivid as a screen, disproportionate, then a shot of his feet, his hands in his pockets as he kicks at the pine cones, or laughing at the kids who see them off from the water waist deep when they're about to leave, tapping their knuckles to make them let go when they hang on to the edge of the boat; and Jacob hears him repeat that expression like a fatal omen, *in two shakes of a lamb's tail*; and when he finally got up, wanting to grab his book, the jinx of dizziness washed over him, he swayed, his legs turned to jelly, he was sweating like crazy – and we should specify that what poured out of him and trickled down his body was nothing like the liquid he secretes in the sweat lodge when he's invited, no, this was venom, a bitter, animal liquid, concentrate of spite and rancour. Once he felt steady, Jacob remained upright for a long time, stiff as a stake in the middle of his house and suddenly – like a match struck – prey to the explosion of his will, he got dressed and left.

JACOB ROWS for another day and another night in the visceral forest. He cleaves the peat moss, parts the mangrove, dodges the waterfalls. Fever and anger serve as fuel and fact and he speeds along, drinking nothing but resinous alcohol from a plastic flask, not eating or smoking, he twists in the rapids, surfs the current; by day catching glimpses of deer, wild boar, but not a lynx in sight; bumping into a group of students rafting who are whooping it up so loudly they hardly notice him, narrowing his eyes at a few Natives gathering stones from the shore, men from other villages, holding his breath at night, when the shadows lengthen poisonous, absolutely inhuman, when he feels he'll suffocate, succumbing to the nocturnal beauty, fascinated, eyes rolling back, lips dry, the desire to scream strangling his larynx. He doesn't sleep. He's gathered the tension in his body as though condensing material into a cannonball – he holds himself slightly forward, concentrating on capturing the smallest flux in the water that could speed his course and carry him forward effortlessly, focused on loosening the energies around him, on recycling his anguish and agitation into each of his gestures, and strangely his exhaustion vitrifies his fury, keeps it intact.

AT DAWN on the second day, when the buildings of Coca rise up suddenly perpendicular to the surface of the water, it's a different man who paddles out of the woods, a man beside himself. The sun rises, ricochets off glass and steel facades, iridesces the shimmering rainbows of hydrocarbon slicks that ring the waters, and the triangular plates of metal festooning the edges of the dugout – like a set of open jaws – sparkle in the light.

Catching a glimpse of the dugout as they pass, drivers speeding along the banks at this early hour widen their eyes in the rear-view mirrors, slowing dangerously, and later, arriving at their offices, head towards the tower windows to watch the guy's progression, call one another over, check it out, there's a strange one down there, see him? And, upon waking, riverside residents raise the window blinds and end up going out onto their balconies. It's not the dugout that shocks them, no, there are lots of those around here – rather, it's seeing him, this livid man who rows with his back straight as a rod, his black tie like an Ottoman sabre across his chest over the white shirt, the dark velvet scholarly jacket, the white socks peeking out of moccasins – where'd this guy come from?

COMING UPON the anchorage sites on both sides of the river, and struck by the enormousness of their surface area and the multitude of machines, Jacob slows, holds the paddle horizontal and throws his head back, throat taut as a bow; he floats slowly on the calm water, minuscule wavelets explode softly against the hull – a freeway over the river, six lanes, the sky is the colour of votives.

He takes a long breath and sets off again, with great strokes of the paddle in the river, *splash splash*, sounds that punctuate his progress, and finally passes the river shuttles, pot-bellied as teapots, armoured with divers and workers who move lively over the anchorage sites, their wake lifting the dugout that pitches, vacillates; sprayed, Jacob reawakens and suddenly spots a large stretch beside the bank that sparkles, silvery, and goes closer to see better. Dead fish float in the dozens, thrown up from the depths by the explosions, their eyes open and staring. Anger seizes him again, exhaustion leaves his body, he glides along beside the stinking, macabre pool, lips pressed together so as not to scream, and each stroke of the paddle injects him with new energy to carry on. Soon he comes in sight of the long quay of the Pontoverde platform, where silhouettes cram together onboard a final shuttle like the ones he passed earlier – same colours, same initials. Here it is, he thinks, suddenly rowing like mad.

He moors his dugout under the concrete mixing plant, beside the wasteland, and drags himself out of the hull. The sky has turned grey from the coal. He clambers up the bank, clinging to handholds, then pulls himself up straight – and surprisingly, he doesn't faint. He's hungry, thirsty, wants a coffee. Summer Diamantis, who at this moment is walking towards her batch plant after the daily site meeting, frowns at the sight of this vaguely disturbed form, crumpled clothes and bare head, and turns as she's passing with a mechanical torsion – who's this guy without a hard hat? – yet doesn't slow her step – what's occupying her mind at the moment are the latest concrete mixing trials. So much so that Jacob is able to walk the entire length of the esplanade with a confident stride, right up to the main building, without being stopped. The rain begins to fall. This is when Diderot pushes open the door, anxious about the sky.

From the top of the three short steps that lead to the door of the building, he asks the guy in front of him, who he takes immediately to be an intruder, you there, what are you doing here? Jacob has come to a standstill at the bottom of the stairs, says flatly, are you the one in charge? His arms rest by his sides but the milky blue of his eyes worries Diderot

just as much as the sky that melts now and coughs up rain
in big warm drops, what a mess. The one in charge of what?
Diderot speaks without aggression but with impatience, and
begins to step heavily down the stairs to talk to this guy – but
he's stopped on the second step by Jacob's hand that comes
up against the centre of his chest, the long knotted fingers
spread wide over the fabric of the shirt that grates, the
palm made metallic by its hardness, are you in charge of
this construction site, yes or no? Diderot freezes. His eyes
scan Jacob from head to toe, rapidly, without noticing any
suspicious bulges where a weapon might be concealed, and he
pushes the hand away firmly, begins to step down to the last
step, saying yes I am, what's it to you, and with these words,
the hand that was pushed away comes back hard against his
stomach, gathered into a fist, *bang*. The blow catches Diderot
off guard as does the storm that he hears rumbling far off
and he folds over, staggers, then collapses against Jacob, who
falls backwards and the two men roll on the ground. They lie
there a moment, inert, long enough for the rain to speckle
their clothes with dark spots that quickly cluster into a single
patch, long enough for the esplanade to become glazed and
transform into mucky clay, till finally they make a move
to stand up. Diderot turns to his side and uses the ground
to press himself up while Jacob, already standing, teeters
on skinny legs, the knobs of his ankles protruding under
the white cotton of his socks, easily visible beneath pants
that are too short. He's the one looking down on Diderot
now, dominating him with his height and a body that's ten
years younger. But in the next second he doesn't stand so
tall – taken by surprise at this primitive move, a punch, a jab
straight to the gut, when all he wanted – he'd swear it – was
to sit down at a table and discuss the thing with this big man,
he seems like a good guy, explain his point of view calmly,
show him how this bridge he's building will bring destruction
and extinction, how he'll be part of tragedy and loss, and how

directing this thing makes him a kind of killer. Instead, as though the rain drumming down had harassed his thought, preventing it from forming into a possible sentence, as though the soaked, muddy esplanade had sucked his words deep into the cesspool, he takes a breath and spits, *bastard!* There's brutality in this hirsute body gripped by violence, in this voice that insults and hurls even though the body is stiff, but it's a brutality that Diderot doesn't calculate, suddenly bristling, seized by fury, this nutso better not piss me off too much, is all he thinks to himself. Once he's up, the pain in his stomach hooks him again, it kills, and this annoys him, he's the one in charge. Head down he ploughs into Jacob like a bison, like a locomotive, a squall of muscles and fat, the blow is violent, Jacob gasps, suddenly breathless, takes a step back, and once again is flat on his back. The spongy ground welcomes him with a hiss of sludge. Diderot steps forward and stands over him now, enormous, one leg on either side of him, you have two seconds to get lost, two seconds before I call someone. But Jacob, who he thought had been neutralized, down for the count, rears up again, grabs him by the ankles with his two tense hands, pulls him forward, and Diderot falls on his ass again, *splash*. It's a fight, then. The two men hit each other in succession, one after the other, an interval of a couple of seconds between each clout, a breath between each slap, one after the other they grab each other by the collar with one purple fist while the other gathers into a ball of force, pulling back behind a shoulder and hurtling forward like a projectile against the cheek, hooking the nose, the ear, the brow; they bash each other, both slow and heavy, clumsy, and it's crazy to see how they resemble each other now, their clothes the same colour because of the mud, eyes blistered, crimson and sweating under the deluge. If you'd been there to see the combat – the bridge against the forest, the economy against nature, movement against immobility – you wouldn't have known who to cheer for. In the end, Diderot, finished, steps back staggering, turns halfway, but Jacob's voice behind him holds him still: look at me, asshole. Diderot freezes, hesitates to turn again, turns, you talking to me? Jacob stands, filthy, holding out a knife he just pulled from his sock, shitty little knife that doesn't scare Diderot but whose blade is rubbed with lemon-yellow sharpening ointment, a thick paste acting on the steel blade like resin on the bow of a violin. You talking to me? Diderot takes a step forward. Yeah, Jacob has lowered his hand and now he states in a formal voice: I demand that the work be stopped – his glottis goes up and down his trachea but his eyes don't blink. Don't be ridiculous, Diderot sighs, now get out of here. He shivers, the rain intensifies, and the air cools off. The guys on the site must be wading in this shit, we'll have to be careful of landslides, risks of rising water levels, he has to go now, pivots to call the guards, he's back to the bottom of the three steps when he hears a noise at his back again and whips around, exasperated. Brilliance of the blade, a burning in his side, blood that spurts, a thousand candles. Jacob disappears.

PUDDLES HAVE formed now, spread out over the surface of the large Pontoverde platform, fairly large and fairly deep pools, these are the ones making the rain sound, making its splat oppressive. One of them stars outward at the base of the three steps of the main building– men's boots had pressed into the ground in this very spot, their heavy soles marking the ground – and it's here that Diderot lies, his eyes on the sky. No one has come out yet to see what's happening outside – can it possibly be true that they haven't heard the brawl? Can it possibly be true that, polarized in front of computer screens where forecasts of bad weather appear, and holding their breath as they contemplate disturbances, they've gone deaf? Barely three minutes have passed since the end of the scrap and Diderot's losing blood – his shirt has blossomed red-violet over his stomach, and is dripping scarlet into the puddle; he doesn't try to extract himself from the mud, doesn't make a move, relaxed now, calm, and his consciousness, floating in the vague indentations of the sky, repatriates large bells above his forehead that ring out: *bastard, bastard!*

THE SAME word that Katherine Thoreau yelled with her fist raised at the bus driver after he started driving again while she was hammering on the door, hey, open the door, please, hey! But the little man paid no attention, didn't look at her: this wasn't a bus stop, it was a traffic light, a red one, at the edge of a seedy intersection on Colfax. A disaster for Katherine, who puckers her lips as she looks at her watch now and flies into a panic: if she's not there on time to punch in, if she misses the river shuttles to the sites once again, she'll take a wage penalty, or even lose her job, for sure, shit, shit. In a rage, she kicks the hydro pole standing there, winces, turns, catches sight of a figure reflected in the glass of a motorcycle dealership, a full-length silhouette, Katherine observes it and then goes nearer: a pretty woman still, forty or maybe a little older, tall, a fuchsia parka too thin to keep the winter out enwraps her abdomen and reveals it heavy – breasts and belly – without much of a waist anymore; acid-wash jeans hug thin legs cushioned by a pair of dirty sneakers, thick brown hair at the roots lightens to flavescent at the shoulders, reddish straw clogged with badly maintained curls, her nails are bitten to the quick and the skin of her hands is dry and lined, a little gold chain with a heart pendant is her only piece of jewellery; it's not that she's ugly, or dirty, no – you can see that this is the kind of woman who only owns one bra but who washes her underwear in the sink, the kind of woman who soaps herself vigorously, tongue pressed between her lips – it's just that when you see her, you sense poverty. Katherine Thoreau stares at her reflection, she's tired, her eyes adhere, wrinkles deepen in her reddened skin and give her a sad look but she doesn't think she looks half-bad in the mirrored glass, she's not done for, with a few dollars, a haircut, wrinkle creams, and some rest, she could still have appeal; but at seven in the morning, she grits her teeth to keep going, to hold on and not get the hell out of here leaving them behind to fend for themselves, the four of them, her depressive husband, her demanding boys, her little girl who's teething. The night had taken a bad turn: at three in the morning when she couldn't take it anymore, she got up from the sofa bed to turn off the TV that Lewis's eyes were glued to, *I at least have to sleep if I want to be able to work tomorrow* she said in a syrupy voice, a voice that humiliated her husband because, brandishing an ashtray, he suddenly spat out, dammit! I don't want you to go back to that fucking site, all those guys checking out your ass, I know that's why you do it, to get them hard, I know it, you think I'm stupid but you better watch it, I'm warning you, and Kate, stunned, thinking of her days – hard hat on her head, visor down over her nose and crammed into a machine for ten hours in a row clearing out the backfill in the anchorage hole, the abominable racket that leaves her dazed when the evening siren finally sounds – had laughed a superior laugh, which conveyed to Lewis his impotence – she might just as well have called him a loser, asked him how he thought he would do it, practically, to stop her from going to work – a laugh that she stretched out with a contemptuous smile, okay sure, I'll stop going, later guys, I quit, but tell me if you're not a complete idiot how you think we'd manage? What would we live on? She was planted with her hands on her hips in her polyester housecoat and couldn't dodge the ashtray when it was thrown against her temple, *bang*, let out a scream that she quickly stifled with a hand to her open mouth because at that moment Matt, her oldest boy, had pushed open the front door and he was drunk, everyone had bellowed insults, and the younger boy, Liam, suddenly appearing in his pyjamas in the middle of the living room had, as usual, thrown himself sobbing against his mother, and the electric atmosphere had not failed to wake the littlest one, it's true that they were all on edge and squeezed like sardines into this shitty condo. Later, when they were lying down again on the sofa bed, the little one between them with her soother in her mouth, Katherine had said firmly to Lewis, say you're sorry, and he'd mumbled sorry then taken her hand across the child, and they held each other like that in the darkness until sleep overtook them.

NOW KATHERINE Thoreau is shuffling along Colfax smoking butt after butt, and when she finally catches sight of the bus she looks at her watch, knows that she's already late, that the river shuttles will have left. She punches in when the first drops of rain shatter on the ground, then sets out to cross the whole Pontoverde platform to the main building so she can report to management – it's humiliating to have to go ask a favour, a late slip, like a late-night college girl, like a slacker chick. The place rumbles beneath the volley of rain, ominously emptied of workers. Katherine Thoreau moves forward beneath the downpour, her shabby, non-waterproofed parka quickly saturated and heavy, water running inside, down her chest and her arms, down her neck, her sneakers fill with water and her socks splash around inside. She lowers her head and her hair hangs in front of her face in streaming strands as the water crashes down, she peers ahead through the strands and then concentrates on her feet in order to avoid the little pools forming quickly all around, it's a long path to the building, it's long and suddenly seeing the water splashing out from her soles Katherine says to herself, this is it – this is my life, it's taking on water, it's leaking out everywhere, it's all going to shit, Lewis and his bullcrap, the children who worry her, Billie in front of the TV all day beside her dad, Matt who stays out all night and hasn't smiled in weeks, and Liam who cries every day, she thinks of them and tells herself she's not gonna be able to hold on much longer – that morning she'd gone to ask the neighbour to check in on the place around lunchtime, the boys would be at school, and her husband was crippled, yeah, an accident at work, she has a little girl and can't afford yet to put her in daycare, would she be able to go check that everything was okay? And the woman, a matronly black woman with an unbelievable goiter and pink eyes had looked at Katherine sullenly and then said, okay, I'll go, and without missing a beat had named her price, ten dollars, and Katherine's eyes had widened, for that price you'll make lunch for the little one, you'll change her, and put her down for her nap, and the neighbour had said, okay, and the bargaining was done, but now Katherine was doing the sums: the neighbour's price was too high – she'd have to change that if she didn't want to hand over her whole paycheque.

From very far off, she'd seen the two figures grappling in the mud until one collapsed to the ground and the other fled towards the concrete mixing plant, and Katherine had parted her dripping hair to see better and quickened her step. Now, she bends over Diderot, groggy in the puddle, kneels to take his head in her arms, and says quietly, it's going to be okay, then screams over her shoulder, help, someone's hurt! Help! Her voice carries, she turns back to lean over him, murmuring breathe deeply, breathe, the strands of her wet hair skimming Diderot's face like Chinese paintbrushes, and, tickled a little, he opens his eyes, stammers, who are you? But people are hurtling down the short staircase now, big dry shoes, men armed with rolls of white paper and blankets. In no time at all Diderot is carried to the first-aid trailer and they turn to Katherine asking what was she doing here at this time, for God's sake, late again, Thoreau?

THE SITE IS IN FULL SWING. A MUTE UNFOLDING at first, clandestine even – no one in the city could have guessed what was cooking on either side of the river; no one could have suspected what was going to emerge from the ground, except perhaps to get up at dawn and wonder about certain buses hurtling past full of guys squeezed in like sardines, that pass again in the opposite direction at the same speed when night falls; except to get an eyeful of the shuttle traffic on the river. There was no fanfare for the placing of the first stone, no Boa photographed trowel in hand and provisional smile before an audience of dark suits and towering half-naked women on stilts who whisper to one another in a language where the *R*s roll over one another headfirst as though they were tumbling to the bottom of a well; there was not a single notice posted on a wall or a telephone pole, in the halls of the subway, nothing, there was no sign. The Boa had taken care to have the immense Pontoverde platform placed south of the city and to forbid any publicity about the work so as not to alert Coca's inhabitants and users – his electorate, his clients – to the disruption inherent in this kind of construction – the disembowelling of favourite views, dust, noise, heterogeneous pollution, traffic jams, resurgence of carjackings, influx of poverty-stricken populations looking to glean what they can at the margins of the site. The bridge began to impose itself in camouflage: the drilling sites were closed off with plywood hoardings covered in *trompe-l'oeil* panels designed to seamlessly match the neighbouring buildings, nearly invisible except for the skull inside its red triangle pirating each doorway.

The percussion of the bulldozers would fuse with the shocks and usual hammerings of the inner city, with the smoke of car motors and the gusts of dust. Lemon-yellow smog soon hovered over the city. The bridge men continued to arrive from all around – they were suddenly in the majority in the bars, where they often left a good quotient of their pay – in this way identical to newcomers who were always looking to buy a round in order to make some contacts, counting on inebriation for business ideas because, dammit, here they were, in the right place at the right time.

NO ONE saw a thing. In the first weeks, the inhabitants came and went in a city that was just as sparkling and fluid as ever, business was juicy with fat dividends, ice cubes clinked together gently at the bottom of bronze whiskies chin-chin while girls with the corners of their eyes tattooed inhaled speedballs – coke + baking soda – before heading out on the prowl in bras and denim miniskirts in the underground parking lots of big luxury hotels; piles of glitz were poured out and sold by the mile, cosmetics overran window displays, sixteen-year-old kids made a fortune at roulette using a system they unearthed on the internet, the bridge was being built, the bridge men and women didn't lift their heads anymore, worked huddled over the necessary gestures, each day fulfilling quotas of square yards, cubic yards, and requisite tons on the phasing charts, yes, the bridge rose up, it began from the lowest point, the deepest, a depth that no one in Coca could begin to imagine, it was anchored in holes calibrated to an eighth of an inch that pierced one by one the strata of sedimentation, rested upon the heart in the mille-feuille of memory, was sustained by the darkest, heaviest glebe, a thick paste that sweated its rivulets of archaic juice, dripped *plop plop plop*, and it echoed as it would in a dungeon, glistened in the beams of headlamps while hard-hatted heads bent down to examine it and then stood again, faces blackened, eyes popping, here we are, here we are, the asshole of the world – this shouted in all the languages, we're almost there, a little lower, another yard, go on, you can do it, teeth gleaming in the darkness, enamelled like so many fireflies, everyone shouting, walkie-talkies crocheted to their ears, farther, farther, go on, keep going, deeper, farther into the hole, while above, way up above, at the surface of the world, in the dazzling sunlight and the glare of deluxe hi-gloss sedans, there were still high heels *clack clack clack*, sculpted rubber tires that rasped the asphalt, moving people who went on living life ignorant of everything that was going on.

BUT IT WAS time to meet, flustered since they'd been caught off guard and losing their heads over the idea that a bridge of such a scale could soon rise up in Coca, panicked at the thought that such a work could change the economy of the city, of the region, and cause their influence to collapse. These are the owners of the four ferryboat companies that cover the Coca–Edgefront routes, sharing the total river transport, and among them, the *Marianne* – created by a Frenchman when the city was founded, by far the oldest, and which holds the monopoly over Coca–Ocean Bay traffic. The narrowness of the old Golden Bridge, its low capacity, has greatly favoured their development, so much so that at the time when it begins to be dismantled and the Pontoverde work site begins, no less than two hundred boats, from the simplest dory to the largest ferry or speedboat, dither daily on the river, incessant rotations chanted by the sirens, foghorns, or toots of the piston horn that call the latecomers to the dock in time for departure or warn of potential collisions – and they're numerous, these shocks, these run-ins of hulls caused by alcohol or a fog, a lover's daydream, a sudden fatigue, Coca's maritime tribunal ruling on its lot of crashes each week. According to the registers of the chamber of commerce, the total river activity amounts to a billion dollars each year – including two hundred and fifty million in net profit – and agglomerates more than three thousand jobs; the average crew of a double-ended ferry has five people: a shift manager, a crew foreman, a mechanic, and two mariners – and then there were docking pilots, helmsmen, deckhands, boat builders; providers of fuel, electricity, lifejackets, buoys, barf bags, paper towels; there were fast-food workers, ticketing agents, administrative employees, lawyers, accountants, marketing specialists, and publicists, as well as medical facilities for all these people. This is a very juicy business. A godsend. A business currently under threat by the construction of the new bridge. Six fast lanes, wide and paved like a racing track, will connect the city to the continent, will accord it its place in the communication loop beginning at the bay with the plains highway and ending at the fertile valleys and mining sites far on the other side of the forest.

SO, ONE evening at the end of October, four limousines brake in synch in front of an Italian restaurant in Edgefront. Four men with dark overcoats that widen their shoulders but cause them to slope down extract themselves heavily from the cars and greet one another on the sidewalk while the vehicles disappear – an unspoken protocol makes them defer to the oldest one among them, a colossal man, white hair gathered in a ponytail at his nape, mirrored glasses, cigarillo, dark jacket with purple satin lining – he's called the Frenchman, a direct descendant of that other one, male primogeniture – then plunge inside, straight to the table at the back. A fine wine is brought to them while they wait for the meat, but they've barely tasted it before the

Frenchman strikes the table with a fist – a gold signet ring, big as a walnut, glints there, vaguely aggressive: all right, we've gotta take care of this. The other guys lean in towards the middle of the table – from far away it looks like their four heads are touching, collusion of thick foreheads and cunning ears – the propositions fly: corrupt the security commission in order to cause the closure of the site, buy the ecological lobby and launch a smear campaign against the bridge, bribe the trade union and bet on the outbreak of a workers' strike. The voices accelerate, it's a question of not letting themselves get fleeced, of giving the Boa a warning, of "settling accounts" with Pontoverde, and now the quartet talks sabotage and workplace accidents, nitroglycerine and trinitrotoluene, the Frenchman whistles angrily between his teeth, striking his index finger against the table, we need guys on-site, a sucker, a Judas, we'll buy one, sort it out. The three others approve, and the Frenchman leans back in his chair and concludes, good, we're in agreement, lifts a solemn glass above the table, arm outstretched, a toast to the success of our enterprise, straight away imitated by his three companions, and with their alliance thus sealed, knots his napkin around his neck – a large square of white poplin – and claps his hands for the plates.

THE BIRDS. THEY SHOW UP EN MASSE IN MID-
November. Suddenly the sky seems immensely vast and
inhabited, flapping; the least flutter of a wing seems to
swell it from within like an inflatable mattress, the smallest
winged creature's passage – including bats, dragonflies, or
the bee-killing Asian hornet *Vespa velutina* – intensifies it.
Propagation to infinity. One morning you lift the blinds
and the birds are there, at rest, floating on the river or
scattered over the marshes downstream from the city.
Hundreds of dark spots float on the milky water like
shadow puppets, hundreds of round heads and beaks
mingle in one great clamour. Watching them, you begin
to count the number of miles travelled, you recite to
yourself the craziest distances – seven thousand miles in
one go for the bar-tailed godwit or forty thousand miles
in six months for the sooty shearwater; you try hard to
identify them, to recognize and name the types of flight
and formation, recalling that most of them have followed
precise flight corridors all the way from Alaska and also
migrate at night, taking their bearings from the stars, the
map of the sky unfurled wide inside their tiny brains, their
sense of direction more rigorous, more mathematical than
a GPS – and researchers at MIT in Boston, in Vancouver,
and in the Atacama Desert study the birds for this, baffled
and fascinated; it's moving to think that even the most
solitary, most asocial among them has migrated in a
group, as though survival depended on finding a collective

solution, and you ask yourself again what would we look like, after sketching such lines in the sky, after gliding on thermal currents so high up, sometimes even thirty-three thousand feet above the surface of the earth, piercing the stratosphere, our feathers knitting the cumulonimbus together, outrunning cold and hunger, spending half our reserves of fat in the slog – and at that moment, you tell yourself that a ruby-throated hummingbird is only three inches long and can cross the Gulf of Mexico in one shot – amazing, truly, that they are so precise and punctual: often it's the same post in the same field where they alight, on the same balcony at the same window, and the children who recognize them charge outside in pyjamas to bring them bread crumbs, rushing, goosebumps prickling their skin, slippers getting muddy but they don't care, and they turn back towards the house and shout it's him, he's here, he came back! They prepare a nest of cotton, straw, and twigs, a shelter complete with pantry and reservoir: a lesson in things.

IN COCA, ornithologists are on the alert. Their binoculars scan the sky or level at the nesting areas: they observe, count, inspect, tag, and untag – wouldn't be good to miss the newborns; they hold their breath, ready to brandish the Convention on the Conservation of Migratory Species of Wild Animals, international treaty ratified in Bonn in 1979 – ready to brandish it, because this year there's the construction site on the river, and even if the cranes provide new perches for the breathless birds to stop, the experts would already bet that the ecosystem has been disturbed. They're worried. A delegation alerts the people in charge at the mayor's office: the degradation of wetlands compromises nesting, threatens the species; a study on the wild swans south of Baku has just proven that the pollution of natural habitats around the Caspian Sea, which forces migrating birds to mix with domestic species, increases the spread of avian flu. These men aren't kidding around, not at all, and the mayor's office makes the mistake of ignoring them, turning up its nose at their duds – lumberjack shirts over white tees, clean jeans belted high over their middle, yellow Timberlands, baseball caps, large cases for cellphones clipped to their belts and Siamese twinned to their thighs, Swarovski binoculars around their necks: it's a mistake to take them for idiots, to make them hang around the deserted halls for hours and then smoke them out with speedy interviews where they're told that the site's ecological standards are draconian and make up 17.8 percent of the total cost of the work; it's a mistake because they're already getting organized. The first findings vindicate them and they attack – forty-eight hours later the International Court of Justice decrees, after a rapid hearing, that work on the Coca bridge must be stopped during the birds' nesting period. Three weeks. At least three, three weeks gone. The ornithologists in Coca can breathe again, while back at head office the financial directors of Pontoverde choke on the calculations of what this farce will cost them, aghast to learn that birds so small, so light, little flyspecks of nature, could slow down their superstar construction site; and the communications directors, proving exemplary in terms of their reaction time, immediately come up with a snap campaign – Pontoverde, ecology is our mandate, Pontoverde for your kids – and demand that the teams in Coca send them photos of kids petting birds under the guidance of the bridge's engineers, smiling at the camera, hard hats on their heads, the company logo clearly visible above their eyes.

THE BOA gets the news instantly, informed by a call from his chief of staff while he's on his way back from an official visit to Dubai – where the birds are more discreet, it seems to him. And of course he explodes. How is it that no compromise with these cocksucking ornithologists was possible? Couldn't we have just promised to finance new studies, new tagging campaigns, new binoculars as powerful as astronomical telescopes, new computers? Forehead glued to the bay window of his gigantic office, he watches the birds floating gently on the river for a long time, then suddenly turns and shouts: and the Migratory Bird Hunting Stamp Act, isn't there a single asshole here who thought of that? Is dealing with these ballbreakers more than you can handle? Acres of marshland in exchange for ecological tolerance on the site of my bridge, isn't it in you to think of a thing like that? He collapses into a large leather armchair and loosens his tie. One of the Boa's secretaries, believing things have cooled off – stupid kid – starts talking, assuring him that he knows about the bill that was approved by U.S. Congress in 1934, popularly known as the Duck Stamp Act, but the risk with that was that hunters in Coca would just see it as an additional tax. The Boa stares so hard at him that the young man's voice shrinks and chokes till he's silent. He says, you, get out of here, leans his head back in his chair, and casts his gaze out the window, far, the farthest possible distance away, into the agitated sky.

THE SAME sky that Diderot examines while he's out smoking a Lusitania – sick of pacing like a lion in its cage in the meeting room, satellite phone to his ear to mollify the bigwigs at head office who bray like donkeys, furious, the birds, what bullshit, what a fucking pain, we've gotta get rid of them, take care of it, Diderot. The situation worries him. Three weeks is a long time. The guys will go bumming around in the city, and the ones who began by hooting about this fowl situation, rubbing their hands together – two or three days to score some cash, to knock about in the city, or play hooky, time off on this kind of site is nothing to scoff at – will soon be disoriented, bodies unoccupied and heads heavy with this idleness, they'll sleep in, laze around till the middle of the day in greasy barbecue joints, or they'll sit clicking away, eyeballs swollen in internet cafés from taking in so many onscreen promises of sex, pussies, tits and ass, half-open mouths, and if there's a glimpse of tongue all the better, they'll click furiously, most of them geographical bachelors from the universal contingent of mobile workers, and, come evening, the same ones will sweat it out in streets along the river, no pay yet, no cash really to burn, they'll end up cracking, turning the mattress over to go get drunk or find something that'll get them high, 'cause it sucks here, we're doing dick all, and while some get depressed others'll split in double time, and there you go – a shitshow. Diderot chews the insides of his cheeks and paces up and down, three weeks of forced loafing around means much more than a delay to make up: it breaks the site's mechanism, interrupts the flow of energy, wrecks the work rhythm. It will be more difficult, afterwards, to reactivate everything; it will be heavier, slower, more painful, like starting to run again after stopping, all the muscles cooled down.

A FORMATION of Arctic tern flies off and nosedives over the river. The bird in the lead suddenly leaves its position, exhausted, and repositions itself at the end of the line. Diderot too feels exhausted: his bandaged side hurts him, a piercing pain bores into him whenever he speeds up his movements and it condemns him to a rigid chest – he moves like an old man, with small steps, torso leaning stiffly forward, and since he's only mobile from the neck up, his cervical vertebrae clang against one another: looking up has become a torture. Whispers fly that he's paying for his stubbornness with this – in the days that followed the attack, he'd kept working with the help of morphine injections, without taking a rest or even the time to press charges – he seemed to be redoubling his ardour in order to stop thinking about his wound, and people press their lips together saying pedantically, he's repressing, not a good sign, but hold back from speaking to him about his convalescence, because he doesn't engage anyone in conversation anymore and turbines around like a madman, the whites of his eyes growing more and more yellow, his sweat more and more bitter and his words more and more rare. Mad – he gets that way at night sometimes when the bells pass over his pallet and ring out, *bastard, bastard!* and he wakes up, breathing hard, the back of his neck on fire, legs heavy; he gets up, distraught, and goes to take a swig of alcohol straight from the bottle, any kind, exaggeratedly, but without any pleasure in being drunk, only hoping to go back to sleep like a log and never managing to before dawn: he's losing ground.

When he gets back to the building, he heads to the meeting room where they're waiting for him. The news precedes him. The team leaders are tense: so what's happening, are we stopping work? We're stopping all this because of a few warblers? For how long? After that it's not gonna come cheap when we have to play catch-up! One of the engineers plays the smartass, exclaims in a loud voice, well, I'd like it too if they protected my reproductive zone! The room laughs. Diderot waits for things to calm down, coldly announces that the site is shutting down for three weeks, and then he leaves the room.

FLOCKING ABOUT the different sites, the workers are assembled on the esplanade and the team leaders line up in front of them. One of them clears his throat and announces the temporary halt to the work. Three weeks of vacation, guys. There're birds reproducing and we can't bother 'em, that's how it is, guys, that's nature. Stirring in the crowd, a hubbub, heads turning and necks outstretched as though the bodies were suddenly looking for air to breathe – some oxygen that wouldn't lie; shoulders undulate, hands fidget nervously inside pockets – and some close into tight fists that soon swell crimson – legs shake, or pace: the air quickly grows tense over the site. And are we gonna be paid? First question to fly. With a worried look the team leaders evade this, they don't know, hazard doubtful orders – take advantage of it to get some rest, to visit the region, to stay with family, or to find yourselves a girlfriend, huh? There are tons of good-looking girls around, eh, whaddya say? But the guys laugh bitterly, nice try: why not say thanks while we're at it, thanks, boss, why not congratulate ourselves and give ourselves a pat on the back, isn't life great? What proof do we have that the site will start up again, why don't we get paid, at least? It's one of the guys from Detroit who speaks up, a guy with an emaciated face, dry skin marred by old acne scars and red patches, blond hair tapering to a rat-tail at the back of his neck. His eyes are very pale, almost white. He's suspicious, says he knows these grand speeches by heart, I'll tell you, I'm not gonna get fucked over twice, and the others behind him nod their heads in approval, yeah, yeah, we're sick of being had. We want our money now, we want it right now or we pass the buck, we ditch this place for good. His voice carries across the entire work site, cavernous and broken, a violent shake of his head punctuates the end of each sentence and he brandishes a smoke-stained index finger at the team leaders, the nail bitten to the quick and ringed with hangnails. The leaders confer with a look, one of them turns to Summer, we've got to send word to Diderot, tell him shit's hitting the fan, they want their dough, then he says aloud, very calmly, okay guys, you gotta be reasonable – we can't guarantee that you'll get your pay today but we'll do our utmost. How much is that? The worker from Detroit doesn't let it go – back there, thousands like him had been taken for a ride, kept in the factories with false promises while everything fell apart, and when General Motors began laying off men in groups of ten thousand, it was too late, it was all over, he's the one who closed the shop and since then has been kicking himself for not leaving before the breakdown, there were fewer guys hung out to dry then and his references were good, he would have got more dinero and been able to get back on his feet faster, and probably would have been able to keep his wife, too, who'd left to go back to her parents' place with their little girl after the house was seized one Sunday morning, the day of their anniversary, the house and the television, the well-equipped and pretty little kitchen, the three-seater couch, the barbecue, her exercise bike and his fishing rod, the kid's electronic karaoke machine; the truck sent by the bank was parked right in front of the garage and it sucked up their life from the inside, swallowed everything. It didn't stop. You couldn't see anything from the outside but you could hear the sound of furniture and things being heaped carelessly behind the tarps, pushed, piled, and for sure there was breakage, it was like a giant vacuum cleaner that emptied the house, emptied out their life. His wife had watched it all, straight-backed and silent, and then once the seal was on the door, had thrown a big suitcase into the trunk of their beige Rover, buckled the little one into the back seat, and turned towards him, glacial, you'll at least let me keep the car? How much is your utmost? he asks again, yelling this time. Summer has taken her place in the ranks again with a message from Diderot: we'll pay them. Once the guys hear the news, some of them form a line to get their cash – among them Katherine Thoreau, Soren Cry, Duane Fisher and Buddy Loo, and the Natives – while the others head for the locker rooms, at a loss. Summer and Sanche are side by side: what about us? Will we be paid or not? It's Sanche who speaks, see-sawing back and forth from his heels to his toes. Yes, everyone, Summer smiles, everyone will get their cash and meet again in three weeks.

LATER, SUMMER tosses her hard hat into a corner of her office and goes to the sink to drink from the tap, water splashes everywhere – for goodness' sake, there are cups, everything you need, plus the water in Coca is polluted, no doubt about that; dries herself off with the back of her hand and goes to sit in front of her laptop: no news from the Tiger, whose face has begun to dissolve, his face and body blinking precise at intermittent illuminations, then suddenly grainy, becoming transparent, and so Summer closes her eyes more and more often, even presses hard fists against her lids, worried to think that one day there'll be nothing left to make him reappear in full force, nothing to counter the progressive erasure of this guy, exactly the way you lift the heavy chain of the bucket in a well of shadows, exactly the way you lift it into the light, the bucket and its fragile, perishable cargo – heave-ho, heave-ho – what does he look like, the Tiger, what is the timbre of his voice, the grain of his skin, the scent of his body, what is the taste of his mouth, heave-ho, heave-ho.

AROUND HER, the plant purrs, the workers – loader operators and mixing truck drivers – labour away, the aggregate flows at a constant speed, well spread out on the transport belts, and this continuous flux of energy gives her security, envelops her like a coverlet, a kind of mental cabin where she now passes the clearest part of her time: the batch plant has become her home, a shelter. With a view of the entire site, she oversees these industrial tools, lowers her eyes to the latest touch screen, follows the production of the concrete in real time, step by step, ready to make the slightest adjustment: at every moment, the variable nature of the aggregate can require modification of one parameter in one of the three hundred and fifty formulations saved on the computer. To those who tease that she's a brown-noser, mocking her record work hours, seeing an excess of zeal or ambition – with Sanche Cameron at the forefront – or to those, far more pernicious and cruel to hear, who imply that the poor thing, she only has this in her life, nothing more than staring at her desk and reacting to the detection of an anomaly in the test results for the mixer, a trending graph indicating the consistency of the concrete, Summer calmly responds that she likes to be here, in her workplace, at her command post, that the metamorphosis of the material is a spectacle that fascinates her, that things do have to move forward – which is not very convincing at the moment, and they stubbornly see her articulate speech as the mask of her solitude.

Summer examines her work plan, evaluates what these three weeks of interruption will mean for her, the one who remains in charge of perpetual movement – what a joke.

Don't stop. We don't stop, this is her first instinct, we don't stop, we'll get ahead, we won't stop until it's impossible to stock the concrete on the site, we just keep on going, that's all she can find to say, her mouth twisting over her charts, when two guys knock at the door and ask if they should stop the centrifuges. They frown at her words, and the smaller of them, a thickset Mexican, points out that the whole site is stopping. Summer turns around, looks daggers at him, not us, we're going to get ahead. The guys back up on the landing and close the door again, she hears them swearing in Spanish the bitch, the *hija de puta*. Then someone knocks again. It's Sanche. He pokes his head in the door. You all right? He's taken off his work overalls and is dressed to go out on the town, a black leather Gestapo-style jacket with visible yellow stitching, pointy shoes, a silk scarf printed with cannabis leaves. Whatcha doing, Miss Concrete?

Summer smiles, *nothing*, I'm not stopping is all, I've got the whole team on my back but I don't care. I haven't gotten any other instructions. Sanche smooths the ends of his scarf with an automatic hand, looks at her, shrugs his shoulders, answers that the whole site is stopping for three weeks. Summer remains silent. The darkness grows in the room. The lamp on her desk carves her a ghostly orange face with grey shadows, a jack-o'-lantern on Hallowe'en night, she's scary, you should stop working, Diamantis, come with me, everyone else is already gone. She shakes her head, concrete is a very complicated recipe, you know, very complicated, we always think of it as a basic material but it's a surprising substance, tricky, and stopping production requires a protocol – Sanche sighs, pretends to beat a retreat, walking into the door, for god's sake, bangs his fist against it, deliver me from this crazy woman; she raises her voice now and accelerates the flow; for example, a concrete formulation must be validated by laboratory tests and then by on-site tests, they check its strength after twenty-eight days, and it takes a long, long time to find the right enunciation, the one that will suit every need, the one that will respond to the desires of the architect, the right tint, the right resistance to freezing, to thaw, the one that will endure shifts in temperature, the one that will ensure the concrete doesn't set too quickly, doesn't set too weak, her voice fades away softly, she turns her back to Sanche, who's placed his hand on the door handle and is getting ready to leave as he says, stop, Diamantis, you're such a pain. Summer whips around. A mixing plant is not a car, it's a process, it doesn't stop when you press a button, we have to be sure of ourselves, is that clear?

IT'S FIVE O'CLOCK IN THE MORNING. A BALCONY, Diderot, and before him, the landscape in motion. He holds himself up, leaning against the icy rail, naked, the blanket ponchoed over his head, his chest inclined towards the street where the snow has hardened into slabs now, filling in the length of the sidewalks in dirty strips. Calm arms and sleepy legs, soles of his feet soon sealed by the cold to the concrete floor, he leans, breathes, seeks, down there, leaning his head towards the river which he knows is within his reach, so close that he touches a section between two buildings, the velvety purpled surface of the water appearing beneath the wintery fog: the birds are still there.

Last day without the bridge, thinks Diderot, shivering goosebumps as the landscape unfurls before him at the rate of the rising day, higher, brighter, wider, deeper, with more contrast; as it's laid out in tiers and terraces – miscellaneous facades and roofs fringed with satellite dishes, underwear, and capitalist logos hung out to dry, raised parking lots, interchanges, triumphal arches, cranes, arrows, domes; as it fragments and assembles itself with the same momentum, which is still the impetus of beginnings, a powerful combination in which, far off in the background, high and grey, stands the great forest of the other bank. His heart, wrung out at the close of a long night, also begins to dilate, in unison with the upward impulse tied to daybreak, which is enough to make the blanket fall to his shoulders, his head out from under the cover, his funny head, the cold sets it aflame like a handful of dry leaves, he feels his heart beating now in his chest, *bang bang*, beating so hard it tears open the day without a bridge on the horizon, goddamn shitty day he knows it already because after twenty days of forced time off without pay, anguish is what seizes him, creasing his forehead and knotting his stomach; calculations are what colonize his cranium and costs are what stack up. *Bang bang.* Quick look at the dry sky and he pivots inside, gets dressed quickly, a gulp of cold coffee and no shower, nothing, not even toothpaste, just a new bandage over his scarred middle, the Velpeau bandage that holds him together, a pair of bike shorts moulding his big thighs, and he dons his cycling shoes, three turns of the scarf, thick yellow wool hat, steps over the mess and goes straight out, down the stairs, grabs his bike in the garage, and there he is – outside, alive and well, the scent of the night on his skin, outside outside outside, because that's the best place to be.

THE TASTE of rebirth. This is the first time he's been outside in a whole week – the last time he felt this weak he was seventeen and had banged up his kidney in a motorcycle accident, pissing blood and unable to get up; the arrival of the birds, condemning him to inaction, had only worsened his state. A low moment. He'd amassed a long string of days spent stewing, when nothing in him knew how to fend off the sadness that infiltrated his frame – came in through the cleft of his wound, he thought, even though it was completely healed over now, didn't hurt anymore, just a purpled line of skin with no swelling – and poisoned his blood. He had spent most of his time suffering, obsessing over the man he'd fought, and was already making a thousand plans for the next time he sees him, while down there, on the site, in the slowed-down offices, the guys were glutting themselves on comments: Diderot, idol with feet of clay, paper tiger, felled oak. Some talked about finding the guilty man – Soren Cry took care to throw his knife into the river as a precaution – and got geared up to organize a punitive expedition into Edgefront, into the shady neighbourhoods, because he could only have come from there, could only be one of those guys. Strangely, no one thought back to the testimonies of Summer Diamantis and Katherine Thoreau, who had both spoken of a white man in a tie. The site's turning to bedlam, dereliction threatens. Work has to start up again tomorrow. It's time.

BIKE ALONG slowly, first rolling alongside the river, then for two miles follow the black paved path that weaves back and forth beside the frozen river, solid and intense as Chinese ink against the uncertain murk of the static waters, pass the juvenile financial district, effulgent, bristling with cranes that are too red, too high, too new, makes him think of a teenager at the peak of his growth spurt, leave the park on the left-hand side, promise yourself to go hang out there when it warms up, to go see if they barter here as much as people say – an HP printer for a Moroccan ottoman nailed together in Meknes, an issue of the *Village Voice* for a set of muffin tins, a water pipe for an IKEA duvet – if they deal here, if they turn tricks as much as people say, if they tire themselves out – martial arts under the trees, kites on the meadow, dodge-ball soccer and running everywhere – if they make love amid the vapours of New California Gold, compressed inside acid trips against a background of mind-blowing music, or breaking away to languish beneath the wide green leaves of the banana trees (so soft and welcoming), if you can hear poets in baggy jeans and fluorescent flip-flops droning the language of owls plaited together with that of capitalists, if people organize politically, if they dance on Native burial grounds, if they pray – if in fact the place creates a utopia at the heart of Coca, a clearing where unbridled words fluctuate, a gap where the world could reformulate itself, and Diderot pedals faster and faster, caressing the foliage with his eyes, leaves powdered with snow, the California black oaks against the chalky bronze and golden highlights of the ginkgos, speeds along beside the stone wall that breathes, snowflaky, and rings this park without gate or fence. Gain momentum and roll onto the boulevard that snakes along the side of the valley, inhale and exhale regularly, above all don't force it, don't waste your strength, don't rush, instead climb in cadence, wait to change speed, and when the slope is at a good angle swing onto the plateau without pedalling harder, take advantage of the bends, pass the McDonald's, the Trader Joe's, the Walgreens, and the Safeways, and once you've reached the top of the boulevard, only then turn right and climb to the circular promontory that advances into space, balcony that overhangs the valley, the city, the river, and the bridge that rises up over the water, dome of the forest behind, get off the bike, unhook the flask, and drink the water that will have taken on the metallic taste that is, for Diderot, the very flavour of Coca, embrace the white landscape, sparkling under the hard sun, and measure how far you've come. This is the first stop.

Diderot huffs and puffs, water dribbles down his frozen chin, his face is the colour of a beet, and sweat trickles into his eyes: he would never have believed he could have such a hard time making it up a hill. He's leaning against the guardrail that drips melted ice, his feet buried up to the ankles in a grimy snowdrift, chin resting in his big paw bundled in a glove, he gazes at Coca at the bottom of the valley: I'm too old for all this, don't have the body for it, don't have the shoulders for the job anymore, nor the legs solid or feet nervous enough, and he soon thinks of the little house in the Finistère and quickly shakes his head, no way, the Finistère, dammit, the name alone makes him want to run because here we are at the edge of the continent – there, there would be only his mother like the crust of the earth, his mother in a blue blouse trimming the hedges, her hands between the leaves moving a pair of pruning shears much too heavy for her, his hunched-over mother in the mauve mountains, blue sky, roses, his tiny mother, all dried out except for her cheeks so red and waxed like apples, so brittle, osteoporosis and memory lapses, they'd go walking along the Bay of the Dead (*Baie des Trépassés*), on the sandy beach where stiffs drowned in the Raz de Sein wash up after eight days, they'd laugh at the macabre toponym and would promptly fall into the trap of the place, its implacable nature, its din; they'd watch the waves forming far off that would swell, powerful, great rolls of rough and nebulous force that pulverized light in their passage and imposed themselves with a kind of absolute fate, like the very first world, the very first proof of days, and maybe he'd even swim naked in the sea, lifting himself up onto his toes and raising his arms with each wave that smacks against his chest, yelling with cold, joy, fear, yelling with his mouth wide open soon smothered with so much oxygen and nitrogen, soon dry and silent, while the little old woman would recite the names of the capes and rocks to herself, her maroon cardigan buttoned to the neck, house shoes buried in the wet sand soaking up sea and crabs, yes, maybe it was time now to go home and set himself up in a part of the earth where there's no more ground to dig, precisely, not many more gestures to make, a place where he could enjoy the world as it is, the simple perception, head on, without there being a need to add any action, without a need to make anything other than what already exists there, tangible as a pleasing flower that we pick with one simple movement, a pure sensation that would still – just like the motion of the waves, like their knowing and mysterious rolling – return him from the inside and shake out his bones, just a sandbank then, a bit of earth and water, animal exuberance all around and the bitter smell of seaweed, just a cape, a simple, rudimentary place, and leave airports behind for good.

At the bottom of the valley Coca dazzles, and it's as though the impatience, the avidity, the rapacious desire have been rendered visible. And this peps Diderot up, reinvigorates him. He jumps back on the seat, *hup*, and in one moment has turned his back on the city and on the future Finistère, spins towards the white plain, his tires whistling on the asphalt again, again the pleasure of being swift, of splitting the air as though it were matter, again the joy of penetrating space headfirst, laid flat over the handlebars in the position of speed, making his body one with the machine, hair and clothes flapping noisily in the atmosphere like so many minuscule flags, and Diderot laughs in spurts, the icy air he swallows dries his throat but he opens his mouth, and his teeth, spoiled by deposits of tobacco, gleam in the sun as his big all-terrain tongue flaps against his lower lip, the air he exhales is exchanged for that of the limestone plateau, it's a strange vertigo, as though his presence were the only thing that made the space around him exist, as though he were at once the centre and the engine. At this point, it's ecstasy: the conjugated forces of his body and his wheels propelling him forward with the firmness of a piece of artillery, every swerve seizing his senses. Diderot takes off, glides, lifted, and his thoughts also materialize, roll in his brain, tangible as stones and precise, he's having clear ideas – it's always on his bike that everything settles, everything crystallizes.

RETURNING VIA Colfax, nearly noon, a barbecue joint, pickups with snow tires outside, and at the edge of the parking lot, an empty swing that grates dismally on a crossbar: Diderot's hungry, he goes inside. Dim room panelled in yellow pine, no windows but Christmas decorations in abundance, club music turned up loud – Jefferson Airplane, "Somebody to Love" – and a phenomenal hubbub that finally covers his internal weather, the incessant come and go of servers with hard smiles, weak phrasing. A girl in a cowboy hat welcomes him with a menu in hand, reels off a commercial greeting in the form of a question – How are we doing today? – turns on her heel, leads him between tables populated with beers and men wearing large lumberjack shirts, two or three tables with girl duos, one with a family. For Diderot, a table in the corner and *andiamo*: triple burger, fries, Coke.

When the door opens, the ray of light whitens the atmosphere and reveals the dust suspended in the room, thousands of particles without mass, without volume, mysteries of matter, and then dark silhouettes enter stamping their feet on the doormat with disproportionate ardour, on the pretext of knocking off the snow that'll soon turn to puddles. Diderot's irritated hearing them *stamp stamp* for ages, bloody racket, raises his eyebrows: a new family has been seated at the other end of the room. There's a little girl in a high chair, two teens, a woman with auburn hair, a man in a wheelchair. The woman captures his attention. She shrugs off a fuchsia parka, lifts her hair from the hood of her tracksuit, and is now studying the menu while the man in the wheelchair drains his first beer.

At the moment when the server brings their plates – three burgers for the five of them, two Cokes, two beers, they'll share – Diderot catches the eye of the woman, who greets him with a nod of her head, murmurs something to the man in the wheelchair who also looks up at him, and finally she gets up, crosses the room, and comes to stand in front of his table, her jogging pants are loose, too big for her. Hello, she smiles, a heavy layer of turquoise eyeshadow on her swollen eyelids, clumsy mascara, lilac circles under her eyes, round smacks of apricot blush on her hollowed cheeks, mouth enlarged with a brown line, is it Carnival or something? Diderot puts down his cutlery and without getting up says hello. The woman holds out her hand: Katherine Thoreau, I work on the site, I'm the one who found you knocked flat the other day. Surprised, Diderot gets up – ah! – and shakes her hand, vaguely vexed by the use of the words *knocked flat*. Now they stand face to face. The woman is tall, her beautiful hair smells like family shampoo and cigarettes, she leans her eyes into his, sage-petal green eyes, softness itself, you're feeling better, then? Her voice gets a little lost in the din of the restaurant, of the music and the cowboy servers shouting orders, but Diderot's instinctively tuned in to the right frequency, and he hears her. Great, watch this – he lifts his arms in the air, would have even spun around – a server carrying a stack of dirty plates passes between them, he places his hands back on his thighs, great, no, really, excellent. I see that, she smiles, an exaggerated pout of admiration, her eyes shining now, you came by bike? Diderot clears his throat, yes – he wasn't thinking of his bike shorts or of his flat little shoes, of his body, and feels suddenly naked and confused, forces himself to round up his memories – the man in the tie, the fight, the pain – but he doesn't remember her, or that her hair caressed his face while he lay in the stinking muck, steeped in rain and blood, who is this woman? So everything's great? she asks again, still cheerful, beginning to retreat towards her table – but I happen to know she's lingering a little, wouldn't even mind spending the whole day on this side of the room with this man, handsome as a continent. They're standing straight as totems in the smell of the deep fryer, they're hot, they shuffle, embarrassing the servers who graze past, held fast in this moment that's quickly draining away. Great, Diderot watches her, twisting his mouth – how long has it been since he talked like this with a girl? Ignoring the three faces behind her and the little one who's bawling, Katherine has put her hands in her pockets, there's interest, she looks him up and down, pretend serious, we start up again tomorrow so better be in good shape, right? She's pretty now, pretty because of her gaiety, a soft look, beautiful neck, body loose, so pretty that Diderot, looking for a way to keep talking, asks her abruptly: which team do you work on? End of the laughter – an end to the cat and mouse, the parenthesis of joking around and the molecular desire – what we have now, face to face, is the boss and the worker, and it's as swift as a cudgel blow. Katherine Thoreau freezes and replies, I'm a driver, Anchorage Three. Ah, very good. Diderot bites his lips, thinks, you idiot, you complete idiot, while the woman takes a stronger step backwards, signifying that she's returning to her table, in a hurry to be done now, but in that instant knocks against the wheelchair, stumbles, spins around. It's a man Diderot hadn't seen who's come up behind her and announces, sugary sweet: your food's getting cold, dear. Katherine lets out a cry of surprise, immediately covers her mouth; she hadn't heard anything either, no one can hear anything in here, then she hurries through the introductions while looking away: Lewis, my husband, Mr. Diderot, the boss of the site – she feels miserable as she utters these words, the boss of the site! why not kneel before him and lick his boots while she's at it! She grows hot with rage, wants to escape for good, but Lewis holds out a cheerful hand to Diderot, oh I see! You're the one who was knifed by a wacko? Diderot nods, stepping back in turn towards his table, but Lewis insists and rolls closer to him, why don't you come finish your meal with us, Mr. Diderot? It's no fun to eat alone, isn't that right, dear? Katherine, overwhelmed, breathes, let's not bother him, Lewis. That is when Diderot, like an amateur actor, looked at his watch and then declined, thank you but you see, I've finished, I must go, after which he paid, picked up his things, and as he passed the family at their table, waved his hand, a wave that only Lewis returned, the boys just watched him hard, and she kept her turquoise eyelids ostensibly down at her glass of water, ignoring the little girl who wailed and held out her arms, demanding justice, they must have argued over the number of fries and sips of Coke, and now, on the plates, there's nothing left for Katherine.

SIZING UP
THE PLACE

WHEN NIGHT COMES OVER THE TERRITORY, Coca takes shape. Darkness suits it, heats it up, drives it mad, delivers it cruel and brutal, sharp edges and an interior disturbed by thousands of rival gleams; night reveals it as an orange, effervescent, vitamin C tablet tossed in a glass of troubled water, a jar of crude oil placed in a sink, a distributor of oxygen, speed, and light.

Then day falls and multiplies its light, abounds its noise, the city doubles its speed, racing tongues rave inside big excited mouths, and this name propagates left and right: Coca! Coca! Coca! The Brand New City! A zone of proliferation with swarms of febrile businessmen, dealers of all kinds, sly teenagers, opium dandies, usurers, ladies of the night, and murderers in wigs. Each week the big coastal newspapers (the first to be enticed by its reputation and fascinated by its rapid growth) publish a hot and nervous image, compare it to a nubile virgin, unpolished and cunning, still a little gawky, look, look at her, her blatant come-on, decked out like a little whore, hand on one sequined hip, ferocious, determined, listen to her calling you, come on in, boys, come see, come taste. They're exaggerating of course, making a show of it, because columns always have to *sizzle snap pop*, but basically they're telling it like it is – and sex is definitely one of the main activators of the big global mix, practised in order to abolish differences (or so they tell themselves) – social, physical, and generational – it's no secret, just driving through Coca at any hour of the day you can feel the frenetic pace of a city doped up on sweat and money, stretched to the limit as though pumped full of Botox, you can measure the formidable Joule effect that's constantly at work.

Coca promises the high life. People come here from all over, bodies impatient, pockets holding just enough to get by for a few days; constant turnover of people and desires, burning cheeks and boiling pupils, fast streets like centrifugal motors and skyscrapers opening onto a sky that dispenses good fortune: the power of the territory in action. Here you come into contact with everything that makes up the great stew of a city, you hear the spasms of concrete and the violent scansion of hearts immersed in a common turbulence. Yet the secret of this incomparable flow that makes the blood pump harder in the arteries and sweat pearl in the small of the back, this secret is no secret to anyone, it circulates through all possible networks like breaking news: don't come to Coca unless you're ready to join the hustle! Don't lay down roots here, and certainly don't come for fun or for some rest. Approach it like an ambitious wild beast, breathe deeply and kick open the door, show up without waiting to be announced, without checking in, go ahead and put your plan into action.

AND YET, it's still hard to understand how people could have dreamed of setting themselves up in such a dented cleft of the red limestone plateau, at the flat bottom of a valley with asymmetrical sides where jackals and lynx descend at dawn, incisors still gleaming with blood. Yes, it's hard to understand how starving fanatics, carried forward solely by their mission to give their cult a piece of land, to give their god a cult, to give their deaths a god – how they had managed to cross the enormous continent, to carve through the prairie and the mountains, along the way finding grasses tall enough to feed their animals; how they cleared a path through the forest of cacti encircling the plain – plants with branches sharp as folding razors or machetes – borderlines of barbed wire as tall as a man on horseback; how they strangled rattlesnakes with their bare hands, walked along the canyon floor; how they got around the murky ponds transmuted into frozen lakes in winter, and into sanctuaries for deadly mosquitoes in summer. How they braved the bestial heat and the beggar's cold. Hunted deer, trapped hares, harpooned carp. Killed Natives. How they dragged their families heaped onto grimy wagons, built houses, raised bison, fattened pigs, fenced in fields of potatoes and corn to feed them all. How many corpses and how many gone mad by the end of the journey? How many horses carved into steaks over primitive fires? How many scalps? Above all, how could they have stayed here, and continued to take wives here, to have children here, to bury their dead here, spring summer fall winter, one year then two then ten, spring summer fall winter, continued to burn brains and put holes in chests, to eviscerate bodies, spring summer fall winter, how did they do it, yes, we wonder in earnest, because to stay here, on this tongue of land flared like a skirt at the river's edge; to grow up between the high plains and the howling forest; to take root here was, after all, to defy Heaven and all of Creation. It was to claim to call the coyote by name and outwit the grizzly, to drink melted snow till they got the runs, to roast scorpions squatting shoulder to shoulder, to spit out sand and rub flint. They did it, though, these bearded men with hemp twine hair, these women in their bonnets, these fevered children, all of them dirty and deathly afraid, chanting canticles with one hand on the trigger, all of them murderers: they founded a city.

AND THEY were not mistaken. The place was worth the blood and the sweat and the crevasses of tears, the putrid lumps, the mad chilblains cleaving their pale feet: the valley is five miles wide, spread between the plateaus and the giant swathes of brush, flat as a palm, and edged by a river on its western side. A harsh but steadfast climate, developing predictably solstice after solstice – music paper, the scansion of their lives, the carrier of their days, monotony which closes on a final note of death; scorching summers liquefied into storms with electric skies and hailstones like Ping-Pong balls, radiant autumns, icy winters, sovereign springs, sweetness finally, the sweetness of a clearing, a thousand nuances of green, horses strolling in the prairie, youth and the strength of the reeds, tartness of the air, and rumbling of the water. And there are these violent winds from the east, carrying loess gathered on the plateaus – this permeates the ground, seeds the valley, fattens the cattle like cream on butter. Arriving here, the men who were still able had knelt on the ground and brought a pinch of earth to their mouths, tasting it with a click of their tongues – because that's what you do – then had risen, weathervaned around, thrown their hats in the air and shouted, we're here! This is it, goddammit we made it, we made it – in any case they didn't have a choice anymore, it was here or never, the horses were fevered, the children had stopped speaking, the women's bellies were covered with eczema, and they themselves were going mad.

IN THE EARLY days, Coca curls up in turtle position. The pioneers are alone in the world, terrified, convinced of their superiority, propped up by their belief that they have been chosen. They settle in, they colonize. They proceed methodically, like the Greeks: mark out the territory, build the sanctuary, trace lines in the earth, put up gates, houses, share the arable land. They don't see the old Spanish mission thirty miles to the south – so regularly destroyed by Indian raids, dysentery, and fevers that only some thirty members are left, and you should see the state of these guys – not one of them would be able to tell the story of that January morning, two hundred years earlier, when three forty-ton caravels with tough black hulls and sails worn threadbare pierced the ocean fog, approached the coast, unloaded priests and soldiers, powder, chalices, pots, barrels, bibles, and censers; not one of them would be able to tell this story: the men had barely placed one foot on the ground before they did exactly what they had come to do – they scattered here and there all along the coast, put up camps encircled by low stone walls between which the ringing of heavy Catholic bells could soon be heard, the spearhead and the backbone of evangelization, cultivated, hunted, sang, baptized everything they came across, Scriptures in one hand and musket in the other – and then began to die of isolation, they literally die, hang or drown themselves, bungling their entrails with grain alcohol; and not one of them would be able to imagine the twenty-year-old Franciscan monk, wild-eyed kid with a capuchin face (the monkey) who, sometime around 1630, went inland following the eastern bank of the river with twenty men behind him, and who, after seven weeks of walking, threw together a hasty altar in a prairie at the foot of the limestone plateau and celebrated the Eucharist, the river mirroring a wooden crucifix: mission accomplished, you are the children of God, you have arrived in Santa Maria de Coca.

COCA LAYS low behind its palisades, its enclosures, its pigsties, and its corrals. It doesn't have the same expansionist rage of other cities on the continent, born in more or less the same way, and never sets foot on the opposite bank, on the other side of the water, where the bulging forest hatches heretical and cannibalistic tribes. Conversely, it works to preserve its perimeters, to consolidate its circumference: a burrow of a city clenched around its assets – weapons, flocks, oppressed women – this is what it is. A hole. A cluster of rough and blunt individuals bustle around, working like dogs by day and growing fearful once night has fallen – because night in Coca is the night at the bottom of a well, a double layer of darkness where fear turbines, because night is in the sky but it is also in those who never lift their heads and limit their world to their own feet and their own stomachs – and so they kill, dance, copulate and rape, steeped in alcohol to the roots of their hair, and finally collapse onto straw mattresses that stink of sweat and humid hay. Who, in the morning, stagger out onto the doorstep in boxers or undershirts, hirsute hair and pasty breath, one or two dogs at their heels, and piss legs spread eyes blinking, point their guns at the riverbanks, target otters or any other half-witted mammal frisking about in the clarity of dawn, *bang! bang!* and, having shaken off the dust, go back inside the house to demand their coffee with a sullen groan. Pure rednecks, say the few travellers who risk coming to Coca by water, armed themselves, pistol barrels stuffed to the brim.

THE NATIVES do finally show themselves. At last. One fine day they come out of the woods and move closer to see, flow into the bushes without even rustling the leaves, and suddenly rise, immense. They're here, standing near the huts, armed with lances and naked. They breathe like people. Terrorized themselves, they cause great fear, heavy rifles are pointed at them, stay where you are, don't take a step, don't make a move. They don't understand a word. Well, we warned them. Shots are fired, bodies crumple, everyone leaps into action, and then nothing – little groans among the tall grasses and the scent of gunpowder. After that, the settlers are scared: they don't like us, they seem cruel, they eat human flesh and drink blood hot from the carotids, like a spout flowing straight into their bestial mouths. What if they come back? Scouts are sent into the woods to locate them, to evaluate their numbers, and to scope out their strength, the dying mission even sends emissaries to give them a chance to finally learn that all men are brothers in the eyes of God. Rare are those who return safe and sound from these expeditions: posts planted at regular intervals appear along the length of the river, at the forest's edge, exhibiting mutilated bodies that attract bronze-eyed lynx (*Felis tigris cocaensis*), speckled hummingbirds, and electric-blue snakes. At night, people barricade themselves inside wretched little huts, weep with terror, twist their mouths, stroke their chins, and finally give up on risking their necks to cross the water, to clear out the forest any more. In Coca, the river does its job – it composes, it separates – and the years pass.

Because yes, there is this river that excites it, caresses its side. Long golden cobra lazing and wild, lying curved like a trigger across an entire continent. Three thousand miles. Deep in these parts, and the fords impossible to find even though scouts on horseback have been sent out on the banks to plumb the riverbed, deep and yet also wide – at least a mile – wide enough that you can see storms roll in from the high seas, and strong, the dark and rapid waters pleated by a powerful current. It's always drawn as a little frozen torrent grown to a lazy giant in the middle, where it touches Coca, and then as a managed national river, canalized for commerce between the city and the sea. People like this gushing of crystalline waters that deepen in colour, opacify, and then grow cloudy with motor oil, disgustingly polluted in certain bends, before mixing with the salty water of the ocean in the gulf. Okay. But the problem is that we don't know where the animal comes from, its source is a mystery, no one has ever been able to pinpoint the precise location, not the GPS coordinates, it's an uncanny thing, and has been the same story since the city's beginnings, not the young Franciscan monk with his hooded monkey face and his expeditionary body devoured by anguish and mosquitoes, not the young aces of the first convoys, not the geologists and the hydrologists from London, Boston, Decazeville, and Lons-le-Saunier who would take up residence in Coca between 1866 and 1925, travelling upriver for months – the last ones to come play the detectives, tell the story of the fire at the Pernod factory in Pontarlier in 1901: the zealous employee who emptied barrels of absinthe one by one into the Doubs to avoid an explosion, the wide river that was instantly alcoholized; the soldiers at the riverside garrison who filled their helmets and drank, who burst into guffaws, splashing into the water to quench their thirst, letting it flow down their chins, spatter on their beards, coats unbuttoned, a miracle, Jesus descended into the valley; and the following day, nine miles away, another river is contaminated, its waters turned opalescent green, the fishermen are pissed off, this better not mess up the trout; and this is how it is discovered that the Loue River, believed until then to be autonomous, original, is in fact a resurgence of the Doubs – astounding the profession – a first colouration in the history of hydrology – no one has found the river's source, no solitary adventurer, no reality-show hero tossed into the forest from a garish helicopter equipped with infrared cameras; all of them eventually turned back, got lost, tumbled wounded into a ravine, or got tangled in thick vines and fluorescent ferns, backed away from the enormous waterfalls that suddenly rise up three hundred miles to the north, liquid walls whose most minor trickle would shatter the strongest steel-hulled boat; and finally all agreed to establish that there was not just one source, but many, and that they would come back later – and later never came.

VERY SOON there was a port in Coca. Dynamited stone from the canyons east of the city moved forward into the river in compact heaps, forming breakwaters where high-tonnage vessels began anchoring in the beginning of the nineteenth century. These are fitted out in the opulent cities of the estuary and travel upriver for seven days, bringing machines, casks of wine, precious fabrics, health remedies, books, and newspapers, and leave again heavy with bricks and anthracite, cattle, skins, and furs. Traffic intensifies, the river becomes the umbilical cord by which Coca grows fatter and then slims down: technical innovations, moral evolutions, musical revolutions, medical progress, developments in fashion, noise of wars and celebrations, all of this surges back towards it aboard these long phosphorescent ships – they make of it a continental lighthouse, a faraway light burning in the dimness of an immense and wild land where only the edges have been civilized. Also, in 1850, an actual lighthouse is built. Joshua Cripplecrow, mayor of the city at the time (named for the darkness of his hair, nails, and teeth, for his lameness and scheming – he's a killer) has only this in mind, this is his life's project. It would be raised at the river guard, where the bed narrows before opening out again towards the south in a rift basin fringed with marshland, and would be crowned with a turning flame beneath a glass cupola: a lookout tower. Soon beacons are placed along the length of the banks, buoys are roped up, a harbourmaster's cabin is built, a dry dock, dockyards, captains are trained, and today Coca is still the last port upstream on the river. Beyond it, the mangrove creeps forward into the water, the islets in perpetual formation threaten to ground vessels, the map of the riverbed is drawn twice a year, and navigating requires a light, flat-bottomed craft – canoes, dugouts, kayaks; farther still, there are only mossy wooden pontoons floating in front of riverside cabins. At the level of Coca, however, if they're well manoeuvred, two giant tankers can pass side by side.

AT THE time the lighthouse was built – let's go back for a moment – gold was discovered on the western bank: three clean nuggets in the mud, three little flickers that quiver in the sun. Gold, gold! Immediate influx – men, mostly, young guys who are strong, poor, and full of belief. A new wave of migrants reaches Coca following the continental path of the pioneers while another crosses the ocean, comes to skirt the black coasts aboard stinking ships; they advance slowly, very slowly, and find the entrance to the bay – such a narrow passage – a tiny door, the eye of a needle – and it is so moving to suddenly come upon the bay, intact, secret, just by craning your neck the way you'd poke your head curiously through a half-open door, it was such a strong feeling – the ship moors deep in the gulf, a troop disembarks and travels upriver, usually on foot, unknowingly following the path of the young missionary, and then branches off towards Coca. Once they've arrived, the newcomers spit into their hands, build boats, rafts, cross to the other bank, transporting what they need to clear the land. There's traffic, a Frenchman sets up a ferry business, charters a first vessel sixty feet long and deep enough to hold two horses, a dozen men, a few cases of sugar and flour, a barrel of hooch, and twenty barrels of powder. By Jove, it works like a charm.

The guys don't pull punches, they charge ahead and make a space for themselves. First-come, first-served, that's the name of the game – you just gotta go for it. They know nothing about this part of the river, nothing about the Native burial grounds parallel to the river, bodies buried with heads towards the ocean and draped in blankets embroidered with shells; they know nothing about the sacred trees, the giant sequoias clustered into cathedrals of foliage, the pines (*Pinus lambertiana*) and the little clay altars with parakeet feathers and clusters of honey mesquite (*Prosopis glandulosa*) burning. They cut, clip, and clear relentlessly, bust through, turn around and dig. They set themselves up and some of them do touch gold – these ones are rare, but they brandish their pebbles, eyes popping, screaming their heads off, a long cry that swells between the trees and thus reactivates the hope machine. Others see them, envy them, tell themselves that they got lucky, and wonder, is luck democratic or are there chosen ones; does fortune smile on just anyone, might she even one day smile on me, just one tiny little smile that would revive in one fell swoop this mass of exhaustion that I call my body.

A NECKLACE of bric-a-brac houses appears in what comes to be known as Edgefront. They're pitched in the mud overnight according to the rule of the *fait accompli* and stand shoulder to shoulder on a band of earth no wider than a mile but at least twenty long, tacked onto the river's edge. Families move in, some of them come down from Sacramento off the train that unifies the interior of the territory from then on. They grow gardens, set out rabbit hutches and all kinds of enclosures for chickens and pigs, dusty paths cross-hatch the large strip; women give birth screaming beside basins of boiled water, and soon there are children playing with sticks, building huts and trapping coypu. Calm returns, the great status quo: no one thinks about the Natives anymore, sometimes you can make them out here or there at the far ends of the strip where the sylva touches the river, and some even exchange words with them. But no one goes into the forest anymore except for the fur traders, and these men are wrapped in a cloak of mystery: they've trafficked alcohol and weapons, squatted beside leathery shamans to chew hallucinogenic roots, learned their language which includes four vowels and four consonants (the women have only three vowels at their disposition), hunted sable and deer, tamed the blue fox and the whiskered screech owl (*Otus trichopsis*); they've tracked that bronze-eyed lynx and played knucklebones with forest men clothed in tunics made from salmon skin and adorned with shells collected from the banks – knucklebones with the debris of skulls, nose cartilage, portions of clavicles, and all kinds of phalanxes – they've followed little girls dragging flat dolls with fish eyes all the way back to their huts and done business with their mothers, then have followed these same women into the immense swampy prairies populated with spirits and magic sounds, and while some of them get killed, others have children. Intermediary men, they've plumbed the thickness of the brush over a range of at least two hundred miles and when they return, when they emerge from the sticky gangue and blink their eyes, blinded, lips dry and green at the corners, skin livid, the people run towards them, encircle them calmly, welcome them with respect and open arms: they bring rare plants and materia medica, bitter berries and leaves that salivate, more furs, and, more rarely, gold and carnivorous flowers.

A FIRST BRIDGE was built in 1912, baptized the Golden Bridge. It's a burly, rustic, but also umbilical and thus ambiguous bridge, as though its primary function was less to de-isolate Coca and aid its expansion to the other bank and more to regulate the flood of poor people who live on the other side from then on, to filter their incursion into the old city and, once night falls, to facilitate the return of those who work in the city's central neighbourhoods – above all, to prevent them from lingering where what's prized is order and security.

In the decades that follow, the city sediments, its grid is etched into the ground, its map – airy, diaphanous, still containing numerous enclosures of high grass – unfolds slowly: temples, schools with bells, newborn civic buildings, flour mills, cart makers, stores, hotels and exhibition centres, a small university, a theatre, a few restaurants, several bars and saloons, all this coagulates gently during the prosperous years that follow the First World War. A way of life develops that siphons all space, sucks areas clean, absorbs and neutralizes them, the day-to-day triumphs, while vernacular fictions solidify – those fictions that will populate the city from now on until they're indistinguishable from it, like a second skin; fictions surrounding Coca's foundations, risen up *ex nihilo* beneath the infinite sky, extrapolated from the virginity of the New World with this sense of accomplishment of communities held in the palm of God's hand; but fictions that also bump up against the city's earthy melancholy, its aphasic silence, as though living there amounted to facing adversity, since humans would never get another chance – there would never be another Earth.

THE RIVER, this liquid wall, continues to draw a border-line in the heart of the city, fixing more strongly than ever this "other side of the water," this area that excites or repels. So silty, so thick along the banks that the children who swim between two fish traps can't see their hands beneath the surface, and their feet have completely disappeared into the red sludge where thin black snakes slither past. But it has also become an integral space of life: people work here, circulate here, draw their subsistence from it. There are hundreds of vessels upon the water each day now. Ferries multiply, crossing the river or descending towards the bay, barges trade and transport; in summer simple rafts are poled along to conclude minor deals, and in winter little cargo steamers fight their way through the greyish ice; canoes fish here – and when the salmon come back upstream during spawning season, boats are suddenly packed in shoulder to shoulder and there are shouts from all sides, screams and laughter, because dammit, fish are spurting from the surface, it's a miraculous draught of fishes, and tonight, it's a party, a festival, a belly-splitting good time, grilled onions and boiled sea asparagus, crispy potatoes; tonight it's violins, a ball, prohibition wine pouring forth from barrels, boobs at attention in the cleft of corsets, pricks in hand, in mouths, and sex all you can eat, tonight it's all-out mayhem – and, racing over the waves like arrows, you can catch sight of loads of Native dugouts.

Because yes, the Natives are here now. Set up at the edges of the forest, their dwellings thicken the border and send up smoke between the branches, a milky-white veil against the black of the woods. People say they were drawn like magnets to Coca because of the bartering on the river, the sparkle of electric lights, and the bitterness of the beer, that they want to read the newspapers, speak several languages, and go to the movies, that they do what they have to in order to follow the path of progress, that they've chosen to evolve. People like to say that they were attracted to the city simply because it was much warmer than their gloomy woods and that the tiniest room with a concrete floor is superior to the dirt floors of their mouldy huts. People like to say that the city was simply desirable, and so they desired it – just like we desire it when we're fifteen and live far from everything, bundled away in the country, in a backwoods town where the church bells keep time, stuck in the bleak countryside dying of boredom, where you sleep with chickens because, shit, there's nothing else to do, though what you'd really like is to bust your eardrums and let loose on the dance floor, or at least watch it rave the whole night long. More rarely, people imagine that they're refugees, and that it's actually fear, violence, and hunger that have pushed them here, huddled together, on edge and lost.

The truth is that the status quo had gone on for too long and the first lumberjacks ended up making their way to the forest. They were newcomers to Coca themselves, guys from the interior, from Montana and Nebraska, but also Europeans, giants with flaxen hair, Slovaks, Germans, Poles; they had short and gnarled arms, empty bellies; they knew how to do the job already and kept costs low for a downtown boss. We know that they would begin gently at first, choosing the youngest trunks, spacing out the cuts, two guys at work while three or four others kept a lookout, and then they'd haul the trunk together, one behind the other, clearing out narrow corridors through the forest as they passed like veins that they would use again the next time they came back to work – all this so as not to leave a trace, so as not to break the implicit pact that had governed life in the area for so long: they poached Native land in silence. But, little by little, becoming bolder, they shrank the space between cuts, began to set traps themselves, and sometimes even got so close to the villages that they mistook domestic livestock for wild game and grabbed them shamelessly. Then they rapidly tightened their hold on the forest, turned the pressure on the tribes up a notch: encampments were set on fire in order to gain territory, animals poisoned with sulphuric acid, girls were abused – a little seven-year-old Native girl was raped and strangled, found floating in the river, body swollen like a wineskin. Still no roads but forest channels that would become a netting of paths in a few years' time for lumber vehicles. So the Natives got scared, and while some of them plunged farther into the immense forest, following the game – their sustenance – others, desperate, walked all the way to Coca. It was a surprise to see them turn up like that – some were even disappointed – so this is what the Natives look like? These are the people who gave the territory its name, who terrorized the early settlers? These are the noble warriors who walk with God at their backs and the plain beneath their feet? Feathered, quivers full of arrows, proud gazes and agile bodies racing through the deep forests, they were objects of fascination and fear – the caricature was helpful for illustrating an enemy worthy of the courage it takes to hunt him; a sexual fantasy for well-dressed women, an aesthetic model for all those nostalgic for the noble savage who would be glad to bring one back to their conferences – fattened up, cloistered in the vapours of rubbing alcohol, chewing rotten tobacco from morning till night and getting swindled by kids – bear's teeth for coppers – it was crap, and no one gave a shit.

A SECOND wave of immigration happened in the 1950s. Although isolated, Coca continued to attract new populations that need to be housed – families driven from the coasts where life has become too expensive, where work is scarce; modest and working families besotted with detached houses and nature, poor folk seeking to remake themselves, lost souls seized by the dream of the West, that stubborn myth that colonizes their minds. They speculate on land to be divided into lots, take over the pasture land, conquer the fields; little by little the tractors are put away and gas stations pop up, wagons are soon replaced by pickup trucks and Fords – and some real property swindles go down. A few roads are rapidly outfitted with motels, fringed with restaurants that serve cheap meat, with bowling alleys and supermarkets, with warehouses. At night, neon signs trace the outline of girls in pink garters, stetsons on their heads, mugs of beer in hand. Because – funny thing – the more the city modernizes, the more people turn to the clichés of the past to attract regulars – in other words, the fewer real horses, the more rodeos there are – in freshly done-up arenas plastered with giant ads, and so people pay their share. The descendants of the pioneers stick together, fold inward reflexively and cement a violent aristocracy whose financial dominance is based in the major areas, or what's left of them – they keep close ties with the police, the courts, and the banks, and the most intuitive ones team up with the unscrupulous wheeler-dealers who operate here. Violence itself changes shape. Where there used to be brutal brawls, settling of accounts and ordinary vendetta, now there's petty crime, drug trafficking, women traded like horses, and sexual crimes. Now there's racketeering, deportation, extortion, and usury; now they use intimidation in order to take their pound of flesh.

BY THE END of the millennium, Coca's getting bored, super-provincial, and so confined. Definitively insular. The youth who mope around here spit in its face. The asshole of the world. The city has nevertheless verticalized with a few buildings. People also say it's a modern city. White city hall with columns, white courthouse with cupola, white chamber of commerce. Standard American decor with large dark-windowed sedans gliding past. You wonder where the people are. Air conditioning everywhere and long bars of automatic watering on the beds of close-shorn grass, of a gaudy green. Indifference towards the world, exacerbation of family powers, suspicion towards foreigners, contained prosperity, sorrow of women whose elegance is lifted directly from the pages of fashion magazines from Paris, New York, and Milan – copied so closely it breaks your heart, truly, it hurts to see – no distance, no delay, the latest lipstick on their dry lips, the right bra, the right panties – people are suffocating here.

  Luckily there's the water. The movement of the water. The light of the water. The deep, wide, fertile river. The frozen river – skating rink that cracks on all sides when the thaw comes, wakes like an animal and shakes its scales of ice, suddenly so alive beside the weary city. Luckily there's this freedom. But on the other bank, the neighbourhood of Edgefront is still nothing but an edge – edge of the city, edge of the forest, edge of the river, thrice marginal, triply fascinating – densely populated strip served by the old Golden Bridge and the cohort of ferries crammed tight with people who are pushed back from the pleasures of the city, them and their motorcycles, strollers, cars, those who live in the shanty towns leaning up against the forest. There's nothing of interest here. Sure, there are factories, harbour docks, a football field without bleachers, a supermarket, a school. But no one puts a kopeck into it. Volunteer associations set up free clinics in prefab buildings that start leaking at the first sign of the rainy season, maintain the church, care for the cemetery. That's it, and the general opinion is that that's enough. It's the land of cobbling things together and small-scale deals, schemes, ploys, all the little survival strategies that keep the mind alert; the land of small gardens, all the yards in fertile disarray; the land of hammocks cobbled together in damp shacks, the latest plasma-screen TVs and fridges full of beer; of trailers where Natives with piercing eyes sleep, depressed; and slapdash houses that won't make it through the winter – the floors warp, the electric wires melt once the space heater is plugged in, the exposed pipes freeze to the front walls. It's the land of the other side of the water, it's the outskirts of the city and the suburb of the forest, it's the land of the edge.

WHEN JOHN Johnson, called the Boa, bursts onto the municipal political scene in the early 2000s, he causes a stir – he is the reform and the new – and by bypassing the elite, supplanting the local heirs and using surprise, he creates a tactical advantage that lasts until his election. During his final campaign speech, he presents himself as Prince Charming, called to wake Sleeping Beauty. The one you've all been waiting for to begin living again.

A THIRD
LANDSCAPE

WINTER GOES ON FOREVER, A SHEATH OF glass. Cold corsets the city. Oxidizes perspectives, clarifies sounds, detaches each gesture, and in all of this the sky plays an exaggerated part. On the river – bleached ashen like the rest – people are at work and the bridge expands. Near the enormous columns that are now like the two indestructible ankles of this whole story, there are now long concrete seawalls reinforcing the banks. Steel is unloaded onto them, carried by rail to the Pontoverde platform, and then transported here aboard barges equipped with icebreakers.

It's phase two of the site, we're switching over to height, colonizing the sky. Diderot, in fine form, lifts his glass to no one in particular during a gathering on the work site, New Year's resolutions formulated by the skin of their teeth on December 31st, mulled wine served in translucent plastic glasses that immediately melt a little – but we know that his glass holds only Coca-Cola. In other words, Diderot's voice smacks, we're finished with the holes, the excavators, and the explosions, terminado the digging and the blasting of the ground, heads underwater and feet in the abyss, eardrums shaken by dynamite and the pressure of underwater chambers, the mud and the mire, done with the dredger – Verlaine packed his bag three days before Christmas – the time has come for cranes and arrows, the time of welders, rock bolters, the time of skilled labourers. We begin the raising of the towers: the Coca tower and the Edgefront tower, seven hundred and fifty feet high. Cheers! Shouts fuse together over the esplanade, and one voice distinguishes itself from the hubbub – a vaguely nasal timbre, probably that of Buddy Loo: seven hundred and fifty feet, yeah, kinda like the Empire State Building, eh – an assertion that's corrected right away by Summer Diamantis – the Empire is taller, ours will be more like the Tour Montparnasse, and she's barely finished her sentence when Sanche's voice sounds in her ear, Diamantis, there's not a single person here who knows the Tour Montparnasse, and without answering him, she migrates towards the wine.

THE WORKERS drink, pace, and comment, glasses in hand, we're gonna have to climb up there, gonna have to do it, with a mix of impatience and anxiety unbridled by the alcohol. Sanche Alphonse Cameron swallows a smile, arms crossed over his chest, puts on an innocent face: his time has come, and he knows it. Four months overseeing vehicle maintenance was enough for him – now he's going to gain some altitude. The Coca and Edgefront towers will be identical, each one composed of two immense steel piers placed thirty yards apart; these will be solidly anchored to a concrete foundation and then innervated to each other via crosspiece supports, sorts of gangways that will also serve as platforms to hoist people and materials. The piers themselves will be composed of prefabricated steel girders, bolted one to the other all the way up – requiring a rhythm of twenty-five girders per worker per day, the guys have been informed. With each tower thus reinforced, they'll rise yard by yard, and the higher they get, the more a mass of cables, pulleys, winches, and hoists will trickle down, and the crane will also progress, unfolding its boom in tempo with the work. Sanche's crane will work on the construction of the Edgefront tower.

He dribbles his way along the crowd to the buffet, lingers over the pot where the liquid churns like a priest's robe scented with alcohol, pepper, and cinnamon, orange zest floating, refills his cup: he likes this wine that rasps his tongue, exactly as this city has rasped his skin from day one. Because in terms of promising the good life, Coca has done more than meet his expectations: it has reinvented him. He arrived in September as a model crane operator, a loving only son, an attentive fiancé, but since then he's had the feeling that each day he's slipping a little further out of his lovely smooth skin, his even skin: it has dried, flaked off, fallen in scraps, and he rids himself of it with a stiff joy, kicking in the shavings, in the slough. Everything happened as though the city, which acted on his skin like silver nitrate on photographic paper, was revealing the stigmata of desire and ambition, the taste for the game, the will to power, and now he enjoys the feeling that another skin is forming beneath the old one, another skin that he doesn't yet know but that is the skin of real life, there is no doubt, and when he looks at his leopard body in the mirror, he feels handsome, yes, and tells himself that the moment has come to let what is inside him come to life.

DEEP INSIDE the multitude, Katherine Thoreau for the moment keeps her distance from Diderot, who verifies her presence with quick sidelong glances – they're waiting for each other. Night falls, the crowd disperses, people throw their glasses into large trash cans and drift towards the locker rooms; the alcohol has warmed them, but it's bonuses they're talking about as they open their lockers, this Christmas bonus that no one has got yet, can't let ourselves be lulled by cheap wine, we gotta sort this out. Trestles, portable stove, and cases of wine packed up, emptied, thrown out, and Mo Yun, astounded by these actions, begins to turn near the pot, there's still enough

145

to fill his flask and this is what he rushes to do, then sets about fishing out the orange peels one by one and stuffs them in a piece of newspaper, a cone he pockets, excited by this sweet deal, and then wanders away – and it's at this precise moment that Diderot makes out Katherine's hair as she moves towards the workers' facilities, tells himself she's leaving and he's going to miss her, tosses his cup in the can, and with hands in his pockets launches himself in her direction – after all, I never really got to thank her, this is what he tells himself to get himself in gear – and intercepts her, almost solemn, hey Thoreau, one thing, I wanted to say thank you – and Katherine, who had seen him, a moving mass slaloming between the last groups still on-site and had instinctively slowed her step so they would meet – choreography of collision, it's as old as the hills and still totally magic – she stops, opens her alcohol-clouded eyes wide, thank you? Thank you for what? She's had too much to drink, Diderot sees it right away, her face is capsized, he gets right to the point: thank you for the other day, the fight, you know what I mean. She rests her naked eyes on him, transparent irises stinging behind the slight swell of her lids, oh, that's all in the past, she pouts, that's behind us; she wobbles on her feet, puts a hand to her temple – I have to eat something, I've had a few drinks, I have to eat, and Diderot seizes the opportunity – a miracle of a chance – to simply say, wait for me, let's go.

LATER, THOREAU and Diderot are sitting in an ordinary snack bar, dazzled and stunned to be there and for it all to have happened so easily – even though they had to perform several circumventions in order to slip away quietly, and even though as soon as they'd been seated Katherine had to get up to go vomit in the toilet bowl, vile, in the bathroom – and, plunging her head into the hole, holding her hair back in a ponytail, she'd wanted to laugh again, I'm drunk, this is ridiculous – then she'd copiously splashed her clothes while rinsing her mouth under the faucet. The room is sparsely populated, only a few individuals lingering, two cops taking a break on their patrol, a man with a very long beard who soliloquizes. Quick, Katherine, have something to eat – this sudden first-name basis accelerates the cadence – Diderot calls the server over and Katherine checks her breath in her palm. You okay? He looks at her, smiling, and Katherine lifts her head, I'm great, and then, as though she couldn't wait any longer, she shrugs off her ugly parka, and, taking off her sweater, crosses and uncrosses her arms from bottom to top, a large movement, her face disappearing fleetingly into the wool collar, then she opens the top buttons of her shirt beneath Diderot's eyes that comb over her, imperturbable, and finally shakes her head lightly so her hair settles – a light moisture dews her top lip and her cheeks are red, and with this gesture she's just made you think she was too hot, but no – and in a rush of unexpected directness she says, I'll warn you, this is all I have to offer; Diderot, vaguely outdistanced, chews the inside of his cheeks and then states in turn, just as calm as she, and direct, that's already a lot, and Katherine, in a trembling voice, says I think so too.

AT MIDNIGHT, AT THE WHIRR OF THE SIREN THAT
signals the end of the second eight-hour time slot, the men
stagger from the Pontoverde platform, skin tight, eyes
burning under flickering lids. While most of them go back
to their digs, a few others head for downtown Coca, zone
of games and pleasures. The single ones value this rhythm
even though it exhausts the organism and disturbs the
nervous system (they get up around two in the afternoon,
work from four until midnight, party till dawn), it lets
them have the nightclubs when they're bumping. They
like night on the work site, night that encapsulates them,
encloses them in pools of light – multitudes of bulbs light
up the darkness like a celebration, vehicle headlights
signal to one another in code, the drivers' cabins are lit
like alcoves – and emphasizes their community, their
solidarity, and their strength: they are comrades, brothers
in arms. So they don't stagger too long, no, they get excited,
a little dazed and impatient to go hit on the easy women,
to drink and gamble, impatient to find, after the difficulty
and the tension of the work, a little simple flow, a little
sweet fluidity. Once they're out, they walk through the
fallen dusk in groups and keep up a good pace all the way
to the shuttles that will take them there; they climb inside,
already jostling one another, a pack of kids joking and
jeering, a gang of electric schoolboys. Soren Cry, with his
skirting-the-walls attitude, usually goes to sit at the back of
the bus, solitary, and leans his head against the window, his

gaze wandering out into the darkness; he likes these trips that are like decompression chambers, floating tunnels where he's taken in, transported, where he can finally let his guard down. He doesn't even see the guy who sits down beside him, who gives him a few taps on the shoulder so he'll turn around and holds out a solid hand, Alex. Soren extends his hand reluctantly and then turns back to the window, but the guy hits his shoulder again, three quick hits *whack whack whack*, I know, I know who you are, I knew you in Anchorage. Soren starts – no one can see it but I know that his heart jolts inside his chest as though he was suffocating and then starts up again in a torrent – he replies slowly, naw, man, you must be mistaken, I've never been to Anchorage, I'm from Ashland, Kentucky; but the guy suddenly leans in close till his shoulder is touching Soren's and lowers his voice, let's not waste time, Soren Cry, don't bother talking shit, you got it? Then, as Soren nearly pukes from terror, the guy spits out rapid fire in a falsely relaxed voice you had a little trouble in Anchorage, Soren, a story of a girl and a bear, not pretty – Soren's catapulted upright on his feet as though on a spring, leave me alone, man, I've never been to Anchorage, I'm from Ashland, you must be getting me mixed up with someone else – but the other gets up just as fast to push him back down with a palm pressed hard against his shoulder, listen up – this is your last warning before I go to the cops, they'd be glad to get the guy who killed someone with a bear, believe me, everyone there was real shaken up – are you listening – hey, are you listening to me? Soren lowers his head, the back of his black hat covers his brow and his eyeballs vibrate in the darkness, strangely liquefied, yeah, the guy comes to press his cheek violently against Soren's as though for a tango and breathes nicotine-gum-scented breath in his face, when we get downtown we're gonna get off together, but you're not gonna take off and play right away, we're gonna talk first, got it – I've got a job for you, a thing you can't say no to, or else, *bang* – he's placed his first and middle fingers together in a pistol against Soren's temple, blows on them like the professional after the clean execution of the contract – and Soren stiffens in place, cornered – and in fact, cornered is exactly what he is. When the guy finally steps away from him to joke around with the others in the front seats like nothing's going on, Soren turns his head to the window again: microscopic islands of light and noise – neon signs, yellow-gold windows inundated with the warmth of kitchens, glowing embers in car ashtrays, blue halo of television sets, dogs yowling, solitary joggers who breathe and hit the pavement in cadence, bikes that zip through the night – perforate the urban darkness, residential neighbourhoods that stretch out, that hold embraces, hold dreams, all this is not for him who will never, it seems, find any rest, never, ever. Soren knows the way, just a few more minutes before they reach the big time bad luck of the sidewalks, deep in the orange belly of the city; he is emptied out, and while the suburbs slide past the window, his past unrolls like a great scroll, just as black and shadowy, and, in a few linear bursts of light, there he is, back in Anchorage.

FROM THE airport onward he had trembled, rigid with exhaustion from the trip and the spectacle of corpses on display on the concourse. A magnificent collection of stuffed specimens from Alaska, land and aquatic wildlife, animals he'd taken the time to gaze at, impressed by the reflective gleam of their pupils – they too had a gaze – and by the shine of their teeth moistened with varnish – they were hungry; among them, a moose with flat antlers and gentle eyes, a strange amphibious and vaguely prehistoric creature, solitary and independent, who crosses large rivers and grazes with its head underwater; a white bighorn sheep with large amber-coloured horns curving in hoops like the rolled coiffure of Madame Bovary; and finally a brown bear standing on its hind legs, colossal: ten feet tall and at least a thousand pounds. Soren is fascinated by the power and the violence – two nouns that, to him, are strangely synonymous, and he has blithely confused them since childhood – that subsist in this furry carcass staged in the airport terminal. A handsome welcoming committee. One that nightmares are made of – and nightmares would come, the animal would come to life on the flagstones.

First there was the boat to build, a hull a hundred feet long with a steel frame that Soren and three other guys had put together over a few months; the owner, a rich restaurateur from Anchorage, is starting up a hunting business and wants to transport hunters and fishers in groups of thirty to the lodges he owns in Kodiak, Seldovia, and Eagle River. It's on this building site that Soren meets his first bear, a hungry young male who pulverizes the empty beer cans left behind after the break and flees at his approach. A few days later, when he sees it again, Soren decides from then on to prepare a bundle of berries, roots, and dried fish for the bear – he leaves it behind the shed, in the animal's path (he does this in secret: taming a bear on the work site is strictly forbidden). Ten days later, when he goes out behind the shed to see, there's nothing left of the bundle, and paw prints are clearly visible in the snow; Soren smiles, quivers with joy. A few days later he hears it growling again behind the fence, rushes to see it finish devouring the enormous bundle he'd brought so carefully onto the site; when it catches sight of him, the bear freezes, and they watch each other – Soren notices the red crescent mark above its eye – this lasts two or three seconds, no longer, and then the animal disappears behind a wall of containers.

Once the hull is finished, Soren finds another job in a factory where he freezes his ass off all day long standing in front of trays of fish to be gutted before packaging. Yet he continues to bring provisions, once or twice a month, until the night when he finds the bundle intact – the bear's not coming anymore. This desertion hits him hard: Soren lies around, gets drunk on weekends, feels himself foundering. When he hears word of a position as a bus driver that's opening, he snaps it up, and, displaying some ultimate confidence, he begins to venture into nature, which is where he meets the woman who will drive him completely insane.

Though he doesn't entirely believe in this thing between them – she's in university, she's travelled, and she speaks French – he lets himself be taken in because they share a similar metabolism, both are solitary, independent early risers, two mute and graceless individuals fascinated by wildness. In the beginning, Soren's not very physically attracted to her – she's stocky and short limbed, with a closed face and dull hair, but he likes her arrogance and her big breasts beneath the aqua down jacket, breasts she lets him enjoy at will, breasts he kneads, licks, sucks; besides, he's aware that she's not clingy, doesn't ask questions, and that his appetite for sex suits her. When she arrives at his place because of some story about a broken heater in her studio, he opens the door politely, specifies with a smile that this is only temporary, right, but he's so transfigured that a girl is knocking at his door, it's as though he's asking her to stay forever. So she makes her entrance, royal and desired, and soon there he is waiting for her to come home each evening, organizing night trips into nature, now he's driving her around, guiding her, and making casseroles for her. The end of the study she's been conducting on wolves (communication within the pack: decoding the cries and the howls) – signifies the end of their honeymoon. The girl returns to university and is suddenly smug about it, doesn't bother answering the questions he asks, is openly bored; soon she brings guys over to his place in the afternoon, students who are a little boorish but flush, who down his beers and drain his hot-water tank. Strangely, Soren takes it, says nothing, holding out – but the girl humiliates him more and more often, refuses to sleep with him anymore, refuses to let him touch her breasts, snickering at his handwriting – are you dyslexic or something? You should get that checked out, buddy, I won't be here forever – or at his job, going out each night under the black netting of new stockings, breasts out in the open, and comes home at dawn drunk to toss used condoms in the garbage. He finally asks her to leave – he's scared now that he might hit her, he knows himself, she's gotta get out of here. But the girl digs in her heels, says she's waiting for a money order from her father; Soren, crazy with rage, answers coldly I don't give a shit tonight you are outta here – but that night, ridiculous, they end up sleeping together again, and it's so intense for Soren that he doesn't know what he wants anymore. This time again the girl screamed her pleasure loudly; gleaming with sweat, strands of her hair stuck to her temples, she looks at him for a long moment with brilliantly shining eyes – her mouth is cruel and disdainful. Soren, it's time I told you clearly: I am not a big dog, not a mare or a goat: I'm a woman, a human being, can you get that straight? Then she turned towards the wall with a sigh, stifled a dirty little laugh, and, with her back arched, presented her ass to him again, and he took it. It was that same night that the bear from the site reappeared, foraging in the shrubby bushes behind his building. Soren is completely disoriented, the girl is asleep on her stomach. Not knowing how to find an outlet for the sexual violence that torments him, and feeling himself losing ground, he gets dressed and takes the garbage out, keys in hand. The animal is there in the small courtyard, resplendent, walnut brown and lustrous beneath an enormous moon; he lifts his head and looks at Soren with his little eyes, they recognize each other, the bear has the same sliver of red above his eye, it's him – Soren is dazzled, spellbound, calls the animal softly and he comes, moving slowly on four paws, swaying with his whole enormous body, and warm, it's magic, Soren climbs the stairs backwards, step by step, holding out the garbage bag to the bear who comes slowly, with no other noise than that of his fur against the walls at the turns, then once Soren's on the landing he opens the door quickly and puts the bag inside, a few feet from the doorway; he leaves the door open and slips out to climb a little higher on the staircase, and as soon as the bear goes inside the apartment, he turns the key in the lock with a fevered hand, closing the door on the bear and the girl.

THE MEN have just got off the bus. Alex immediately places himself behind Soren – who moves ahead reluctantly, desperate – and pushes him forward with a series of jabs to his shoulder. They plunge into a gleaming, oily neighbourhood, following narrow alleyways and finally enter an ordinary bar where a Frenchman is waiting for them. Have a seat. Beneath the grenadine bulbs that light the place, Soren learns their faces – Alex's intrigues him, he recognizes him vaguely. As though this conversation was just a pleasantry, an interlude of sociability in good company, the Frenchman points at both of them with a whirling index finger, what are you going to have? The minutes that follow are exactly like a hand squeezing the throat. The Frenchman, silver fox with prominent Adam's apple, says you'll receive a package at the midnight change of shift – Alex will bring it to you, but he won't come onto the site – you'll have to pick it up outside and then stash it in your locker. You'll still have time to catch the bus and have a drink with the guys. Soren looks at his hands trembling on the table: and then? Then you wait for instructions. Soren doesn't blink, he lowers his head again, his eye is reflected in the bronze of his beer, he exhales: what's in the package? At this point Alex plants himself against his shoulder again and practically licks his ear whispering, shut up, while the Frenchman lifts Soren's chin with the signet ring on his fist, listen up – you don't ask any questions, you just wait for instructions and everything will work out fine. But Soren insists, tears in his eyes like glue, and if I say no? If you say no? If you say no we may just find ourselves a bear and lock you up with it.

RALPH WALDO WILL BE STOPPING OVER IN Coca for twenty-four hours – this is what he tells Diderot in mid-January over the phone in a mild and international voice. Since the Boa is off in Dubai, Diderot and he will meet alone. Rendezvous in the Four Seasons bar, the last luxury hotel to open in Coca, a popular spot, built in the old prison like the one in Istanbul: the cells of the defiant Natives and the area's worst crooks have been redone as deluxe suites that go for two thou a night, after the walls have been scraped of all the rebellious graffiti, racist insults and threats directed at the judges – when I get out I'll stuff your balls down your throat – after sanding off the caricatures relegating the heads of these same judges to the darkness, cheeks colonized by scrubby sideburns, fur of corruption or intransigence; the visiting rooms are converted into meeting rooms for all kinds of conference calls, the workshops into business centres, the refectory into a jazzy lounge bar, and the slammer courtyard into a tropical garden with a mosaicked pool and beds of eternal, undying roses.

DIDEROT IS late by an hour at least, but Waldo smiles at him, fifty years old, tall and slim, without a paunch, splendid hands – slender wrists, but a singular width of the palm and thumb, fuselage of muscled fingers – placed on his hips, elbows thrown back spreading the tails of his jacket, billiard-ball head haloed with a glory still sharp: they say he won the Coca bridge contest by drawing the bridge right in front of the jury, pencil in hand, a double-edged ruler in his pocket, this is all I need he said right off the bat, presenting his meagre supplies one after the other like the magician who shows the audience the inside of his hat before pulling out a flock of turtledoves, all I need is an idea and a strong philosophy. Then the oral part of the presentation, the dreaded challenge, had mutated into a master class, Ralph Waldo beginning his talk with murmurs whispered into the auditorium as though he was pondering aloud: how is a bridge conceived? How does its shape appear? Is it determined by the context, or does it define itself according to the stated needs? From there he had launched into a virtuoso demonstration led by his hands that suddenly inhabit all the space and by his voice that explains each detail on the board, nevertheless allowing himself a few fumbles, a couple of hesitations while he tears white sheets from the large board, pantomime of the violent and inhabited genius, and even though it is false – even grossly hypocritical – this work in progress becomes something daring, sassy, that captivates the judges: they will award the prize to this choreography, as well oiled as a number by the Bluebell Girls.

WHISKY LIGHT and fluffy carpet, willowy women swaying between tables, golden dimness, the men start drinking. They get to the bridge immediately: how is the site going, Georges? The man scrutinizes Diderot from behind his fine, round, polycarbonate glasses; he's dressed in black – polo shirt, Italian suit, and leather running shoes with rubber soles, the latest trend. Diderot takes off his jacket, mumbles, it's going fine, we've dredged three-quarters of a million cubic yards of silt and sediment, a whole shit heap that we dumped back into the ocean, not a pretty picture, I'm not sure we're totally within the lines, have to watch that the eco gang doesn't crack down on us;

then we had to dynamite a channel and level the shoals – we've prepared the bed for the beast, the anchorage phase is almost done, we're raising up the towers, everything's on schedule.

Ralph Waldo smiles. His question was intended to evoke a general impression, an emotion, some interiority – not a technical report. A dialogue of the deaf ensues: while Ralph Waldo extrapolates on the question of the bridge, touching upon the aesthetics, the intimate experience of crossing over, and that of nature – he's the man who returns from a great theoretical distance, the one who invents the form – Diderot delimits it, handles it technically, numbers it, sizes it, and finally gives his progressive rectilinear view of the crossing; this goddamn bridge, like all kinds of works, is nothing more than the calibration of a form we all know inside and out, and to talk about it means simply isolating a problem and breaking it down, breaking it down, always breaking it down, one more time, and then once more, and it's in this methodical way that any appropriate response will arise – this is his method, his way of thinking.

RALPH WALDO versus Georges Diderot. Two men face to face, deep in their armchairs, the alcohol going to their heads; the bar is closing, last call, they have one last stiff shot and then go, hugging themselves in the rain, Ralph Waldo teetering with his glasses in hand, my aim is always to intervene the least amount possible he shouts with his arm extended in what he believes to be the direction of the bridge, one must always find the lightest, purest, most modern form, an interpretation of the landscape – his glasses fall to the sidewalk as he stumbles in the gutter – an interpretation of the landscape, that's what I deliver, he streams water and belts it out, happy in this moment, and Diderot inwardly visualizes the giant mechanism of the site, the deployment of forces, the physical expenditure of the men, haggard and dirty by day's end, the deafening noise of the machines, the bundles of bills counted and recounted one by one in filthy hands before being folded into small squares at the bottom of leather wallets, the accidents that threaten and those that happen, the closed faces of the Natives and the violent movements of the men from Detroit, suddenly making out Summer concentrating on her concrete and Sanche, minuscule at the foot of his crane, holding all this with Katherine right in the middle at the controls of her excavator, he lets himself be overcome with emotion – an interpretation of the landscape! – a silent laugh shakes him as the architect takes great strides towards the river, chest slanting to the ground as though he is charging into a strong adverse wind, Diderot clings now to Waldo's voice that cuts through the wind and declaims: a third landscape – not the welding together of two areas, Georges, but a new landscape! Waldo has put an arm through Diderot's, and, hooked together like this, they make their way towards the river, drunk, spirited, magnetized by the banks, the tree-lined path, the little benches, the bushes, and soon hypnotized by the roar of the waters, the curvilinear signs traced on the surface, the bubbling filaments – illegible chalk messages on a blackboard – that disintegrate in a space of seconds.

The unfinished bridge is massive in the night, a monstrous presence, very dark – Waldo stares at it in a low voice, the lighting at night shouldn't be too bright, too spectacular, Georges, I don't want flame sabres, beams that slice, bulbs that carve, all that grandiloquence junk – the towers won't be lit right up to the top, that way you'll be able to imagine them extending into the night, the deck will be a simple stroke like a vanishing line, and we'll regulate the balance between shadows, between different qualities of shadows, we'll let the materials, the river, the city, and the forest touch, and, for the bridge, all I want is for people to sense the strength of the cables. Diderot listens to the architect's voice flowing through the murmur of Coca and that of the forest, and holds Waldo back as he leans dangerously far out over the waters, seeing nothing; he turns him around gently so they can go back together, and whispers in his ear, about the lighting, no problem, I've got a plan for that too.

SANCHE HAS A COUPLE OF MINUTES LEFT before the day starts up, before he has to decode the workers' hand signals as they prepare and balance the loads to be lifted – standard gestures outlined on professional charts, official crane operator language learned by heart and hard-hatted silhouettes drawn on white paper on the day of the exam – and then hoist each load of reinforcing steel that must be placed within a half-inch degree of precision. A few minutes left to enjoy his position. Sanche turns towards Coca, his gaze grazes over the city, stops at an intersection where silhouettes rush along, says to himself how much he'd like to turn his boom towards that tower on the river's edge, thirty storeys high in aquamarine blue, and maybe he would be able to touch, with the end of his extendible arm, the window of that girl who welcomed him in Coca, that twisted, splendid caller at the square dance of life.

FIRST FORMIDABLE hours of his arrival in Coca, the girl who's all legs who lifts his name up on a placard, the car that rushes towards the city, the radio turned up blasting international pop. This impression of crazy speed and light that spatters, this incredible feeling that life is racing ahead. Shakira croons, sings loud on the choruses, shakes her head, her hair coming loose, taps her hands against the wheel, pressing the accelerator at the same time so that they move in rhythm with the stereo, smokes red Dunhills, slants a look at a text, and once they're alone in the middle of the plain says to Sanche in a husky, ironic voice, don't worry, sugar, I love to drive in heels, and he grimaces a smile, a smile of panic and enthusiasm, that will need to be elucidated; his mouth is dry, now, the reverberation of the sun exhausts his eyes so thoroughly that he finally lowers the visor, tells himself he has to buy a hat right away, a black one, a stetson with a leather band, promises himself he won't go cheap; and then the highway that cuts through a desert zone with powdery ground, white as a lake of salt, occupied here and there by little groups of shacks, by thirsty coyotes – Sanche imagines them lingering around the oil wells – and by cacti with arms outstretched like Christs in glory. Suddenly space gaping open before him, a lateral scope, the faraway hills at both ends of the plain, shadowy forms floating on the haze of the heat, blue, drowsy like dinosaurs, while here, right beside him, the girl is another mountain who adjusts the A/C and pays attention to the vibrations of her cellphone; Sanche, stunned by their communal presence in this mercurial racing car, shivers, rubs his hands together, smiles again that same smile people like about him, head held high and facing the windshield; he says to himself in this second, here I am in the latest Mercedes beside a Russian girl with legs to die for, I'm twenty-seven years old, I'm a crane operator who just flew fifteen hours to come to this site, my first bridge, and I know like everyone else that anyone who wants to build a bridge must first make a pact with the devil, and before him, the highway is like a fatal funnel he dives into headfirst with her beside him.

LATER THEY reach the end of the high plain, the highway ending bluntly at the edge of a precipice beyond which, crouched in the valley, the city of Coca shimmers – a camo moth, thinks Sanche, leaning closer to the windshield, it must show up best at night. In the middle of the day, the sky reflects its serene grammar in the facades of the towers, and the entire landscape is absorbed into them while the cranes, cranes by the hundreds, planted close together, augur the city's power to come. They merge onto a street that's fairly wide but fissured, pavement eroded by couch grass; it winds along the side of the plateau in sweeping bends grossly hollowed out from the limestone plateau, and once it reaches the valley, blends with the interchanges and other fast streets, the way a white strand sneaks into an otherwise vigorous head of hair. Later, when they reach the heart of the city, Shakira Ourga's large hand makes excited deferential gestures as she points out Coca's riches, her face tense with a restless rictus. She makes a point of slowing down in front of the giant aquariums inside which he can see the gleam of luxury racing cars, check it out! Ferrari, Mercedes, Porsche – they're all there, Sanche nods his head solemnly, leans forward to see, whistles, and in so doing gives Shakira great pleasure; soon she tosses the keys of the Mercedes to a Filipino valet, dark as a spectre in front of the door of a restaurant on the first floor of a mirrored tower – for seven years he's been standing here, in his narrow redingote and tasselled cap pushed back on his head; seven years since he immigrated to Coca, seven years, you have to stop and imagine such a sequence, counting on your fingers, the faces of the wife and kids fading inside the pages of his passport, a monthly money transfer sent to the village and the crumbs of his paycheque gone to pay for a room without windows in a basement somewhere, very rarely a woman with him, and candied tangerines that he sucks in front of the television, he says only thirty words a day, but the same ones a hundred times over.

They eat lunch quickly once Shakira has put down her phone and taken the waiter to task for serving the table beside them first – she speaks to him in a hard tone, face closed, the nail of her index finger tapping the gold-plated face of her Swiss watch. Face-on, close-up, the relief of her face is brought into focus, and Sanche follows its line, rising and falling, a route that unfurls its black coil behind the table where the girl devours her meal, citizen of Coca, new and jewelled in an irreproachable body, cared for like a precision tool, behind this avenue where she works for the city, behind this tower where she sleeps with the director of the powerful chamber of commerce (who happens to be the owner of the Mercedes), a route that unlaces dirty bus stations and the fear of being killed, the back of covered trucks where she knocked against others like her, baggage holds, trunks of cars, train toilets, robberies, the joy of coming upon a half-full can or a sweater at the bottom of the garbage, freezing your ass off and filthy. And behind her curving back that's already been through so much, things are fidgeting, stirring, shouting – behind her is Russia, the war, and Youri, her little brother the soldier, the one who was posted to Chechnya, the one she didn't wait for. The one who left as a young man without knowing, not a war lover, no, more like a lazy sun-basking snake or a clever monkey, who left in January 2000 without knowing, in just the same way you'd get up from the couch to stretch your legs – and who is now charging into suspicious buildings in a suburb of Grozny, breaking down doors with great kicks, submachine gun held firmly against his hip and pointed inside at hypothetical enemy bodies vanishing into dark corners, staked out in the rubble, or covered in mud, and who freezes in front of the apartments, waits, listens, keeps watch, and at the least noise sprays a heavy shower, sprays a ton, sweeping the space with the gun *rat a tat tat tat tat*, sprays like a madman, and after a while he doesn't even go to the trouble of listening first, nor of casting a look inside – he breaks down the door and machine-guns straight away without waiting – he's that scared, he's seen that many of his buddies in agony after being ambushed by surprise gunfire, and then have their throats cut post-mortem – he's that terrorized, broken, out of his head, and that's how crazed, deceitful, and fanatical the other side is, that's how much they want his scalp, and through all this there's the waste, there are drops, it leaks even, dammit it drips, blood and guts, there are cries and screams and old women and children, through all this he leaves a hell of a trail of carnage, that Youri, he spends his time machine-gunning, he's the kamikaze of the squadron, he doesn't know how to do anything but this anymore, and when he stops, it's to drink his face off with other guys who, like him, left without knowing, or it's to go to the brothel – but he can't even get it up anymore, there are too many little noises in the room, too many suspicious breaths – or to write to Shakira, his beautiful sis. Shaki, wait for me, wait for me to get back to Moscow, we'll get out of there together, I'll have the cash. But Shaki left without him. And behind her, Youri breathes down her neck with his fraternal breath, a nauseating stench of gunpowder and hot blood.

AFTER THE meal, Shakira steps away to compose a message on her phone and then suddenly does an about-face, decides to take a trip to the beach stretched out along the length of the river north of the city, and Sanche lets himself be carried along even though just the idea of a beach seems bizarre to him right now – a beach! – it hadn't even crossed his mind – all he's seen so far of Coca is an assembly of towers arranged in a geometric cadaster.

On the way, they pass other sedans that are as powerful and drive past other buildings that are as dazzling although still unfinished. Shakira sums it up: here, the rules are simple – if you have money, come on in, and if not, well then, bye-bye! – her hands leave the wheel to illustrate the words – inward/outward flaps – and Sanche, gobsmacked, contracts his buttocks on the seat as the car plunges full speed ahead in the fast lane that hugs the river's edge.

Water-level parking lot, new cafés, patios, umbrellas with logos, cheery soundtrack, and always pop, synth versions of old standards. At this hour, a high-rolling sun varnishes the surface of the water and the sand of the beach sparkles like sugar. They walk to the shore. This is the only place where I feel happy, Shakira breathes deeply, sends her thongs clattering with a kick, walks towards the water, hikes her jeans up to mid-thigh, and enters the river, calling out to Sanche, come on! come on! and Sanche has the feeling that things are becoming clear. They're becoming clear in a strange way, because his gaze abandons the girl to move farther off, towards Edgefront and the opposite bank: greens of all sorts mix their shades into a sonorous and profuse border of vegetation, tall as a man, a few roofs of sheet metal emerging here and there, shacks, motor boats anchored beneath the branches, rowboats, and pontoons floating on tires, and farther still, in the depth of the field, the rise of a forested mountain devours the sky loudly. Then, Shakira's voice again, come on! come! She smiles at him from the riverside and he smiles back, shaking his head no, hands in his pockets and feet scraping the minuscule stones; and he's sweating beneath his shirt, he's thirsty, wipes the corners of his lips. So the Russian stepped from the water and walked straight towards Sanche with long strides, thighs streaming, hair floating like feather dusters, stopped right in front of him and commanded: take off your clothes. Weighed up like this, Sanche rubbed his chest with an indecisive hand: he hated to disappoint. Right now he's wondering if he'll have to carry out the lubricious actions appropriate to the situation – in other words, contained as they are within a limited perimeter and subject to high temperatures, he, a Russian girl, and green water bathing the length of a city given over, mouth open, to a future bridge; asks himself if the time had come to, if he was being watched, if this tall chick straight out of the taiga was a test, a lure; he unbuttons his collar, loosens his tie, suddenly catches sight of a guy combing the sand with a metal detector, warns the girl, careful, he's going to get you – Shakira lets out a stunned whinny of a laugh and picks up her sandals, Sanche mops his forehead, and they leave the beach.

Before starting the car again, Shakira had carefully wiped the sand off her feet with tissues slipped between her toes and then curtly crumpled and tossed out the window one by one, the whole box soon squandered. Sanche's eyes had followed the white Kleenexes that floated in the air, fluttered softly, deformed by the slightest breeze, and finally settled on the ground, little by little smudging the entire landscape.

THE SIREN sounds, Sanche gets into position. On the ground, carpenters, welders, and rock bolters press together, having stepped off the river shuttles. They wear hard hats, they're getting ready, heavy-footed. They pace without getting anywhere. At the second sounding of the siren they remain aggregated, their shoulders move in an abnormal wave, and suddenly one guy steps away from the group – the others encircle him – he speaks for a long while, brandishes his fist, shakes his head no, and it seems like the others are with him. Sanche calls an engineer on the platform, the walkie-talkie crackles, there's a lot of noise down there, shouts, stirrings of anger, what's going on? A circumspect tone responds, things are heating up, the guys won't go to work, there's a commu-nication breakdown. Sanche presses against the window to see better – an abnormal restlessness prevails below, the guys who try to head towards the crates are prevented by others who grab them, hurl abuses at them – features change in an instant: mouths that open wide, circumflex eyebrows, red blotches. The crowd has become a body shaken by spasms,

Sanche thinks to himself someone's gonna end up in the river, thinks the water's freezing, doesn't understand anything, and decides to climb down. Once he's on the ground, what strikes him is the raging commotion, the tumult. The guy who set himself apart tries to keep the crowd calm, a white guy, torso narrow as a playing card, shoulders like a coat hanger, pointed, a kind of gypsy; he lifts two knotty arms to silence the crowd, hey, hey, two black sideburns lie like Arabic daggers along clean-shaven cheeks, and when his thin lips – a dark stroke – finally open, they spit out words one by one: no one goes to their station, no one – we want a daily raise, and until we get it, we don't go back to work. His voice furls in the brief silence that follows, then spurts out again, playful for the first time, we didn't get a Christmas bonus – well, we're gonna get something better than that.

Men are now forming a barricade across the platform, linking together, arms like basket handles threaded through one another, they align themselves solemnly. Sanche walks among the workers, curious, a little marmoset come down from his branch fishing for information, irresistible and a pain in the ass, smiling brightly, he doesn't pass by unnoticed. After some time steering through the crowd, he finally comes upon the man who was speaking and asks him, what's happening? The other scans him with a suspicious eye, what's happening is that we want to be paid starting when we set foot on the work site, and not only from the time we fasten the first bolt, get it? Sanche nods his head yes and the other continues, speaking as though he was spitting with anger, they deduct the time it takes for us to get here, but the thing is it takes thirty, sometimes forty minutes between punching in on the platform and arriving here – so multiply that by two, coming and going, and that's at least an hour extra per day – at least. We will not be exploited. The man is cold, rubs his hands together, looks at his ancestor's watch on his wrist tattooed with barbed wire, we'd better not take too long or they're gonna lose their temper in the back. At that moment a group of workers approaches, worried, we don't want any trouble, we can't afford to lose our jobs; and the man with sideburns slashes them with his eyes one by one, coldly, his mandibles pulse beneath their fur, *baa, baa,* so we're sheep then? *baa, baa* – he scowls, terrifying in his anger – Sanche follows the exchange with fevered attention, wonders how this is all going to play out, already wants to be a part of it, when suddenly the guy with sideburns shouts at him with a jerk of his chin, you management? Sanche assents without blinking, and specifies as though apologizing, I'm not under local contract; the other looks at him contemptuously, well you've done well for yourself then, and turns back towards the men all packed together, stamping the ground, some of them smoking with hands cupped around their mouths as though to warm them. Sanche stands frozen in place, terribly alone.

The workers are trying to organize themselves now, talking about defending their interests, tongues are loosened: untenable pace, sketchy safety measures, shitty salary. The story of the twenty-five box girders per worker per workday – this means three assembled per hour in the deafening noise, discomfort, and glacial cold – is brought up again: the guys shout that the box girders have been badly assembled in the prefab workshops, that all too often they have to weld in order to make sure the steel pieces fit, to standardize them, to make them watertight, and that this slows the rhythm – and not all of them are trained welders, a certified skill, a craftsman's job. The man with sideburns walks among them, introduces himself – he's a carpenter, from Ontario, and Seamus O'Shaughnessy is his name. From time to time he casts a glance at his watch and eventually comes back towards Sanche, you – you're management, so call the bosses and tell them to step on it, we're cold out here. Sanche nods okay, steps away from the group – happy to be the messenger – calls Diderot, who picks up, listens, asks him to specify the number of guys and the causes of the walkout – you can just see him twisting his mouth and stroking his chin – says okay, I'm coming.

DIDEROT'S ARRIVAL on the Edgefront site causes an awestruck silence, a mixture of reticence and curiosity. They all know his form by heart and step aside to let him pass. Who's the spokesperson? At these words the silence grows thicker, and then Seamus O'Shaughnessy steps forward from the ranks, his lips pressed so tightly together that they are no more than a notch on his disturbing face: I am. The two men size each other up. Seamus restates the demand – always this same clipped phrasing, lips that pull back to reveal his gums: a raise of one hour per workday. Diderot looks at the guys, says we can't do it: an hour a day is six per week, twenty-four per month, etc., multiplied by the number of salaries, I don't have to spell it out for you, it's pie in the sky. Oh yeah, what do you mean pie in the sky? Seamus grows tense, body like a tight fist pushed deep in a pocket, and Diderot says drily, you'll never get it. Seamus turns towards the others, okay, so we'll put the strike to a vote: if we don't get a raise, we stop working. The guys start to get riled up, swell slowly in a great collective movement – it's quite beautiful to behold – and now some of them address Diderot directly without any more protocol, some of them call him by name – Diderot doesn't have superpowers, he's just a man with two arms and two legs and a hard hat on his head, and he too is in deep at the moment – they repeat, we wanna be paid for the travel time, or we walk out; their voices overlap and comfort one another, one guy takes it further, yeah, and we'll occupy the site. The hot flame of anger is reawakened in their eyes all around, the feeling of power, yeah, we'll stay, we *are* the bridge. Sanche has stepped up onto a crate, we're in a power struggle now, he trembles, excited, and watches Diderot evaluate the situation, weighing the seriousness of the crisis, knowing he has to work something out quickly, has to find a solution. Diderot states slowly, almost solemnly: I agree with the principle. Some of the guys shout, applaud, someone lifts a woman up by the waist, everyone starts pushing against each other; Seamus throws them a wrathful look, what are they thinking? We're not here to celebrate Santa's generosity, we're here to put pressure on the boss. Diderot quells the crowd again immediately by announcing, with a lift of his hand, hang on, now we'll have to do the calculations. Gust of silence and ebb of enthusiasm among those facing him, you won't get rid of us with a few extra crumbs, we won't let ourselves be walked all over, says the woman who was just lifted up in triumph.

DIDEROT PICKS up the pace now, points to Sanche, you, come with me; and turning to Seamus O'Shaughnessy, asks him to also choose a witness – he picks Mo Yun, petrified in the front lines and whose excessively large hard hat half-closes his agitated eyelids. Diderot elucidates his method: synchronize your watches, we're going to take the trip together, the weather conditions are normal, we'll time the exact length of the trip from the locker rooms to the site, and when that's done, and only then, we'll negotiate.

  The quartet sets out in the shuttle back towards the Pontoverde platform, moving farther away, leaving the workers a little lost – some raise their hands and wave as though they were heading off on a long voyage. After a few minutes, Seamus points out to Diderot that in fact this is a speedboat and not the slower river shuttle that transports the workers from one end of the site to the other – he specifies, tensely, I'm telling you because we need to be meticulous. Diderot nods, that's true, and asks the driver to adjust his speed to that of the workers' boat.

The bow streams along the corridor in the frozen river, conquered that very morning by other ships, the layer of ice hasn't closed over again, and they can hear the water splashing against the hull, no one speaks on-board as though they were all thinking only about the time that passes, that materializes in this spray, thick and white, exploding in heavy pendants and then slowly dissipating into greyish strands. Diderot thinks: this is not the first time he's been confronted with a crisis, nor threatened with a strike – but the previous times, the guys were organized, represented by unions, negotiations followed an official protocol, discussions moved along a clear track, bolted step by step according to a pre-established timeline, each emissary with a few cards up his sleeve. But in Coca – which is, after all, a remote nowhere – the teams mix several different nationalities, the projects require the workers to split up on sites that are far from one another, and, moreover, everything was thought through so as to prevent their coagulating forces: at least half of those hired are under short-term contracts, weekly gigs that, even though they are automatically renewed from one week to the next, thus creating identical linear presences, still instill a sense of profound difference in status among workers on the site, maintain a feeling of precariousness in some – that of a vacation that could end at any moment – and in others, some of whom were lucky enough to have a year-long contract, a feeling of privilege, of a security that should be protected at all costs, the naive sense that they are sitting on a sack of gold, and that there should be no false moves, easy, Tiger, no point in trashing this incredible luck for nothing. And so the conflict had immediately taken on a primitive aspect – a gust of wind whipping, a fire spilling over, a fist in the stomach – it is sudden, confused, unpredictable, gathered up into a single violent desire for justice that shines a torchlight on all the faces; and it is exactly this that shakes Diderot.

Fifteen minutes have already passed in the trip. With his face turned towards the prow, delighting in the frontality smacking him in the face, Sanche prepares himself for his first conflict – so happy in this moment to be in the heart of the action, recollecting as best he can the greatest moments in the labour movement as told by the man from Nouakchott over the long nights when they had sweated together – while Mo Yun, not used to being singled out from a group, is standing circumspect. Once they arrive at the Pontoverde platform, they walk towards the workers' facilities, crossing the esplanade at such an absurdly normal pace that Sanche stumbles, he's trying so hard to control his ankles. At the door of the building each one of them reads his watch face aloud, elbow lifted to horizontal, and Diderot concludes: the trip took twenty-six minutes, are we all agreed? The others nod. All right. We can begin negotiations.

ONCE AGAIN the overheated room, once again the schoolroom table and chairs, once again the tension partitioning the room into two camps – the bosses (Diderot, Sanche) – before the workers (O'Shaughnessy, Yun). And they're off. Seamus, diving right in, restates the demand for a raise: fifty-two minutes of supplementary wages calculated in proportion to an hour of salaried work and multiplied by the number of days worked. Sanche, who volunteered to be secretary of the meeting, scrupulously notes the demand, and after a few minutes Diderot presses the speaker button on the telephone and begins to read this paper to the board members who, practically ulcerated, pass the words along – you have to handle the troops, Georges, the CEO scolds him thoroughly – a raise of this much is impossible, and I'll remind you that the work just got extended by at least three weeks because of these bloody stupid sparrows – and suddenly there's nothing more idiotic on earth than these voices, these little authoritarian gullets that, through the intermittence of the satellite connection, become vulnerable, quavering even, mixing in with the static and the inopportune echoes, the satellite delays – it becomes completely staggering to think that these nebulous packets of vocal waves could have a part in this story, that they'd be granted room to manoeuvre, and even crazier to think that they'd be obeyed – it was all such a farce – and Diderot tried to hold back the hysterical laughter that rose up in him. And when he summarized the conflict for them, he kept to the essentials: the workforce is paid for eight hours of work even though they're here for nine hours, so either you stretch out the dough or we tighten up the shifts – in any case you've gotta move fast or the guys won't go back to work, the strike will be put to a vote at noon, and then we will have lost the whole day.

SIX O'CLOCK strikes now at head office in Bécon-les-Bruyères, a crisis committee meets *chop chop*, and already the financial directors are in violent opposition, those who are for a raise arguing that a reduction in work time will lead to paying much higher lateness compensation to the municipality of Coca, and those who are for a reduction in work time panicking at the thought that the bridge's budget will explode if they pay this additional hour. Calculators heat up between impeccably manicured hands. Some of them, zealous, frenetic, compare the cost of laying off the troublemakers to that of importing dependable workers, and others imagine the worst – what if this spreads like wildfire and contaminates the whole site? They're so worked up they don't even notice night falling like a slipcover over the Héraclès tower, while thousands of miles away, in another latitude, closer to the equator, a winter sun forces its way behind the clouds, bleaching their dirty whites, and they sweat it out in the meeting room, it's almost twelve o'clock.

SEATED AT his desk, Diderot scrolls through the reverse schedule for the umpteenth time. Lifting his head to the three others, he suddenly says: okay, we'll work it out between us. Seamus starts, immediately mistrusting this "us" that stinks of trouble, mafia collusions, secret deals, familial scheming, everything that disgusts him – and he has reason to be mistrustful: Diderot is not on the workers' side, doesn't know a thing about a guilty conscience, and if he speaks about an egalitarian "between us," it's out of pragmatism, to find the solution that will put everyone back to work the fastest. Seamus resists, demands a proper agreement, an official, signed document, a guarantee: there's no "us" here, Mr. Diderot, we just want our extra hour. For his part, Mo Yun nods his head and tries to remain invisible, worried that this confrontation might be hiding certain stakes that his rudimentary English could miss, worried it will go to court – and then, he's certain he'll be the accused who's forced into a public confession before ending up in a hole somewhere with a bullet in the back of his head; he thinks back to Datong and all those he saw marching in the People's Square, dunce caps on their heads and signs on their backs, and although he thinks long and hard he can't figure out how he could have been noticed, he who always keeps his head down, stammers and trembles – now he looks for a pretext to be able to leave the room while in front of him Sanche holds his breath – his first social conflict can't just pass by right under his nose, he's got to really feel the thing. This is when Diderot gets up, massive, swings forward with all his weight to slap his hands down flat on the table – they're enormous, stretched out like that, fingers spread out from one another, like great paws – and leaning forward, he looks Seamus in the eye, brows raised so high they're lost in the creases of his forehead. He speaks in a confident tone, without yelling: the balance of power is not in my favour, the site is already behind schedule, we absolutely can't allow a strike – I deliver on time, I've always delivered on time, it's a question of principle. Sorry, but that's not my problem, O'Shaughnessy shakes his head and he too leans forward over the table, *my* problem is a fair wage. He shoots Diderot an inflexible look and remains tense when he answers, the directors will never budge, you're wasting your time: I propose the following agreement, you can take it or leave it: compensation for the transport time, per worker – twenty-six minutes multiplied by two and multiplied by a hundred – now it's up to you if you want to enter into a conflict with Pontoverde. Why a hundred? Seamus asks, suspicious, because in a hundred days we will have finished raising these goddamn towers. Diderot gets up to open the window. And what if the work drags on? Seamus's voice behind him. Diderot whips around: you'll get nothing more on the salaries, they can wait for weeks, but you guys can't and neither can I. I'll talk to the guys, they can decide – Seamus is already getting up from the table and leaves the room holding the written proposal that Sanche, deeply moved, has just handed him.

TWO HOURS later, while Diderot was calling the board to tell them about the agreement and the amount of the bonus – a done deal that illustrates how his is a regime of exceptions within the consortium and betrays his power – not a single executive bats an eye, you want the work to keep going, right? – the guys on the tower carry Seamus O'Shaughnessy and Mo Yun in victory and snap away at them with their cellphones – Mo Yun in an absolute panic now, agoraphobic and desperate to escape these arms carrying them, these hands touching them – and Sanche applauding what he calls the workers' victory – swift conflict and baptism by fire in which, in his mind, countless future promises can be seen.

AT THE BEGINNING OF MARCH, A PONTOVERDE delegation arrives on-site for an official visit commentated by Ralph Waldo himself, a squadron of senior executives with great potential, to which the Boa adds his own contingent of loyalists, as well as some councillors from the opposition who he hopes to neutralize, placing himself at the head of the group – twenty men and three women – and once they all have their hard hats on, this tribe strolls from one end of the site to the other after Diderot has greeted each of them with a handshake and an offer of coffee and cookies in the meeting room of the main building – some are surprised at the destitution of the place, at the insipidity of the coffee, but they approve of the heating system which they study as though they were potential buyers when in truth they're just dawdling, because outside Coca's continental climate continues to assert its brutality, a biting cold darned with blizzards stings the cheeks, assaults shoe leather, penetrates gloves: when they leave, they'll step out backwards.

FOR DIDEROT, these visits are nothing but a big pain in the ass – people will scrutinize his way of doing things, will ask questions, will wait to catch him out: this business of the transit bonus is still fresh in their minds, a *fait accompli* that he has not yet been forgiven for; Héraclès had had to convince the other parties that make up Pontoverde (Blackoak Inc. and Green Shiva Co.) to pull out their pocketbooks, which prejudiced people against him; and the

South Asians, among others, had taken malicious pleasure in mocking these screw-ups, threatening to send in inspectors.

The delegation is invited to come quickly to the site because now there's something to see – the towers – and they get moving. The Natives, warm inside appropriate clothing – thick canvas, fur mitts, fur-lined waterproof boots – stand out from the rest, relaxed, movements loose and smiles on their lips. The executive directors of the consortium, on the other hand, collate their active lightweight shells, bottle-green or sea-blue jackets with corduroy collars, waterproof but not very warm, which they wear on family sailing regattas in the summer offshore from Trinité-sur-Mer in France; they blow on their hands, stamp the ground with their trekking shoes, letting fall a fine clay powder stuck to their soles since Easter hikes on the Pyrenean slopes, when they went valiantly from shelter to shelter with a walking stick in hand, pulling a recalcitrant horde of kids behind them who beg for a Coke each time they stop, never lifting their eyes to admire the sublime peaks, the mountain sheep, and the unparalleled beauty of the wildflowers. These ones had just boarded the rapid shuttles splitting through the squall and already their extremities were red, especially their noses; their lips turned practically the colour of eggplants, the circles under their eyes deepened, retracting them into the back of their sockets – but not one of them dares to speak about the glacial temperature – virility will not allow it, and after all, the guys on the bridge work outside all the time.

WHEN THE large river shuttle comes into view of the bridge towers, a few men whistle, suggesting that the site is much further along than they would have thought, and, reassured, grimace their contentment. It's all taking shape, one of the Héraclès legal counsel concludes. The towers are indeed impressive already, slender and vigorous, flagpoles without any fanfare besides their scarlet verticality. Since their elevation progresses at a constant rhythm, the joke is that they are building themselves, as though their form, their shape is only the consequence of a congenital movement – as though they are actually developing from the inside. But behind the steel walls, it's an insane mechanics that proliferates upward, a labyrinth of box girders where workers could get lost looking for the one they were working on the day before; it's the din of welders echoed, multiplied, boring into eardrums amid the smell of hot metal, it's the explosive atmosphere of a blast-off.

But for Coca's inhabitants, the most striking thing has less to do with the towers' construction than with their sudden presence in the city. An event that affects time as much as it does space. A split. We can never go back. From now on, *never* and *always* would come up in office conversation, in hallways and lobbies, and the higher the towers grew, the more thoroughly something was erased, relegated to the past – and all the more swallowed up, all the more lost since this past was so close and intimate, that much more irretrievable since this past was just yesterday, it was the city "before the towers" that would soon be the city "before the bridge." Something had died, and so what did it matter, the idea of progress attached to the work, what did modernity matter and the need to get with the times, thinking about it dealt a wicked blow.

Getting used to these red metal towers wasn't easy – nothing in their shape or their material helped them to blend into the landscape, to infiltrate it gently. They tripped up the gaze, these superstructures, while at the same time – a paradox that provoked hours of discussion – they stood with a disconcerting simplicity, nearly enigmatic, like elements of a decor that had been waiting in the wings and whose hour had finally come to appear onstage, rising up in exactly the spot where two crosses on the ground had marked their places, sure, incontestable. They rose from the water and the inhabitants oscillated, lost souls without any points of reference anymore, and many were those who urgently set about recounting anecdotes that traced the story of their lives against that of the area, scanning backwards across the urban temporality to unearth lost pathways; tongues came unknotted and spoke of meeting places that don't exist anymore, travel times that have been shortened, walks that have become dangerous, ferry routes that have disappeared, and the subject of horses came up often; then they would blink in the direction of the bridge, and in a grand gesture of appetence they would suddenly argue that really, it was as though these towers had always been there, or at least as though we'd always been waiting for them, and that they had only come to occupy a designated space already carved out for them, and wasn't it all so strange.

AMONG THESE folks, a group of resisters speaks up more and more often, inhabitants from old stock who argue that they've been in Coca long enough to have extra legitimacy; these are individuals who know the area by heart and remind everyone in the preamble to each public speech – in the municipal council, in press conferences, in assemblies of their associations – that, as children, they ran free in fields as vast as the ocean, parting the tall grasses that scratched their pale foreheads; that they swam in every fissure of the river (they can cite the name of each rock and of every smallest pasture before it was converted into a building plot), and that their ancestors mixed the dust of their bodies with this very earth. These ones, who include landowners, families of the first merchants, and ferryboat operators – such as the Frenchman – form the majority of the municipal opposition; they're affected by these towers that make them visible to the world, adding Coca to the list of potential terrorism targets, as though since the attack on the World Trade Center, their imagination has become contaminated by the threat and as though from now on, seeing vertical lines become firmer in their skies, they can't help but envision these masses collapsing, tumbling down in a morbid cloud, a vague paranoia whose corollary, in architecture, boils down to one simple line: we don't want any trouble.

IN THE SHUTTLE, the discovery that the towers are already so tall provokes several questions – some technical (bolting or welding?), some financial (cost of river transport = fuel + crew + cost of wear and tear on the boats), and finally some aesthetic (the red was decidedly unpopular). When they are almost at the Edgefront tower, a member of the municipal opposition – a short man with grey hair in a brush cut, cozy inside his sheepskin coat with fur collar, seizes upon an interstice of silence to criticize this arrogant project, this provocation that will surely invite the vengeance and deadly schemes of terrorists. An embarrassed silence falls over the boat as it slows, approaching the structures. Ralph Waldo sticks his head out from under the awning to better see the vertebrae of the bridge and then concedes that indeed – he places a hand flat against his chest – like most bridges, this one will incarnate not only technological excellence but also a certain idea of democracy; producing a territory that is wider, richer, and more open; integrating dissimilar areas that up until now have been poorly connected; augmenting the volume and the speed of traffic: it will create a new communal space, a strong space, where victim tendencies and apocalyptic predictions – he's become an orator now, defending his oeuvre, eyes sinking back in their sockets and rolling with intensity – have no place. Then, setting aside his formal composure, and vitrifying the stunned assembly with one look, he says: what you have before your eyes is a unit of raw energy, part of a creative impetus whose completion eradicates the dark ideas that will henceforth sully the work of architects. It will emblazon the city with an avenging optimism, a new affirmation – one hell of a number, the Boa laps it up, totally impressed, and Diderot lights a Lusitania. And then the Pontoverde execs lean their heads out to visualize the progression of the work, blinking their eyes momentarily against the wet snow that has begun falling from the sky, and the boat docks at the foot of the Edgefront tower.

THE DELEGATION is brought inside the tower, and rises between the box girders to observe the work of arc welding and to congratulate themselves on the excellent productivity of this technique – one of the directors asks a worker about the thickness of the filler metal, trying to impress, and Diderot answers him curtly, cutting short the puzzlement of the man who puts his mask back on to continue his work; they examine the security, hard hats and harnesses, safety cables – a woman from the delegation stipulates in a loud voice that any disregard for safety guidelines will result in immediate layoffs for serious misconduct, it's simply a question of insurance, and all the heads nod in agreement with the intransigence of such a procedure – they shake hands at random, many of which they have to wait for – Seamus O'Shaughnessy refuses to interrupt his work and keeps his own hand gloved, we're not animals in a zoo, dammit – and anyway it's freezing, the mouths of the officials sink into their collars beneath their scarves and they decide to make a U-turn and head back to the platform. On the way, the adversary of the project stops Diderot, says, I'd like to know your feelings about the bridge – you are the builder – tell me something concrete – he has a determined face, very white and perfectly aligned teeth, and the air of a retired GI colonel. Diderot looks at him and articulates very distinctly, I don't think about hypothetical threats and fantasies, I don't have the time, my concern is for the execution of the work and the safety of the workers, which is threatened by insane deadlines, impossible specs, this shitty climate, and the fucking cost-effectiveness of this whole mess.

IN TRUTH, DIDEROT IS CONCERNED ABOUT Katherine, who he hasn't seen since the night when they sat face to face in that banal snack bar at the corner of Colfax and Arapahoe, centred on short fake-leather banquettes the colour of oxblood, between which – frank, square, and welcoming to elbows and palms, as though created expressly for dialogue – stood the table, champagne surface with rounded corners just the length of an extended arm – an arm that, indeed, had to be extended, unfolded to horizontal, so that the bodies waiting behind could begin to move forward, conjoined at the shoulder, and so they could come along softly, gaining territory, their slow approach; and this carnal arm that would seal the alliance, and which was at present the very measure of what separated them: something still has to be crossed, and that is the table, which is also a river, and Diderot calls the waitress over, Katherine needs to eat soon so she can sober up.

And in this bar, with its flat obviousness and crackling jukebox, on this ochre linoleum shaded with dark rings, between these dirty windows muddled with paint, beneath these globes of white light laid out on the ceiling like the dots on a domino, not far from the counter where fluorescent cupcakes and three-day-old doughnuts sit drying under glass, where fake-leather stools veined like ground beef stand waiting, the Formica table is their greatest ally. With its quotidian power in action, it becomes the great equalizer – of sex, age, social status – an egalitarian playing field neutralizing hierarchies and presences – and if they had thought of this, they would have thanked it, this table, they would have kissed its flat surface with its residue of grease and ammonia, upon which they had unfolded the present. They speak to one another on level ground, as though they had just suddenly turned up face to face smack in the middle of a clearing, or in the way we throw ourselves at one another's heads – like elk that clash antlers, all decorum aside – short-circuiting introductions; Katherine takes off her sweater directly, and watching her, Georges encloses them together in the heart of the matter: the only backwards glance they'll allow themselves is to speak of the path that led them to Coca. She bites into a slice of bread, announces, lucid, I live with my husband and my kids in Edgefront, I have two boys and a little girl, Georges nods, smiling, I know, I met the whole troop the other day, she lifts her eyes to his, right, that's them, she's spreading mustard on her bread now, and you? Georges tilts his face towards the south, I live in Cherry Creek Valley near the river on the Coca side, by myself, no kids, and Katherine smiles, oh it's pretty out there, you're right near the water, and he nods, yes, for the duration of the bridge – he too is lucid, calling it what it is. The waitress puts the drinks down on the table at this exact instant – a beer for Georges, a coffee for Katherine – thus diverting the impact of these last words, and also giving them the gift of a few movements to make – he picks up his glass, she plunges into the mug – then Georges begins again, still calm, three kids, that's a lot of work, eh, but Katherine's gaze slides to the guy in a white hat and long dirty apron who's walking towards them now, pancakes and home fries, kids, that's my thing, she passes a hand in front of her face as though to close the subject, and Diderot moves his belly back from the table: the food has arrived. And afterwards, do you know where you'll go? Katherine asks while considering the contents of her plate, afterwards? he answers, afterwards I leave again, we'll see. There aren't many people left in the place at this hour, the waitress is wiping tables, the old guy with the beard mutters, the duo of cops have gone back to cruising, Katherine splashes maple syrup over the pancakes, and tells him – obstinate in this moment, forehead rounded and very white in the light of the bulb: Lewis, my husband, had an accident last year, a fall, twenty feet; he was redoing a roof for some people south of San Francisco. The insurance didn't work – she swallows her coffee in one gulp – why? Georges interrupts, and Katherine, forehead leaning over her plate of syrupy potatoes that she mops up till the last drop, says in an expressionless voice, he'd had a few beers with .lunch, they said he was drunk. She hadn't worked since Matt was born, it didn't make sense with how much daycare cost, and she'd had to find something real quick and so, for her too, the site, a godsend, she liked it, yes, really. And afterwards? Georges asks. Katherine lifts her palms towards the ceiling and leans her head towards her shoulder, repeats, afterwards? Afterwards we'll see, we move all the time. So we're the same, then? Georges murmurs while they both eye the beer, yes, the same, Katherine smiles.

NOW THEY'RE alone in the restaurant, two towers of light facing each other, and outside night has fallen. A systolic joy clangs in their chests, painful, and traces in a single movement the thing that rises between them and that which sinks quickly, the upsurging of the present and the erasure of their lives before, they're restless and vaguely sad – love is what tears at them. Feeling better now? Georges, serious as the pope, points to the plate that sparkles and she laughs with mock shame, lines folding into suns at the corners of her lids, swollen with fatigue, and at that moment the waitress reappears stiffly, filthy rag in hand, and says, excuse me, we're closing in five minutes. Then Katherine leans towards Georges, forehead pale beneath her mass of tobacco hair, her irises dark now and shining, nearly black, and suddenly she reaches out her arm, advancing one hand towards him and placing it flat against his cheek – a strange gesture, thinks Diderot, touched – and says, we have to go, time is running out, but he takes her hand, folds it like a fist into his own, turns it over, *hup*, a kiss: we have our whole lives ahead of us.

Outside, the cutting cold sent them reeling at first – actually, finding themselves suddenly without a table, they were thrown off-kilter, clattering about like spinning tops – and then it stiffened them as they stood face to face, statues of flesh. Is someone waiting for you at home? Georges turns up the collar of his coat and Katherine zips up her parka, without answering, cheeks on fire and shivering already, you trying to say I should go, is that it? Serious now, and on the defensive, she begins to walk away along the sidewalk – you think I haven't sacrificed enough? – vaguely aggressive while simultaneously weary, on the edge of dropping it completely, but Georges interrupts her, firm, I don't think anything at all, it's you that knows. Let's go.

THREE BLOCKS away, the Niagara Motel on Colfax, and a coarse room where they won't turn on the lights. They arrive out of breath: they ran here. A little hundred yard dash, Georges suddenly pointing out the finish line to Katherine – see the door with the red neon sign over there? – and the two of them got into position side by side, one knee on the ground between their gloved hands placed flat on the pavement, don't you dare cheat, Katherine murmured, and then Georges shouted, go! without warning and they set off like sprinters – clatter of their soles against the nocturnal asphalt, their forms (no longer quite so young) bundled inside heavy coats, the beanpole and Ms. Messy Hair, breathless with the effort – he's in front, she catches up with him at the second block, and then they run heads down, exaggerating their strides, arms pumping like Olympic champions, and she passes him, touches the reception door first, and Diderot, touching it three seconds after, shakes his head, hands on his ribs, and spits I don't get it, they call me Carl Lewis, and Katherine, calm, her hand held out over the counter for the key, it's simply a question of mindset, darling; still breathing hard they stroll through the shadows between buildings till they find theirs, then skirt the doors till they reach their number, a room that is one among many, absolutely like all the others, exactly the way they are a man and woman among thousands of others, and once they're inside there's the sensation of a rebellion, a chanted uprising; they undress in silence, seated one on either side of the bed but they keep glancing at one another over their shoulders – it takes a long time to remove all these clothes, these thicknesses of T-shirts, these laces to undo, each movement liberating epidermal odours, above which floats the scent of the site, like a shared fluid; they're naked now and their skin, merged by darkness, takes on the same temperature and the same carbon nuance. Each one stretches out a hand above the bed till they touch the other, till they move closer, one against the other, and then it's the great trial and error, the tactile opera, and their bodies in multiple fragmentation that know perfectly well how to find their way in the dark.

THEY HAVEN'T seen each other since then, not the next day, not in the weeks that followed. He knows that she works on the levelling sites for the freeway approaches, far from the platform, while he is required to be on the tower sites. And if he's concerned, seated in the powerful superintendent's speedboat among the Pontoverde bigwigs, it's less about seeing her again, touching her, pushing her hair back again from her forehead – they don't miss each other and they have faith – and more about knowing how she's managing to hold these lives – these territories – together.

That night, she was singularly calm and serene when she whispered to him, I want to go home now. He was stretched out on his back, could make her out searching for her clothes in the darkness, had said I'll take you – it was late, the buses would be few and far between, he would drop her off in Edgefront. They got dressed, joking at the thought of getting their clothes mixed up, then once again the space of the motel, Colfax, the frozen car, and the heart of Coca, abuzz like it was every night around 2:00 a.m. They crossed the frozen river, venous and unstable, and once they reached the other side she said, stop the car, I'll get out here. Georges parked without a word and, abbreviating the separation, Katherine got out quickly, then bent down in the doorway, we'll be in touch, and he nodded, take care of yourself. He didn't start the car right away, instead he watched her walk up the avenue, very slim now, not so tall, a silhouette that was out of proportion with her mane of hair. He followed her with his eyes until she turned the corner of the block and until even her shadow had disappeared in the deserted and luminous street, certain that he could still hear her, walking now in another territory, a space that closed itself behind her with every step, a space that belonged to her, that was her home, and he admired for a moment this ability to go home, to go on to the next thing; while she – accelerating now towards her prefab shack with its whitewash mildewing at the corners, getting ready to open the flimsy door to her front hall, sure that the kids are sleeping, breathing cozy beneath gaudy quilts, but that Lewis will be waiting for her in front of the television, eyeballs staring, umpteenth can of beer in hand – she sped up, swelled with a strange desire, and she may even have been smiling softly with her head tucked down into the collar of her coat that hissed like fire with each of her movements, because everything was happening as though she was already recreating herself.

THE ACCIDENT HAPPENS A FEW DAYS AFTER
the debacle – time is running out and the men on the towers
accelerate their cadence. Some of them attach themselves
only once they've reached their posts to save time during the
ascent, which is slower if they're wearing safety cables. But
the ascent and the descent are delicate manoeuvres, each
a sort of rush hour that demands order and vigilance – the
descent is especially worrisome: they tumble onto the deck
sections, down the ladders, they hurry so as not to miss the
first shuttle back to the Pontoverde platform, they're in such
a rush to be finished with the workday.

This particular day, the mild spell had delighted
the troop of workers who went bare-armed, in overalls
or T-shirts. Already in the river shuttle some of them had
babbled excitedly about the return of girls in short skirts,
whistled at the joggers running along the banks, and the few
women on the teams had piped up, cheeky, calling out to the
guys who cut through the air in satiny shorts that they were
waiting for them, whenever you want it, honey. This new
gaiety congests their movements, all of them stammering
the most ordinary gestures, getting excited as they imagine
a boat trip in the bay or a fishing session in the branches of
the river upstream from the city, as they plan carpooling
from one box girder to the next, yelling over the noise of the
welders, and at lunchtime there are a lot of them squashed
onto the deck to eat their sandwiches, and each one has a
story to tell, the transparency of the air sets winter tongues

stirring; just as, far below, hundreds of feet down, the river thickens its slow and unctuous course, the last sheets of ice stuck in the branches on the banks have long dissolved into the very green torrent, and here and there, enigmatic whorls curve the surface of the waters, the seals of some pearly white gastropods, genies of the river who shake themselves off in the eddies – it is once again the time of great liquid mobility.

So now the light too has returned. It splashes off the bend of a crossbeam, a crate, ricochets off rivets, and when a ray of sun passes through the frame and hits their faces, it's blinding, it makes bodies vacillate. The fatal accident happened in just this sort of glimmering: it was a little after noon when, moving forward onto the deck after eating and drinking, his safety cable detached while he mimed the bowling session that led him to a strike – three quick steps followed by a slide, the arm carrying the ball lifted to shoulder height – a guy in his fifties, blinded by the sun, slipped and fell to the side, his right knee hitting the steel deck while the other slid into the void; the big boot at the end of his leg acted as a weight, there was nothing for his hands to grab – and plus the left hand, the one supposed to be holding the invisible ball, was hanging on the wrong side from the rest – and there was no net, no cord there that could save him, he fell to the side, body in a tailspin like a big bag – and if you saw the scene, you might have thought of those stories of pirates, of the guys who were thrown overboard, trussed up in a blanket or a sheet, their bodies nearly parallel to the ship's planking at the moment of the fall: a shout like gauze tearing, the sky half-opens, the sound of the water being pierced, the splash stifled by distance – only a few workers could hear it, too much ruckus, too much banter.

THE ACCIDENT happened at lightning speed, a reflection in the eye, a flutter of lids, a sputter of Morse code, and several conversations continued after the splash, the guys teasing one another with their noses in their lunch boxes and then mechanically lifting their heads, blinking their eyes, themselves blinded or too stunned to believe it – so much so that a few seconds passed before the workers reacted, and suddenly those who had been laughing a moment earlier at the replay of the bowling move stand frozen, pillars of salt; then, having double-checked their harnesses, they approach the edge, slowly, holding on to one another. One of them threw up his meal, deathly pale, he had to be carried back to the ground; others were hot, dizzy, scared to go down – finally the siren was activated. The dead man was found mid-afternoon downstream from Coca, his body stuck beneath the roots and brambles festooning the bank on the Edgefront side. Disentangling him was a delicate procedure.

SINCE IT was a workplace accident, there would be an investigation. This began the next day, and the question of the safety cable left undone during lunch hour would be dissected first. It seemed to be common practice, a lack of rigour or excess of confidence dominant among the workers on the Edgefront tower, those in charge not doing their job well enough, their books showing no fines, no reprimands, it was said without irony that the men held the reins, that sanctions were necessary, a diagnosis that infuriated the workers – Seamus O'Shaughnessy modulated the daggers of black hair on his gaunt face once more and promised to bring up the subject of the infernal pace again if a single worker – a single one – got any shit during the investigation – they would plead an isolated incident, while Diderot would pull out the climatic argument before the investigators, the warm spell, the light, and finally, in order to keep up appearances, and by way of making a compromise, he coldly decreed that alcohol was forbidden on all work sites, and warned them one last time that whoever was seen without a hard hat and a harness would be fired immediately.

Diderot didn't know the man who fell, didn't play the grieving role, just did what had to be done – sent a funeral wreath to the family, people in Missouri to whom the reassembled body was sent in the hold of a plane with the Pontoverde insignia on the side – but the fall affected him, gathering as it did in its fatal trajectory all the confusion of the site. This entanglement of bodies and materials that struggled together on an unstable front, this mixture of slackenings and tension, this parcelled-out calendar, these composite procedures – this fragmentation, finally, that was at the heart of his work and the handling of which was his method – all this suddenly seemed just barely enough, precarious, infinitely friable in the face of the bridge that each day rose higher and more solid than the day before, but each day more monstrous, and in the nights that followed the accident, he thought he could hear again Jacob's shout, *bastard, bastard!* and when he got up to open the window, trying to find something to breathe out there, all he saw in the blackness was a turbulent landscape, exorbitant waters constantly swollen with alluvium, and their endless ringing flow.

IT'S 3:50 P.M. ON MAY 13TH AND THE COCA tower is now seven hundred feet high. Duane Fisher and Buddy Loo have their hard hats on and are properly harnessed but nothing can contain their desire to mess around. Only ten minutes to go before the siren; they've got eight hours of work behind them and are suffocating inside the box girders, sweating under their visors.

They learned to weld in three days, some backup was needed up above, they were hiring young guys, strong ones with skills, and the notion came up again that Natives don't get vertigo, that they possess a unique gene that exempts them from the fear of working at insane heights, funambulists with iron muscles walking fast along steel girders – the legend of the Mohawks always comes out, they who were discovered to be acrobats in the sky as early as 1886 by the foremen of a road bridge over the St. Lawrence, astounded to see them gambolling into the heights, agile and with grace, and from then on they were the chosen ironworkers, imported in groups from their reservations in the northeastern United States or from Canada to flesh out the contingent of workers on skyscrapers (including the Empire State and Chrysler Buildings in New York); and it was said that after the destruction of the World Trade Center towers, Mohawks – descendants of those who built them – were the ones who came back to the devastated site to dismantle everything, and it's certain that it was all the more satisfying to distinguish them in this way – precisely because they had previously been debased to the lowest extent. Duane Fisher and Buddy Loo didn't know about this election, not being Mohawk themselves – they are Ohlone – and yet they too are psyched to be sent way up there.

THE FIRST time they found themselves at the top of the Coca tower, they were stunned at the vastitude of the sky, got a violent smack; the air was iridescent, rapid, billions of microscopic droplets diffracted light and movement, euphorizing space that suddenly dilated to the full extent, and they laughed, intoxicated. It didn't take them long to learn how to provoke danger as you might provoke a dog – they quickly figured out how to pierce the gangue of the prohibited, within which they performed a select repertoire of actions. The void with the river beneath, the red bay that divided the landscape, the others who looked on in amazement, all this made for a kind of theatre, articulated a field of action where their desire for thrills exploded – and so they began the leaps. The first time, Duane had checked his harness a little before four o'clock and turned his face towards Buddy, ivory white teeth and anise pupils, had said flat out – hey, wanna bet I won't jump? – and Buddy, a hand shading his eyes had cast a quick glance down, evaluating the height, yeah, I'll go after you, we'll be like paratroopers, *yes*, we're fighters, we're Indian warriors, and he let out a whoop that Duane echoed before adding, we'll show the new boys on the block how we party – and for sure they got off on it. It was break time now and the guys were coming out of the locker rooms, Duane waited till they were assembled and then placed himself in starting position like a parachutist about to exit, one leg bent in front, the other stretched out behind, then he let out a cry – the classic Tarzan cry – and threw himself into the void, the cable unrolling behind him at a mad speed, like a lasso, like a crack in the wall of time; the harness squealed in his ears while his yell lost itself, naked, no echo anymore, and suddenly the landscape rushed into him, tearing at his chest, cutting off his breath, and then he crashed into the sky without bouncing back – the cable wasn't very elastic – but his body swung back violently towards the column and he had to bend his legs, knees to his abdomen and feet vertical to soften the shock of crashing into the structure; he pushed himself off the steel surface like a tumbling alpinist pushes the mountain away, once, twice, three times, until it diminished to a gentle swinging; he remained suspended in the air, stunned, tipped his head back to look up at the top of the tower where the workers on the team were pressed together, heads leaning over, backlit, a necklace of black beads – he couldn't see their faces but could hear their applause, and then Buddy jumps, he too with the shock and the cry of the warrior, he too the assimilation into the sky.

These stunts became an attraction – the rumour of them spread throughout the tower – and it's certain that Diderot heard about them, and possibly even right from the first jump; word spread quickly on the site and certain residents on the Coca side would have been able to tell him, those who were positioned all day long at the window and saw plain as day all that happened on the tower, who enjoyed making reports to the site foremen, informing themselves about pollution statistics and the construction schedule, and formulating complaints about the dirtiness, the noise, the pickpocketing that was steadily increasing and which they blamed on the workers; and they began to report all this at the end of the day when the bosses were coming back to their makeshift offices at the foot of the tower, they're messing around, they say, winning themselves a few rounds and songs on the jukebox, since the site was in a paradoxical time: the heaviness after the man's death on the Edgefront tower was now rolled up into a new tension – the preparation of the cables, the placing of the bridge deck.

THEY'RE UP top, the siren's gonna go in ten minutes and with a quick glance at each other, Duane and Buddy have decided on a leap. They stroll up to the deck, exaggeratedly relaxed, roll their necks, rotate their torsos as though spinning hula hoops, chewing gum buzzes in their show-offy mouths, they haven't heard the engine of the shuttle that let Diderot out, haven't seen him ascending the levels of box girders using small archaic elevators; and once the workers are gathered for the show, they throw themselves into the air to the sound of shouts, cheers, sputters that Diderot hears too, speeding up, and once he's on the last deck section, stupefied, moves to the edge of the structure, making his way between the hard hats stuck together, and his head is now an extra bead on the necklace that adorns the tower. No one sees him arrive – the workers have their backs to him – but they all jump and turn as one when they hear him exclaim, dammit to hell! They clear the way immediately, then back off, leaving Diderot alone with the two boys who sway in the air, about to light up a smoke since they're off-site now, since they're swinging, since they're braves. Diderot whips around to the workers grouped together at the back, and what happens next? You haul them up, is that it? Yeah, that's it. Diderot leans over again, the two boys have tipped back their radiant faces, surprised their audience has disappeared, all except for this one head, a head they don't recognize, they call up, hey guys, start hauling! Straightening up again, Diderot orders the other workers to leave, get out of here, I don't want anyone else here. A slow movement can be seen, a shuffle of workboots towards the stairs, one woman is worried, turns an anxious face over her shoulder, you're not gonna leave them there, are you? Diderot doesn't answer. He's livid with rage. Once the deck is empty, he leans out again over Duane and Buddy, who grow worried as they hear the sounds of footsteps in the tower's staircases, as they see their friends descending and calling out to them once they're at their level, Diderot's up top, the boss is here. The two boys think oh shit, then hear Diderot's voice shouting at them, you have five minutes to get back up here before the siren, move your asses.

They look at each other, then up at the length of the cable with alarm – more than a thousand feet, at least. And then, without exchanging a single word, they start swinging. Using what sway is left to regain momentum, to increase their oscillation so they can touch the structure again and use it to climb up – they manage, and once their feet are solidly against the metal plate, dark still at this hour, crimson almost black, they tense the muscles of their arms, hard as they can, and haul themselves, inch by inch, up the entire side of the tower; it's long and exhausting, they're liquefied by the effort, clenching their faces and hardening their stomachs, they climb, using little jumps to gain a little more height on the cord, and once they've hoisted themselves onto their bellies at the level of the deck, hair plastered with sweat to their muddy foreheads, hands bleeding, they grab the first bar at the base of the guardrail and pant hard for a few seconds, cheeks resting against the steel deck, still warm, and then Diderot's shadow falls over them and cools them off. He holds out his hand and with a powerful motion lifts them one last time, one after the other; they stay collapsed for a few moments, exhausted, shipwrecked sailors washed up on a beach, survivors, eyelids closed, catching their breath, while Diderot tells them curtly that they're fired, tells them to collect their things from their lockers and then go to the administrative offices for an envelope with their final payment.

TOO LATE. SOREN SEES ALEX WAITING FOR HIM in front of the doors, recognizes him in the shadows, tries to back away towards the work site, casting quick lateral glances to find somewhere he can fold himself away into the dark, but it's too late – Alex has seen him and comes forward, thrusts the bag into his arms whispering don't tell me you forgot about our little deal, it's on for tomorrow, the instructions are inside. Soren staggers under the weight of the bag and lets out a cry, makes a half-turn towards the locker rooms but in the same moment a hand grabs him by the neck: a word of advice – no funny business. Soren shrugs him off with a movement of his shoulder and hurries towards the workers' facilities, those he passes headed in the opposite direction barely nod, no one questions him. Once he's inside, he rushes to his locker, unlocks it, puts the bag in, at the last moment unzips it, plunges a hand in, feels a piece of paper folded into quarters, stuffs it in his pocket, closes everything up again, and rushes to the bus that's waiting outside. Later, sitting alone at the back, head against the window, he catches his breath – how could he have believed they had decided against the sabotage – he uses the small overhead light to read the paper, typed, and turns pale – the bag contains four dynamite cartridges equipped with suction cups – no seepage of nitroglycerine, the explosives are stabilized, reliable – the cartridges are to be stuck to the four sides of the upstream pier of the Edgefront tower, at the point where the base narrows, so that the whole tower, suddenly one legged, will topple; and their explosion will be set off by activating a programmed detonator from the opposite shore – not a sequential ignition system, and not a delay system – through a remote, which will allow him to act at the last minute.

Of course, he thinks of running – nothing could be more simple, he could go back to his digs, pack his bag, pick up his cheque, and disappear on a night bus headed south, any old bus and no one would be the wiser – but he abandons this idea, sure they would find him, these guys always find their man and when they find him they kill him, he's been warned. This is why, tonight – a beautiful night too, odours of mud and detritic ground are a reminder that Coca was built on an alluvial plain, a breeding tank teeming with worms and coypu – he doesn't stray from his routine, stops in for a game of pool at a bar in Edgefront, and then goes home.

HARD TO describe the day that follows when each move-ment, each word, each intention is obliterated by the sabotage to come, by the conviction of such precariousness that nothing else really matters, as though the future was only a hazy aureole, the cigarette hole in the film, disintegrating time. Soren floats, cottony. He gets to the Pontoverde platform half an hour before the first siren sounds so he can be alone in the locker room. When he opens his locker, the bag jumps in his face like a fierce animal: it's a small black knapsack that weighs as much as an eight-year-old child. He stuffs in a sandwich and a sweater, and goes to the river-shuttle dock, forcing his form not to fold under the weight, making sure that this bumpy mass on his back doesn't alter his walk, and keeps his expression steady.

IT'S NEARLY midnight on the Edgefront site and Soren is waiting for the lights of the last shuttle headed back to the esplanade to disappear. He didn't have to pretend he had forgotten something inside a crate, didn't have to tell the others not to wait for him, he'd go back and then take the next boat, no, he didn't have to say a word, because no one here asks him anything – and you could even bet that Diderot himself, who professes to know every person on the bridge, wouldn't be able to hail him by name or even recognize him if he passed him off-site – similarly, no one noticed the bag from which he ostensibly pulled a sandwich and a bottle of water at break, exposing a pile of dark clothing inside. At the moment, Soren is cold. He shivers under the pier, a few steps back from the water's edge, and nature rumbles, the torrent is large, each sound amplified by the presence of the steel column standing behind him. Once he's alone, while the site foremen go back to their portables (Algecos with kettles) giving themselves a break before the next batch of workers, Soren, dressed all in black now, quickly places the dynamite cartridges all around the upstream pier that's sheathed in concrete at this height, making sure to stay hugging the sides, in the shadow of the tower – the rest of the site is lit up like a fairground, a village dance, garlands of tiny lights, he has never performed these movements but he's studied the diagrams on the folded paper, and as it turns out, it's dead simple. In less than three minutes the cartridges are suctioned onto the pier, Soren breathes hard under his hood, picks up the bag, throws it over his shoulder and, camouflaged silhouette already fleeing, he veers towards the brownish, lumpy-looking bank: he has a hundred and fifty feet to cross in the river. A break in the levelling of the pier, a gash three feet wide, Soren squats and slips into the water silently, terrified at the thought that the noise of his specific splashes – the body of a man penetrating a liquid – multiplied here, could alert the site foremen who, in a few minutes, will put their hard hats with headlamps back on and go out to meet the new contingent of workers, while on the other side of the river, on the twenty-seventh floor of a waterfront building, the Frenchman and his posse are opening bottles of champagne, filling crystal glasses, and moving to the picture window, ready for the fireworks.

SOREN IS in the river up to his waist, water so cold that a painful cramp crushes his shins, penetrates his bones, he's sure it reaches all the way to the marrow, corroding his strength, he's suffocating, can't move anymore – stands for a long minute without being able to let go, without being able to launch himself. It's the sputtering of voices behind him that pushes him forward into the fuliginous waves, he falls in, stifling a yell with a tremendous effort, keeps his head above water without really having any coordination, like a panicked dog fallen overboard, then manages to calm down, getting used to the temperature, regaining control, and, synchronizing his breathing with the movements of his body, he begins to swim silently towards the bank, immersing himself completely at regular intervals in the current that carries him downstream. This is when excitement and fear, the fact of being swallowed but conscious, make him believe that a bulky animal is swimming along beside him – he can make out its mass and its phenomenal strength, there are new underwater currents that accompany him, he lifts his head out of the water without seeing anything but the licorice river that grips him and far off the lights of the river shuttle coming back with the night teams – inside they're probably joking around, having a last smoke, daydreaming – he dives under once more but again the animal is there, escorting him, brushing against him with its thick, dense fur, a colossal beast that could well be a bear, the bear from Anchorage, it's wild, it's hungry, hunting whatever it can to feed itself, he's delirious, he speeds up without being able to turn around or cast a glance to his side – terror has so paralyzed him – he hears a growl at his neck and nearly sinks like a stone – there's no fear more terrible than an open jaw behind your back – the bank comes nearer now and the lights of Edgefront press large gold squares of light onto the water while the reflection of the vegetal gangue on the bank lengthens: tall tough plants, bristling black and sharpened lances, they form a barricade, holding Soren back inexorably from all human life. He speeds up till he touches ground, grabs a root, pulls himself out of the river and collapses in a crevice of mud. The bear has disappeared. He breathes, spits, half-dead, and now he still has to take the remote out of its watertight case and press the button that will make everything blow up, he's out of breath, rummages in his bag, drooling bile, can't see anything, droplets form stalactites from the arch of his brow, obstruct his nostrils, block his ears, he hurries, body shaken by opposing pieces of information – he's alive, he's dead – numb fingers suddenly touching the little hard-plastic case, shivering violently – shakes that tear him apart – he adjusts his gaze to the pier where there is no movement yet. The boatload of workers has passed the river bend, it's heading for shore now, begins to slow. On the Edgefront tower site, still very brightly lit, almost festive, three men stroll out nonchalantly, walk to the edge of the quay, cross their arms over their chests, and stand there, posed, waiting, like actors caught up in the pursuit of theatre. Soren has never heard the sound of their voices but he can see the pink of their cheeks, the steam that clouds as it leaves their mouths, three little fellas just doing their job who stand at the edge of the river, the boat is still two hundred feet away, he has to press the button, he has to press it now.

ON THE OTHER SIDE OF THE WATER

IT'S A CHILD, BARELY THREE YEARS OLD –
little Billie – who finds Soren's body five days later in a
vacant lot behind the soccer field in Edgefront, where she's
wandering, teddy bear in hand, left to her own devices.

Billie likes this grassy wasteland a lot, lumpy, with
dirty edges, begs to go there more and more often, and this
morning while Katherine was getting her dressed, standing
her up on the kitchen table before leaving for the site, while
she was adjusting the elastic of her little canary-yellow skirt,
the child took her face between her two soft hands and said,
I want to go to the garden, so determined that Katherine
suspended her gestures, admiring, looked at her and then
hugged her close, whispering into her neck, I promise, my
little chicken, you can go there today. Lifting the little one
to the ground then, she rushed to the boys' room, Liam had
already left for junior high but Matt was still asleep – he
had come home late again last night. The room stinks, an
odour of livestock. Katherine sits on the edge of the bed and
shakes Matt by the shoulder, wake up! He lets out a long
groan and, since she's still shaking him, pushes her away,
eyes closed – she can feel that he's almost as strong as she is
now – then turns onto his side facing the wall, but Katherine
persists, walks to the window and pulls open the curtain;
streams of sun sweep through the room revealing heaps
of crumpled, indistinct clothes, worn-out sneakers, dirty
underwear, mistreated school books and binders, cookie
wrappers, empty soda bottles, and crumbs over everything,

and Katherine, discovering this mess, this filth, gags and asks herself how long it's been since she came into this room; it comes back to her like a boomerang that Liam has been doing his homework at the kitchen table for a while now and only comes in here to sleep. Her own feeling of guilt, even more than the state of the room, is what throws her into a rage. She comes back to the bed, shakes Matt again, hard this time, channelling all her anger into this action, wake up, you little shit! Gets nothing but a loud snore. Unhinged, she charges to the kitchen and fills a pitcher with cold water and back in the room throws it in Matt's face – he bolts upright yelling, Augh! Are you fucking out of your mind? Leaning back on his elbows, he drips, waxy circles under his eyes, mouth grey, skin bleary, stunned to see his mother standing straight and immense at the foot of his bed, pitcher in hand, and to hear her gunning him with these words: you have ten minutes to get up. Then you're gonna clean up this room – your brother can't even set foot in here anymore! When I get home tonight I want it to be spic and span, and this afternoon, instead of just skipping class, you're gonna make yourself useful, take Billie to the garden after her nap, I want you to take care of her and talk to her, I want you to play with her, is that clear? The boy sits on the edge of the bed, head in his hands, and grumbles half-heartedly yeah, and if I don't? Katherine hesitates, then, casting maternal reason and good role modelling to the wind, responds from between clenched teeth: Matt, if you don't do it, I'll break your face. She slams the door, looks at her watch, and goes to find Billie, who's already watching TV on the pullout couch beside her sleeping father, passes a hand through her curly hair, I'm off, my little warbler, Matt will take you out later to play in the garden. The little girl, absorbed by the screen, doesn't answer and mechanically holds out a cheek for her mother to kiss. As she passes through the front door, Katherine feels herself wobble, her eyes burning, her legs weak. She does a U-turn and swallows a big glass of water in the kitchen, breathes a long sigh with her arms stretched out on either side of the sink, then comes back to Matt's room, pushes the door open gently, the boy is standing bare chested, getting dressed. His body's changing, his shoulders are broadening and he has the torso of a young man now, he's not a kid anymore. Matt, she begins, Matt, I'm sorry. The boy pulls a T-shirt on without looking at her. I got worked up. He turns his back to her, goes to open the window. I'm leaving you ten dollars for lunch, okay? She takes a step towards him, places a hand on his shoulder. His smell has changed too. He pulls away, Katherine's hand falls. She begins again in a stronger voice, okay, take care of your sister. And in the doorway she hears the boy murmur I will, don't worry. Later, in the bus full of tremors, Katherine bursts into tears without thinking of anything in particular, and to the woman beside her who looks at her questioningly – a very young woman full of solicitude – answers simply, I'm so tired.

WHEN MATT reaches the vacant lot there's a girl there, sprawled in the grass, waiting for him with beers. What's this? she asks, pointing to Billie in the stroller, little canary with pink heart-shaped sunglasses. This – this is my little sister! Matt releases Billie and she jumps from the stroller. The girl pouts, disappointed, I thought we were gonna be chill, I'm not crazy about kids, and Matt hastens to answer, don't worry, she's not a drag, you'll see; already he's kissing her with eyes closed squeezing her breasts, and Billie walks off quietly.

In the beginning, the little girl meanders along, picks up cigarette butts, drinks the last drops from discarded cans of beer, squats to pick dandelions. Hard to say what stories she's telling herself, it looks like she's talking, wandering in the sun, stepping over the carcasses of rusted bikes, gas cans busted by rifle shots. Soon she's fondling a sole, unlacing a shoe, pulling at a sock, scratching the skin that's revealed with a little wooden stick – she concentrates, her little pink tongue poking out between pursed lips – all the while shooing the flies hovering around, lots of them here, and noisy, then behind the leg she sees another leg, the same shoe and the same sock, and lifting her eyes discovers the rest of the body. She stands still for a long moment, above the head where half the face has disappeared beneath a black crust. Billie, surprised, leans over to ask, hey, are you sleeping? You asleep? When there's no response, she begins to play with the hair, wiggling the head back and forth to unstick it from the ground and holding handfuls of hair at the back of the skull, but as soon as it comes unstuck, a swarm of flies, very dense, swells and surrounds her like the mesh of a net; the little girl hides her face, looks at her fingers covered in brown paste, doesn't understand any of it, and at that exact moment a dishevelled Matt grabs her by the wrist exclaiming, oh shit! They back up. The horrified boy looks at the body, then looks at his sister, she's disgusting, hands bloody, he calls out get over here to the girl who has stayed at the other end of the lot, and when she too is standing in front of the corpse, Matt yells at her, take the little one, take her, but the girl, seeing Billie's hands, lets out a shriek and steps back, are you crazy, she's covered in blood! So Matt sits Billie down roughly: hold up your hands, don't move, stay like that, you understand? And Billie bursts into tears, then her face slowly deforms and she begins to scream as Matt leans over the body again, he too shooing the flies, it's carnage, only the legs are intact – the head, the abdomen, and the entire back are lacerated, torn, ravaged.

THE BOMB hadn't gone off. Unless, in the end, no one had pushed the button to detonate it. Short-circuit in the remote, bad electrical assembly, or a last-minute defection.

The packs of dynamite remained stuck to the pier until they were discovered shortly after the men had arrived for the third shift. From the top of their building, standing neatly in a row before the picture window and looking at their watches, seeing nothing happen, the silent partners grew impatient, and finally the Frenchman yelled dammit, he fucked me over, and while Alex was admitting his failure, his fault for having chosen such a sucker, the Frenchman set the hunt in motion.

AFTER A brief moment of panic at the foot of the Edgefront tower, and once the explosives were neutralized, the guys called Diderot, who immediately whipped over to the site and then spent the rest of the night examining the apparatus, what is this mess? The quantity of dynamite was shocking but the ignition system was rudimentary. The work of an amateur, he concluded.

Soren, for his part, had bolted long ago, shivering in his heavy clothes, soaked with miry water and mud, terrified, not knowing if he had pressed the button on the remote or not, only that he'd thrown the case into the river and had run, looking for some shelter for the night, sure that if he went back to his place the Frenchman's gang would find him there – he had run breathlessly towards the forest, the ultimate refuge for him, he would know how to survive there, a revelation, hit by the smell of the woods, racing along a dark road, faster and faster as the forest approached, with more and more joy to be coming back to the place where he belongs, but suddenly at the edge of the mountain range, headlights that flash on, beams that capture him, men who block his way. A wild growl. There's a bear missing from the city zoo.

TOWARDS THE MIDDLE OF JUNE THEY HAD TO
speed things up even more. Diderot stroked his chin in
front of calendars and work plans and the insides of his
cheeks grew raw with wounds. The men from Pontoverde
were harassing him now, daily phone calls, messages saying
they'd already exceeded the projected budget and that the
only way to not lose money now was to reduce the duration
of the last work phase.

The towers were ready, solidly set in the riverbed,
powerfully held in their protective concrete sheathing,
but no matter how tall and red they were – acrylic paint
developed to respect air-quality standards – they were
stupid, didn't signify anything besides the absence of the
bridge to come – the main component was missing: the deck
that would allow vehicles to cross from Coca to Edgefront.

GOTTA GET a move on now, gotta get to the other side
of the water! This is what you'd hear if you left your ears
lying around in the site offices, in the locker rooms, on the
jogging paths stretched out along the banks – the runners
took advantage to stop for a breather, hands on their hips,
red-faced, some of them still bouncing as though possessed
by St. Vitus's dance, and talked about the progress of the
work between two panted breaths. But in the end, more
than urgency, more than deadlines to meet, it was the
imminence of the last phase of the site, that of the forming
and the placing of the deck, that excited the bridge men

and women, the city's population and the few columnists from the coast who cast a glance now and then at what was happening in Coca: everything would soon make sense, everything would finally become reality. For Diderot, on the other hand, this last phase was not a completion: it fit into the whole as a brand new experience, and once more it was a matter of plunging ahead, of running the risk, in a single sweep, and the cables incarnated this new situation perfectly.

We're going to put a phenomenal tension system in place, a magic system of force transmission, we're going to attain finesse itself! Diderot filters these comments through his teeth while drawing diagrams on the white board, tracing dynamic arrows ($\rightarrow$ and $\downarrow$) over capital Fs, and soon these become slogans called out in a clear voice: the suspension bridge is cutting edge, the cream of the crop of human ingenuity, of problem solving, a matter of distribution of power and mass, the ingenuity of balance, without which there's only wear and tear, degradation, tugs-of-war, collapses and ugliness. He overflows with ardour, the engineers love it – they recall their years of advanced calculus, the problems and the exams, the experiments on freezing lab benches, the water cold and dirty at the bottom of the sinks, the grey smocks; they see again the halo of their desk lamps on graph paper, this yellow circle cut out in the darkness of their rooms, their mothers' worried heads around the half-open door, did you figure it out? Almost finished? Go to bed! and the celebration it is to solve the problem in the hollow of the night, the sudden perception of their own naked intelligence when they nab the curve of the suspension bridge, define the famous catenary, the hyperbolic cosine, rub their eyelids once they've figured out the formula – and all of them suddenly had the feeling of being in exactly the right place, all of them, including Sanche and Summer who sit in on these meetings side by side and throw each other complicit, mocking glances when Diderot plays the ham.

AND DIDEROT may well have celebrated the suppleness of a hammock and the lightness of a nest, but this is still about labour. A hell of a job. High technology revisiting the archaic motion of spinners at the distaff, because overall it is a matter of spinning cables exactly as you spin yarn on a spinning wheel, the specialized work of the cable layers who have already been working for several weeks. The plans had two main cables passing through the summit of the two towers like successive mountain crests and linking the structure to each riverbank. So two titanic ropes had to be built, each composed of 27,572 strands of galvanized steel, divided into groups of sixty-one bunches of strands and assembled by twisting them into a helix around a central longitudinal axis. The cablers gather, twist together, and then compress everything to make it round. Once it was built, the enormous strand would be nearly three feet round and one and a half miles long, a lasso that could capture Ursa Major; a journalist from the San Francisco *Chronicle* determines that, laid out end to end, these steel strands could circle the earth three times at the level of the equator, and it is this comparison, this scale of proportion, that will inspire the Boa's municipal politics from now on. He is jubilant, the fishnet of the bridge is most definitely the net he has used to catch the city, an arachnidan webbing where each knot solidifies his influence and increases the intensity of his desires and ambition; he envisions great celebrations for the inauguration and begins to count down the days.

ONCE AGAIN the teams that swell with acrobats where the Natives take the lion's share, once again the international agencies that windmill through their candidate files, driving a specific, calibrated workforce towards Coca, tightrope-walking workers, almighty men who are hard to pin down once they're there – they run on challenges, confront death with the murky innocence of those for whom working at these heights is a feat as simple as drinking a glass of water or brushing their teeth – but once on-site, they work like gods, cable the bridge accurately – first the two long main cables, then the 250 pairs of vertical hangers, one every 70 feet, each one a hell of a clothespin, and over the weeks they devise an astonishing system of supported steel beams with a total mass of 25,000 tons, and capable of holding, while also stabilizing, a deck that will weigh 150,000 tons.

Reporters show up, cunning guys who want their chance at catching the spectacular image, the girl in a bra and hard hat suntanning on her break, beer in hand, sitting above the void, the guy who lifts his sandwich and looks at the camera, a laughing munchkin under the belled sky, an alignment of shoes in close-up with the river far away beneath, crackled like an oil painting or the glaze on pottery – but this wasn't the time for monkey business, Diderot was shouting now, absolutely furious, the meters are running, still another few weeks to go, stay focused.

SOON A footbridge links the Coca bank to the Edgefront bank, a provisory suspension bridge whose line plays in the air like the fibre core of the cable, the interior thread around which the whole work will unfold. On the night it was finished, the workers advanced towards the centre from either side of the bridge, as was the custom, and broke bottles once the teams touched, they couldn't believe it, the suspension bridge swayed, the wind rumbled under their hard hats, but dammit now you could cross, there were shouts, and finally, each one turned to go back to his side, most of them staggering.

The same night, happy, Georges phones Katherine: come on, let's go cross it together. His voice gets lost in the silence, from which an answer flows back without conviction, okay. They agree to meet on the Edgefront side in the spot where they left each other last time. Diderot, at the wheel of the Impala, waits for Katherine who finally arrives, walking fast, head down, a nervousness about her that doesn't seem like her, gets into the car, and without even looking at him orders, let's go, let's get out of here! They drive towards the river, and, crossing the old Golden Bridge that's living out its last days, they reach Coca. You okay? Diderot asks, when Katherine, opening the window, removes herself into the outside. Ashes fly about inside the car, they race towards the site. What's going on? he insists, showing his badge at the electronic gate and later, standing opposite each other over the hood, he finally discerns Katherine's face: a dark crescent stretches from cheekbone to brow. He doesn't say anything but places a hand on her waist and leads her towards the quay. The path seems endless, they walk beneath the bridge and delicately accost the Coca entrance to the footbridge by climbing the banks, high here, and coffered with concrete blocks between which a little rudimentary staircase has been built. Diderot unlocks the double wire-mesh door and here they are stepping forward onto the provisional catwalk. It's night, their steps resonate on the detachable floor of metallic slats. So, it's almost done? Katherine asks, and Diderot answers, yeah, it'll go quickly now, we'll be finished by mid-August. She doesn't react, asks him about the placing of the deck concrete, the next step, and Diderot explains, getting technical, two methods were in competition, always the famous controversy of concrete versus steel, and finally the solution of an orthotropic deck made of flat steel with two inches of levelling concrete was chosen, the question of the weight of the deck being a crucial aspect.

Katherine, falsely cheerful, nods, she's elsewhere, Diderot gets frustrated: all right, can you tell me what's going on? Beneath them, the last ferries slog from one bank to the other, chockablock with laborious silhouettes squeezed in tight. This thing between us is going nowhere. She looks at her feet. Diderot pauses, could have expected anything from this woman, anything except that it could deflate like this, he points to the end of the bridge, actually I had the feeling that we were headed somewhere. Katherine's face that lights up – he can see it, even in the dark – it's true, she says, we're walking towards Edgefront, and that's home for me. Diderot softens, and so? We can stay a little longer, we can do what we want, right? No, Katherine digs in her heels, I can't do what I want, I don't live like that. I know, Diderot shrugs, I know, but she closes herself off, hard, I don't think you could possibly know. They stand, unmoving. Because of your husband, your kids? He's aggressive, furious with her in this moment, furious for having uttered these words. She hasn't moved, says simply, nothing to do with them, I'm free, believe it or not, and I like my life. She takes out a cigarette that Diderot lights for her with a curt gesture, a gust hits the bridge, he doesn't look at her, leans against the guardrail – fine, so what next? – suddenly in a hurry to be done with her, wanting to avoid murkiness, endless conversations pierced with sticky silences, sad banality, all this while they're on their bridge, together, dammit, not just anywhere, and suddenly after a long silence he says, taking a gamble, okay, come live with me. She laughs right away, a radiant laugh, bad idea, I'm a piece of work, he feels like he's finding her again, takes her in his arms out of joy, pulls her to him, I am aware, brushes a thumb over her tumid temple – the day before, she wasn't able to dodge the metal stapler Lewis had thrown at her face when she was taking Matt's side, accused by his father of stealing cash, his habit of grabbing objects within his reach and whipping them at her face, but this time Liam had risen up and threatened his father with a knife, I'll kill you, quickly held back by Matt, and they had shouted, gone ballistic; and after placing a cold cloth on her temple in the microscopic bathroom, Katherine had come back to say to them all, let's start over, we are not victims; throwing a hard glance at Lewis she'd repeated, there is not a single victim in this room, and later, while she was smoking under the awning outside in a rocking chair about to bust, while Billie was dressing her Barbie for a ball, Lewis had said very calmly that she was free to go, and she had looked him in the eye and shrugged, I know.

Diderot and Thoreau have started walking again, you scared me, Diderot says quietly when they reach Edgefront, and Katherine answers I was scared too.

BETWEEN MARKET AND COLFAX THERE'S California Street, parallel track that's narrower, high concentration at its midpoint – at the level of city hall – of pubs, bowling alleys, bars – all of them large rooms with giant screens placed high against fake mahogany panelling, always the same dimness with a cherry shine. Sanche heads into this area around one o'clock in the morning on the nights when he works. He pushes open the door of La Scala or Sugar Falls, finds the rung of a barstool he can stand on, periscoping his neck around the room, and then, spotting the table, joins Seamus and Mo, two or three others – sometimes even Summer. He's waited all day for this moment.

BEER, WOMEN, a jukebox – paradise! It was in these terms that Seamus took possession of the table the first time they came in, only a few hours after the workers' vote in favour of the bonus; that was almost three months ago already, and Sanche sidling in behind him had admired his virile nonchalance, the sexual authority that emanated from his body; people moved out of Seamus's way, a barely perceptible step backwards that showed the effect of his aura, and in these overpopulated places, no one would think of picking a fight with him; many were they who, on the contrary (like Sanche), would have liked to share his table – baptized "the Irishman's table" at the end of one night even though there was another always tagging along now, and that was Mo.

Sanche rushes to the table, zigzags through the full and humid room, among the streaming foreheads, mouths moistened with alcohol and crazy allegations, he comes the way you'd throw yourself headfirst into the pirate's treasure chest to touch the gold, to make your skin glow with the gleam of precious stones and feel their sharp edges against the flesh of your thumbs, he has stomach cramps, a painful abdomen from impatience and apprehension, and he's barely completed the rounds of greeting, heart lifted and pumping hard in his chest, before he pulls out a chair and sits down, already observing those around him, crazily exulted to be in their company, uprooted, plucked and placed among these heads that are totally unique in the world, to be beside their callused feet, Seamus, the fox character from children's books, fuzzy cheeks, long thick yellow nails, hard skin, one of his grandparents having disembarked in New York around 1850 – the Irish famine, human corpses rotting in piles in the hollows of embankments, hamlets that empty out and are abandoned – no education, no talent, no money – migrates towards the north with a rudimentary compass in his stomach, looking for enough to live on, subsistence, that's all, not a destiny or even a new beginning just something to eat and drink, something to take shelter under, and something to clothe himself in, to occupy the strength of his arms, and then the scattering of a lineage, genealogical absences, empty spaces in the forms, names noted wrongly sediment in their misprints; and at the end, this head, on the alert, this something hirsute and irreducible, and these feet that will soon be on the road again, well versed in the acceptance of loss, definitively eccentric: and glued to his side, clever Mo, who's obsessed by the screen like a possible space of isolation in this plurality of places and paths, a sphere of relaxation where he can unwind a little, release his effort; a woman undulates there, hair swelled by an artificial breeze and skin rounded within the confines of a bikini, she's very blonde, in perfect health, he stares at her, imperturbable, ready to duck out at any second, to veer elsewhere, on a new line segment, a new tangent, why not Africa; and sometimes, but more rarely, convinced by Sanche to rejoin the table at the cost of long minutes of telephone negotiations, there's Summer, with her ponytail trapped in a triple elastic twist, Summer with her cold feet who gets drunk methodically – who comes there to get drunk, doesn't quite know what to do with herself when she's not working – flushes when teased and called "Miss Concrete," ebbs back in her chair when Seamus brings his scarred face towards her and shows her the black interior of his mouth, stop it, she says without smiling but soon it's she who sways forward seeking that same mouth that scares her, an oscillation that makes her dizzier than the alcohol and saws away at the invisible tether that joins her to her country of birth, this cord stretched to the limit that Sanche had cut brutally, with a gesture that was even more sudden than the process to accomplish it had been slow.

THE FIRST part was a regular exchange, although it had been agreed upon, that lasted all autumn, it was letters along with telephone calls, his mother – and his father behind her – invariably soliciting positive responses to questions he doesn't care about – are you eating well? Are you well respected? Have you written to Augusta? Are you putting money aside? – questions, questions, always questions. As though their common language couldn't break free from the regime of the interrogator, asking signified a reminder of his mother's hard-earned right, her enduring right to be informed about his life, to possess him; and replying signified similarly the proof of his filial love. Soon, Sanche – who knows their conversation inside and out before even picking up the handset, and can't stand being forced into this positivity – grows aggressive, he mocks them, he tells them off but always runs into this wall called his mother's radical worry, this frenzied bias she has towards him. It comes to a head in December: despite his efforts to talk to his parents about the site and the people he's meeting here – it was Christmas Day – here he is again irrevocably driven into the ever narrower and more pitiable groove of reassurance. His jaw locks, he hangs up, and never picks up again – too stirred up to compose the phrase that would express, without harshness, the tiniest bit of the violent pleasure he feels living here, far from her, far from them. He feels remorse, has a guilty conscience – reading their name in the messages on his cellphone; his chest is suddenly compressed upon finding a letter or a package in his mailbox, his saliva gets heavier, he sweats, horrified – but doesn't regret a thing. Something has been broken. That's life, he sometimes thinks, during the daily commute home.

One day in March, however, someone comes to get him in the locker room while Seamus is talking to him about a site where he'll probably go after Coca, a uranium mine in Canada, and Sanche, vexed, follows the messenger back towards the administrative offices, who is it? The guy answers, I don't know, it's a woman, and Sanche logically assumes that it must be the owner of his studio apartment who has pursued him all the way to his workplace, some story about a water leak that has nothing to do with him, he scowls, the messenger says into the handset, here he is, and then Sanche holds the phone and recognizes, crystal clear, as though uttered from just a step away, the voice of his mother: Sanche, is that you? Sanche freezes, doesn't answer. His mother is here. She came all the way here. The ground opens beneath his feet, chasm of claustrophobic Sundays and the viscosity of lace doilies on the television, the voice repeats, Sanche? Sanche, it's me, it's Mom, is that you? Once again he'll have to answer yes – yes, Mom, yes it's me – but Sanche doesn't want any more questions, doesn't want to say yes anymore, so he says without trembling, no, it's not me, but the voice attacks again, at once stronger and more fragile, Sanche? Sanche is that you? and Sanche catching his breath one last time says very distinctly, bringing his mouth close to the receiver and almost in spite of himself modulating a definitive voice, no, no, ma'am, no, I don't know you, cuts off the communication with his index finger, slowly hangs up the receiver, turns, and now goes charging down the hallway banging into others as he does, hurtles down the small stairway, crosses the work site, running till he's breathless towards the locker rooms, running with all his might, nothing is more urgent in this precise instant than catching up with Seamus, and Mo, and the other guys from the site, and when he sees their silhouettes getting ready to leave the platform, he speeds up even more till he gets to the bus and mixes in with them, very agitated, his brain like a full tank on a boat that pitches and heaves, a tank of methane or gas, a highly flammable tank in any case, and from that moment on he's full of a new intuition that something extraordinary is going to happen to him now, is going to transpire, here, in a few days or a few seconds: right now nothing is irrevocable because he has no link to anyone anymore – everything is within his reach.

WHAT HAPPENS to him, what comes into arm's reach with the return of the good weather, could very well be Shakira, for example; she too is a night owl, she too has powerful feet and a befitting body, rushing through the city like a snowball, each day growing thicker and more friable than the day before. When she arrives one May night at La Scala or at Sugar Falls, she doesn't need to climb onto the rung of a chair to see who's there, all she needs to do is throw a quick glance around the room to untangle the aggregated silhouettes, and in the middle she recognizes Sanche, remembers the airport and the dip in the river – he's not the one she's looking for and who she'd like to kill at this moment, but his table offers a target to aim for so she heads there. Sanche nearly falls off his chair when he sees her coming towards him, like the lid of the treasure chest lifting slowly: here it is, the pirate's gold.

SUMMER WALKS TOWARDS THE QUAY AT A good clip, full dawn, brilliant skin, cool nape, optimistic girl overflowing with verve, this day is mine and I dance for it *blah blah blah*, she's steady, goes without rushing, crosses intersections on the diagonal so as not to deviate from her initial idea: today I will cross to the other side of the water.

In less than twenty minutes she reaches the banks: the sky is suddenly wide, flared like a basin, the clamour breaks through, and the light whitens. Summer reaches the dock, there, a vending machine, she buys a bottle of water and empties it in one gulp, elbow raised to vertical, she's sweating, takes her place in the short line of people waiting to buy a ticket for the journey, and once the price of the crossing is settled, goes down the steel gangway, jumps into the barge, and, following the wave of people boarding, finds herself in a large room, clammy and sonorous, the windows are dirty, the ceiling low, the odour heavy. Most of the people who boarded with her have spread out along the benches and settled themselves against the walls, chin to chest and arms folded into pillows, eyes soon closed, they worked the night shift in bars, hotels, casinos, gambling dens, and nightclubs in the city, and will soon collapse into unmade beds, shivering, shirts bunched up at the foot of the bed – dirty collars, ties knotted still, just loosened and pulled over their heads, cuff unbuttoned with weary hands.

THE SIREN bawls, the ferry jolts sideways from the dock, and Summer gets up, strolls along the benches, those who aren't sleeping cast hostile glances towards her; she reaches the upper deck, looks for an observation post, finds one at the prow in front of a pickup full of worn-out tires, two guys – Natives, stocky, wide-brimmed black felt hats, turquoise jewellery – smoke cigarettes and parley in low voices, indifferent to the deafening motors, indifferent to the odour of rot – wood, fish, fruit – that clings to the hull. Summer wants to take advantage of the view for the less than twenty minutes it takes to cross from one bank to the other. At this hour, the river is mauve, languid, large and oily folds, no reflection. She looks at the city as it softly grows distant, revealing itself whole as it shrinks, leaning over the greyish eddies that coagulate and dissolve against the hull, while before her, in an opposite movement, the forest rises, rises, huge and black, devouring space. At the exact moment when she passes the median of the river, suddenly close to nothing, far from everything, her heart tightens, tears rise to her eyes in a handful of seconds; the smell of fuel, she thinks as she closes her eyes, it stinks, it's going to give me a headache, and suddenly breathless, she nearly falls over backwards. An immense fear. She knows the one. It's Sunday on the Porte Dorée lake, at the edge of the Bois de Vincennes. Late afternoon. She's five years old. There are four of them in the boat. Her father, her mother, her brother, and her. It's the end of winter and it's a sunny cold. They're rowing. They pass temples, grottos, mills, rotundas. The light on the water is magnificent. Her mother has reflections of gold on her face and she closes her eyes smiling above her shawl. It's her father who's in action. He leans forward, back, to the rhythm of his legs bending and unbending, the oars held firmly in the ring of the oarlocks. They move slowly. They glide over the lake. Little splashes fly into the air while the water creases here and there against the boat. Everything seems easy, beautiful. There is soft laughter in the air. The perfect postcard of a happy family.

The boat is named *Marianne*, like her mother. They were glad to get this one, it's a sign, honey, said her father as he held out his hand to his wife to step in. The *Marianne* is red edged with blue, slathered with thick paint that shows the trace of the brush and the drips solidified along the planking. Suddenly her father stands up, right in the middle of the lake. The boat rocks abruptly, her mother lets out a cry, her father bursts out laughing and grabs her little brother by the waist. He lifts him and holds him out over the lake. Her mother opens her eyes huge and stammers, what are you doing, stop. Her father laughs, he's playing, don't be so silly. The boat pitches in fits and starts. The little boy gesticulates, his thin ankles and his shoes with laces kick in the void, his father heaves him back and forth above the water as though he were going to throw him in. The little girl is petrified, clinging to her mother who's screaming now, screaming at her father that he's crazy, while he stands there, before them, immense, legs spread wide in the bottom of the boat. He laughs, opening his mouth wide. Then an oar slips from the oarlock and falls into the lake. Her father puts the little one down carelessly, swears, shit, then leans over the water and stretches out his arm but the oar is out of reach. The piece of wood floats for a moment on the surface, then disappears. Silently, they head back towards the wharf. The sun has set and it's cold. Everything is sombre. On the banks, the naked trees bend frozen branches towards them. Her mother wraps the little boy in her arms and silently holds back her tears. Her father is out of breath trying to make the boat move with only one oar. He grows tired. The little girl is worried they'll never get there. Once they're back on land, her mother bursts into sobs and stammers incomprehensible words. Her father sighs, the evening is a disaster.

THE OTHER bank disconcerts Summer. The large public square that meets the dock is still in shade, and it's much colder and wetter here than on the other side at the end of

May. A little crowd of poor folk – mostly Natives – come and go between shabby stalls, banged-up vegetables, frilly underwear, used tools, kitchen knives and machetes riddled with rust spread out on little braided rugs, bottles of fake spring water, everything drowned in a smell of boiled cabbage, fatty fish, and soap. Here and there, people toss offal into large cast-iron pots heated on makeshift stoves, cook them over low fires in a spicy sauce, then stuff them into a sheath of big bread sprinkled with lemon, disgusting thinks Summer, nauseated, crossing the square, goes into the first greasy spoon – a mosaic of compressed Coca-Cola cans wallpapers the facade – orders a coffee, the guy behind the counter looks her up and down without a word of greeting and mechanically pours bitter liquid into a plastic cup, turns his back, and picks up his paper again. Summer glances at her watch, almost seven o'clock. She takes a quick look over her shoulder and, through the half-open door, sees the ferry, already at the dock and ready for boarding. The excitement of this trip "to the other side of the water," as everyone says here, dies away all at once, she's cold, what an idea to come here, alone, without a plan, without anything to do. Indecisive, she sips her coffee, soon lukewarm, and while she's counting her change, head down over her open palm, the guy at the bar calls, you looking for something? No, nothing, I'm fine, I'm gonna catch the boat back, she pushes her strap farther up her shoulder, turns towards the door, and behind her the guy continues, so there's nothing for you here, you don't like it? Mocking smile – translucent enamel at the edge of teeth that are very yellow and very straight – in contrast with a cold glance, transparent as a cat's eye marble, Summer, uncomfortable, heads for the door, reconsiders and says simply, I'm looking for Sugar Falls. The guy joins her in the doorway of the greasy spoon, you go to the edge of the square on the left, the path that goes up from there, it's straight till the pavement ends, then you're at the viewpoint, keep to the left on the forest path, take it a little farther and then you're there. His voice mixes in with the noises of the square that have bulked up now, just like the crowd that's growing, the market is opening. Summer asks, it is far? An hour and a half walking, double that if it's been raining. Oh. Summer looks at her watch. You're in a hurry, eh, miss? He considers her, sarcastic, spiteful. You're from the bridge, right? She nods her head. He takes a pack of hardened tobacco out of his pocket, rolls it quickly between thumb and index, lights up a skinny little smoke, props it in his mouth and tosses out, you should get off that site, take the time to go see it up there, it's gonna shake up your identity, Miss Cannibal Bridge.

SHE BUYS oranges, Coke, and bread, climbs the slope of the road, the river at her back, the forest before her. The little lopsided apartments and stone buildings that border the market square have disappeared, she's now walking along beside wooden houses tangled in with one another, some of them in complex and ambitious shapes – Chinese pagodas, Swiss chalets, thatched cottages from the Auge region of France – most of them like western movie falsefronts, walls askew but with an abundance of decorative details. At this hour, children are slamming doors and running into the street, schoolbags dangling from their shoulders, women in worn old slippers lift a crocheted curtain to watch them, and, suspicious, stare at Summer who peels her first orange, we can hear dogs barking behind the hedges, the air smells of detergent and babies.

Soon the sun is beating down, the pavement heats up beneath running shoes, the houses line up poorer and poorer, bricked-up windows or broken panes, garbage and scrap metal heaped up here and there in unkempt yards. Soon unmovable trailers with dusty windows alternate with crude wood cabins, done up with tires or tarps coated with tar, and (always ingenious) outdoor showers through a gleaming slotted spoon, a roof of nailed-on planks, one or two deboned mopeds in the grass, red, yellow, and blue plastic kids' toys, an atmosphere of shacks on the verge of becoming junkyards, a smell of boiling iron, surprised insects bouncing off old axles, grilled instantly, no more children, no more shouts. This is the last section of the road now. Apparently uninhabited, not a soul in sight, but the forest like a bellows, the roots of young trees smashing the pavement open, grass infiltrating every corner and waist-high ferns on the sides of the road, the last huts, a tire-marked porn magazine forgotten on a stony berm, the last bits of trash, more cans, a bunched-up T-shirt, worn-out sneakers, finally a sign that indicates the viewpoint and Summer reaches a little bench graffitied with dicks and sexual insults, a phone number or two. She sits down, heart beating, out of breath, and suddenly discovers Coca silver-plating itself in the juvenile sun, on the other side of the river, the metallic brassiness of the financial district, the shattering whiteness of city hall and the bridge work site; she struggles to assemble the landscape, a light suffocation seizes her, a faintness she recognizes and she forces herself to breathe slowly, images pass – the Tiger who's fallen off the face of the earth and whose eyes are disappearing, the Blondes who laugh on Skype with large movements of their hair, her father – she breathes deeper and deeper, thinking I've got to get a hold of myself, without being able to, submerged by her internal cacophony, displaced, unable to attune herself to what's around her, she sways forwards, spits on the ground, finally closes her eyes. Then lifting her head again looks at Coca, looks at the edge. And suddenly enters the forest.

FIRST THE undergrowth, penetrated by a multitude of wells of light, the coolness that falls into indistinct space, then darkness.

It's night in here, a green and humid night, the clamour of a fairground. Summer is surprised that the path is so wide and the earth so well packed, traces of tires, of paws, of soles, soon she passes two children following each other on skateboards, is this the freeway or what? She feels good now, back on her feet after the weak-kneed episode at the viewpoint. Around her, sequoias like gigantic stakes, ferns in compact masses, fluorescent mosses that cushion the roots, long sharp sedges, and all over the embankment are black holes – Summer shudders, imagining putting a hand in there and the prehistoric beast that would bite it, a cross between a wild boar and a red-eyed otter, some kind of duck-billed platypus that she would be waking. Little by little the forest grows more dense, the light doesn't pass through the canopy anymore, you'd think you were at the bottom of an aquarium, and actually Summer does hear the sounds of water, turn in the path, a stone shaped like a rocket that reminds her of the ones in the Bois de Vincennes, and immediately the acrid smell of a fire from a berm on the river, she goes closer, two guys, both standing with a stick in hand, are watching a patch of earth perforated with holes that let out smoke, the smell is heavy, bloody flesh is visible here and there under the screed of earth: Duane Fisher and Buddy Loo are smoking game, and chewing tobacco from their own harvest.

They recognize Summer who doesn't recognize them but quickly spots, against their dark skin, the sparkling yellow bracelets they wear on their wrist, a plastic strip with a barcode, stamped with the company logo, beeped each morning at the entrance of the site, an open sesame. The two guys throw each other a look that says, what's Miss Concrete doing coming over here? Can't stay where she belongs, "on the other side of the water"? She's got to turn up out of the blue, naively play the tourist? What is she deluding herself with? They all sit down cross-legged around the fire and munch on a nice piece of the meat, telling one another jokes, as though they weren't one girl and two guys, one white and two others, a black guy and a Native, one senior exec on the bridge and two workers who aren't even skilled, who were immediately assigned to cleaning out the canal; in other words, one engineer and two garbage collectors, so what does she want, coming to see them up close? Since when do white folks come and barbecue with blacks in this country? Buddy Loo is cautious. He's had problems before – in January 2006, a Friday night, fifteen degrees below zero, a girl is passed out drunk in the parking lot of a bowling alley on Colfax, Woody's, Buddy picks her up, she had thrown up on her cream-coloured down coat, her eyes are rolled back, he hoists her into his car, leans the seat back, thinks it over, gotta go to the hospital, no desire to keep this girl in a full-on alcoholic coma in my ride; later, at the hospital, he signs the forms and hits the road, but the next day the cops turn up at his place while he's at school, search his room, twenty-seven dollars are missing from the girl's wallet, when he gets home Buddy is nabbed, sent to the hole, held in custody, they verify that the girl hasn't been raped, no, nothing, Buddy makes bail, a month in reform school and community service for stealing, he's sixteen, swears he'll find that girl again and roll her for real, once he's out he starts hanging around the bowling alley again, one night that same bitch staggers out accompanied by a giant with a bull's neck, empty eyes, they've been drinking, Buddy holds himself back from head-butting the girl right away – she can't recognize him, of course – he springs up from the darkness between two big cars, pulls out a gun, threatens the two of them, the girl laughs and then cries when he orders them to get undressed, but for Christ's sake keep your panties on, I don't wanna see your little white asses, your snitchy asses, empty your pockets, *oh-ho*, forty-three dollaaars, makes a pile with the clothes and puts the two pairs of shoes on top, sprays it all with mineral spirits, strikes a match, and leaves them naked and poor, feet in the snow, he took off and never went back to the bowling alley on Colfax, they say there's a price on his head, set by empty-eyed bullneck. So he tells himself he should limit his contacts. Summer intercepts their stare, clears her throat, asks where Sugar Falls is – to have something to ask 'cause she doesn't know what to say, there's nothing to say – she sputters, the smoke stings her eyes, Buddy Loo gestures limply towards the heart of the jungle without even looking at her, while Duane Fisher turns his back and throws stones harshly into the water. She's not welcome here, no, not at all. Buddy Loo doesn't make another move, silently uses a giant rhubarb leaf to ventilate the coals. Summer nods her head once more, bye, takes a step or two backwards and then turns and picks up the path once again, keeps moving forward because she can't turn back now, the falls are there, she can hear them.

DISSOCIATE THE light from the noise of the water. The clearing is vast, bathed in an electric whiteness, so brilliant that it takes Summer a few seconds to filter through the jumble of her perceptions, to distinguish the waterfall that bubbles, the high grass of an intense green colour – a soccer field lit up at night; to discern the bare-chested children armed with little yellow plastic water guns, the women, fewer men, all Native. She walks towards the falls, the little ones come running, their eyes shine, they laugh, call to one another in a language Summer doesn't understand, they make a cortege around her all the way to the stone pool; she casts a glance at the adults who stare at her, greets them with a nod of her head. Then she crouches to drink, plunging her hands several times into the water, splashing her neck, her forehead, her forearms. Suddenly not a peep is heard in the clearing, the hubbub has gone silent. Noticing a large wooden signboard headlined Sugar Falls, she gets up to go read it, but a voice behind her stops her – don't waste your time, it's just propaganda, she turns around, the guy is white, the only white guy here. They look at each other. Sugar Falls! What a joke! the man says with irony, then says to her, you shouldn't have drunk the water from these springs, it's special here. Summer responds simply, I was thirsty. Looks around at the space that grows sharper now, perfectly spherical, but can't pick out the beginning of the path she took to come here. Where are we?

THE WATER in the falls isn't sweet, not even a little. The young Franciscan monk who founded the first Spanish mission had not changed it into syrup by some miracle, contrary to what was written in a few tourist guides or other books given to children. But for the Natives, these headwaters are a blessing, a place populated by spirits, they like to meet here on the solstice, the most well-off among them leave their four-by-fours gleaming at the entrance to the uplands, at the level of the viewpoint, and come the rest of the way on foot. All of them know about it, the path. The guy has thus logically chosen this clearing to teach them archaeology, botany, their pharmacopeia, and their language. He counts on the women, the most regular ones, some of them coming all the way from the other side of Coca to listen to him. He has his theory: teach the Natives to be their own archaeologists so that they can claim ownership of their burial grounds – thousands of them scattered along the shores of the bay at the far reaches of the high plains, beneath supermarket parking lots, along freeways, in the foundations of buildings – and rename their territory, learn how to use the technologies that kept them isolated in order to reverse the situation. He was both full of passion and worn out, operated in a sawtooth rhythm alternating between surging forward and sinking back in depression; his violent fervour cut into the quiet of the clearing, the peaceful atmosphere of this Native picnic.

During the lessons, they listen attentively to the man, some women get up to give evidence, unfold signs, pass documents around. Several times someone comes up to Summer, brings a black coffee, a cheddar-cheese sandwich, offers her cookies and cigarettes. Children come to flop down beside her at naptime, and one of them even puts his head on her knees, she looks closely at the inside corners of his eyes, flat and smooth like the interior of a shell, asked herself again how her eyelids work, drunk with sensations, and calm, inside an absolutely porous solitude at present, she simply sits there, listening to this man whose voice carries louder than the falls, dozing when he refers to the idiots at the university who had decreed the forest tribes extinct – Ohlone, Muwekma – their language, their ceremonies, and reviving when he concludes his talk: we want to take back the burial grounds to compare the DNA of the dead and the living – he points to the children who chase and squirt one another – and it will quickly become clear that these tribes are still alive and well! Suddenly his face grows tense and Summer recognizes the guy she passed on the site, the one who attacked Diderot.

She decides to head back before dark and there are children to accompany her, they are heading back to Edgefront themselves, the parents will follow later. All the way down, they whirl around her, fiercely playful, constantly changing speed, stopping for long moments only to catch up to her again, passing between the rays of golden light that sabre the woods, whistling in the zebra stripes that hide them and reveal them all at once. She can spot a head, an arm, sometimes a whole body, she points them out calling found you! When they get farther away, she can still hear their exclamations, without really knowing if they are joking or fighting, but soon she can understand their language again: their Native language gradually disappears the closer they came to the city and Summer admires this way they have of matching the world.

IT'S NOW WEEK FORTY-TWO, LAPPING WAVES on the river, the sky slumps, it's evening. Coca lights up slowly, Sanche watches from the top of his crane, never gets tired of watching it, a hundred and fifty feet – a height that truly suits him. Dashboard at rest, indicator lights on green, and joysticks raised, a mickey of Jack Daniel's, cookies, a CD player, Sanche is at the footbridge and he's waiting for Shakira.

He called her before starting his shift at four o'clock this afternoon – more precisely, he sent her a text, prefers to communicate by SMS, lapidary signals or a quick joke without preamble, distance conserved, risk management – are you afraid of heights? No, she answered after twenty seconds. Meet at midnight? Okay. Sanche immediately put the phone down and rubbed his hands together because he had to do something, he was trembling with excitement, then three running steps knees to chest, one full spin, oh baby it's yes, tonight's the night and a little later, knees to chest still, he went to buy the whisky in a little joint beside the supermarket in front of the entrance to the site, and, on his way back, met Diderot who was at the wheel of the Chevrolet, about to leave, told him through the lowered window that he would be staying late tonight, two or three things to go over.

AND NOW he's perched in the night, and the stars and the electric lights get all mixed up. But Sanche holds himself back from any nervousness that would cloud his attention and keeps his eyes fixed on the river that snakes towards him, a path punctuated with light, powdery halos, upon which long shining leaves move, a magical view from so high up, this river that, in less than four hours, will carry Shakira to the foot of the crane – she'll arrive on time, 10:55 in front of the main entrance to the Pontoverde platform, welcomed at the door by a contact who's been paid to bring her across the diagonal of the esplanade to the quay, where another accomplice will take care of her; they'll board the management shuttle and head for the Edgefront tower at full speed, where Sanche (who will be keeping watch) will phone her cellphone to guide her along the pier to the elevator door, and while the shuttle does a U-turn to go back on the double without passing the large shuttle of the night team, Shakira will rise to him along the length of the lit-up crane, a golden-yellow projection, and as soon as she steps into the cabin, Sanche will be amazed: this tall body enlarges the cubicle, it makes room.

The machinery of the elevator has been set in motion, mechanical buzzing of cables and promises, and when the doors finally slide open, Shakira is there – stepping over the doorstep, superhuman-beauty spike heels dangling by their straps from her hand, and once she's there she turns in a circle, amazed by the immensity that's so close, I'm taking the grand tour, curious, takes the time to look at everything, the indicators, the buttons, the joysticks, the stickers, the knick-knacks, the CDs, and each movement of her body increases the space in the cabin, it's beautiful here, she concludes, is it dangerous? Sanche devours her with his eyes, he yammers away, the problem with cranes is the wind. The wind in sudden gusts, the wind in blasts. I hate the change of seasons, there are violent breezes that come off the ocean, squalls that form on the plains, swell, and then come hurtling over the river, explode against the woods, then the birds flee and the water starts to turn like in the circus, he mimes the actions: stretches out his arms to say the birds, draws circles with his index finger to say the circus. Since she's listening to him, he goes on, exaggerating: the crane towers sway on their barges, the cabs get the shakes, the loads swing like a pendulum at the end of a long chain, and each lifting operation becomes a risk that shouldn't be taken, when the load is a hundred and fifty tons and the counterweight is twelve, that's why I'm here, to avoid that risk; he points to the anemometer: every morning I monitor the wind speed, if it goes above forty-five miles per hour all operations are forbidden; and above all I watch, I see everything! He's finished talking. The silence thickens.

Shakira takes off her coat – it falls to the floor, reveals her in a black velvet bustier dress, a shape and a material that show her champagne-glass figure, the outline from her enormous breasts – did they grow again or something? – to her ultraslim waist, the chemical platinum of her hair, and the calm pressure of her very white skin, she is nearly naked and better than naked, a goddess and a little bit like a whore, goes to the window, watches the outdoors intensely, narrows her eyes as though she's looking for geodesic landmarks, multiplied now in the panes, precise reflections of faces against the unstable night, spins suddenly towards Sanche, you see, I'm not scared of heights, I feel fine here, she sees the bottle of whisky, and I'd love a drink. They drink. Sanche comes to stand beside her, now he also appears on the glass walls, crowded in here, eh? He smiles, feels handsome beside her, he likes that this woman overcomes him like the outside overcomes the capsule, gobbles it up, reconfigures their presence, and unbridles both their movements and the free flow of their fantasies; he likes the relationship of their two bodies that grow and shrink like in a fairy tale as they touch, as they set in motion all the usual gestures of a first time and he likes that the glass cabin becomes the scene, ceaselessly renewed, of love affairs. He slips a hand sideways beneath her hair and pulls her to him while his other hand slides up under her dress, along the surface of her very real skin – it was phenomenal to touch her, like being the first witness to her existence, and perhaps even more to his own existence, as though it was the touch that created the body; she leans down to kiss him, taking him by the throat, then they undress each other without once bumping heads, no, on the contrary the cabin is exactly the right size for them, its walls provide support, offer them something to brace against or lever themselves with: she raises herself from the dashboard just enough that she can slip her panties over her ankles, lifts her arms just enough that he can slide her dress over her head – she touches the ceiling – he backs up just enough that she can unbutton his jeans and bend down to roll his boxers to the ground, then pulls his shoulders just far enough back that she can push the sleeves of his shirt off his arms, an obstacle course that accelerates the rhythm of their breath, increases their sweat, and soon the windows of the cabin are covered with steam, the carbon dioxide they exhale and the Joule effect of their naked bodies encloses them in the vapour of a sauna, a cloud of condensation that removes them from the gaze of the owls, bats, and moths, from that of the aviators and of teenagers who mess around at night on the rooftops of buildings, a halo that holds them together, sheltered in the heart of the shadows, when in fact the cabin is dilating, swaying, pliable, a limitless erogenous zone; they're standing now, face to face – she had to lower herself a little – and when the moment arrives to enter her it again gets just complicated enough (she does, after all, have to be able to separate her very long legs, and in order to do so must press her back against the window without tumbling over backwards, and then lift her pelvis; he must after all place himself at the right height and be able to slip his hands behind her back, place them on her hips, and find enough amplitude to pull her towards him) that they are required to pirate some new solutions.

EVERY TIME DIDEROT SHOWERS, HE COMES upon the scar from Jacob's knife, a diagonal line along his side, two inches long. It's been almost ten months that he's been living with this crimson segment that screams *bastard* every time his eyes fall on it, and that marks the day when Katherine Thoreau crossed his path. Sometimes he tells himself that without this knife wound, he would never have met this woman, and with the tips of his fingers he traces the imprint. But he can't let go of the insult of the thing. He promises himself he won't leave Coca without having found that man again, the one he rolled with in the dust of the road.

For the moment, though, the site is pushing him hard. They still need to find some solutions for placing the flat deck of the bridge. They have to provide for thermal effects on the steel plates that make up the deck – in Coca, the variations in temperature are extreme, it's a continental climate. Under the effect of a heat wave, swelling the steel, the length of the deck could increase by twenty-seven inches in a span six thousand feet long, and then retract again. So they need expansion joints every hundred and fifty feet – after some discussion they choose a system of modular expansion joints that will allow for movements of any amplitude, in three directions, and rotations on three axes. Deciding on the interval between them keeps the builders occupied for a few days. Diderot loves these crystal-clear technical demands; he orders tests, evaluates, compares, and decides. It's the very movement of the bridge itself, its supple and living nature that's at play in the pure reality of the steel, and he pores over this question with the zeal you put into finishing a project. The teams of ironworkers set out horizontally and assemble the span, plate by plate, six thousand feet long by a hundred across, it's a mechanical job, weld, bolt, bolt, weld. Seamus and Mo are part of the team and work without talking to each other, they've synchronized all their movements with precision, it's a choreography. They work fast in the lead and have quickly covered their strip – and then the river is crossed. They too feel like they're almost at the finish line. A slackening that worries Diderot, it's always in the last days that people mess up the most, careful, he warns them, all the more since in the last few days the heat has been torrid, the guys' heads boil under their hard hats, and there's hardly any shade to take a break in; the steel burns like the concrete that covers the whole span now, the site has become an inferno and it's during the trips along the river that the men become reanimated, they're already imagining themselves in the future, sharing a few leads. Seamus will skip the inauguration of the bridge and leave at the end of August for the northwest of Canada, Cigar Lake, the future's in nuclear, he laughs, compares the wage he's been offered with that of the workers on other sites, while the bridge guys grimace, I'd never do uranium, never, got no desire to become radioactive. Mo watches the banks parade past, he's hesitant to leave with Seamus, who assures him that it's a good contract, but he has a link in Zimbabwe, in a platinum mine where one of his cousins, who he found on the internet, is already working, there are hundreds of us here, he wrote. Mo doesn't know yet what he'll do, he's always gotten by but one thing is certain, he wants to see the opening of the bridge, the lights, the jubilation. Three more weeks to go.

AND THEN one morning Summer knocks on Diderot's office door, and in a stroke of luck he's there, lifts his head from his computer screen: everything okay, Diamantis? Summer will be the last to work hard, he knows it – the levelling of the freeway approaches, including six lanes that must be connected at various points from the bridge to the road system, requires an increased production of concrete. On the Coca side, the bridge freeway flows perfectly into the system, converging towards an interchange which, past the toll booth, will redistribute the lanes in all directions, two of them bypassing the city to head straight for the plateau; but on the Edgefront side, past the toll booth, the six lanes remain connected, and then the hundred-foot-wide channel narrows to look like a simple road that stretches along the river downstream. Summer has to prepare the ground for future construction: the mountain range road, once it's open, will wreak havoc on the neighbourhood of Edgefront, dividing it into two equal parts before reaching the forest. This forest highway is bullshit, Summer blurts as soon as she sits down in the chair facing his desk, hard hat in her lap. She'd hesitated for a long time before knocking on Diderot's door: she'd been working alongside him for nearly a year, and while she respects and admires the way he has of fulfilling himself in human action, connected to a materiality that exists outside of him, she's also cautious of this man for whom living amounts to flowing with the flux of the world, with all its movement. Diderot leans back in his chair: what's going on, Diamantis? This freeway, she repeats, this freeway they want to build, it's gonna wreck everything. Diderot, curt: that's not our job, Diamantis. But Summer shakes her head, but my job is also the freeway approaches and the grid connection. Silence, then Diderot nods softly, that's true, but there isn't a grid yet in Edgefront, we're connecting to the road along the shore, we're easing up the traffic in the centre, that's all. Then, since they're suffocating in the little room, Summer opens the window, turns around, I found the man who attacked you in November. Diderot shudders, his scar burns under his shirt, oh yeah? Yeah. Two minutes later, they're on the way.

THEY STREAKED along in the Impala, silent, zigzagging between vehicles, taking as many risks as fugitives with the cops on their tail, and once they reached the Edgefront side they climbed the road up to the viewpoint, a path that Diderot is seeing for the first time, Summer's driving. Once they're out of the car, he doesn't take the time to contemplate Coca, marvellous, buildings piercing the heat haze, no, they go straightaway into the forest and the undergrowth does impress Diderot, disorients him, fragmentary, the day occupying the same proportion of space as the darkness, he walks for a long time without knowing whether he's inside or outside, incorporated as he is into the frenzy of vegetation, with Summer silent at his side; and later, with the shade increasing its share, the light dissipates into slivers and a silhouette can be seen at the end of the path, ghostly but becoming steadily more incarnate as it draws nearer, Jacob is walking to meet them.

He stops a few yards from them – they too stop, and then the silence swells, swarms, a breeding ground. All three of them are covered with the same patches of light, clothes and skin transfigured. This is the meeting, Summer says simply, staying back while Diderot moves forward. The two men are now face to face, inches apart. They know each other by heart. There is so much noise that Jacob has to raise his voice, I knew you'd come, and Diderot answers slowly, dragging his syllables, I wanted to break your face – and also, I wanted to say thank you. Their timbres are expressionless, they size each other up, without affect, Jacob says, skip right to the thank-you, arms crossed over his chest. Critters of all kinds populate the luminous pastilles, pink flies, poppy-red butterflies, bronze beetles; then everything grows quiet and Diderot's voice vibrates, all right, thank you for the knife wound. Jacob uncrosses his arms, dumbstruck, puts his hands on his hips, and kicks at a leaf; Diderot hesitates, thinks about dealing him a quick fist to the face, Jacob wouldn't have the time to protect himself, he'd hit him in the nose, make him snort blood, the forest swirls around him, it accelerates, he smiles.

Summer paces behind them. A butterfly flutters about her, electric and delicate, she follows it with her eyes for a long moment, then crouches to look closer as it creeps into the corolla of an unknown flower, she concentrates. It's a mission blue butterfly. A super-protected species. On the banks of the river they had to plant entire areas with flowerbeds so these butterflies would have something to live on and decreed that the boat speed and that of the cars on the freeway approaches would be limited to five miles an hour from March until June. The forest is saved. She exults, eyes closed. Then, lifting her head, pulls the elastic out of her ponytail, it's the very first time – suddenly her whole look and face change, she calls to the two men, so is the war over now? I have to get back to work.

THE DAY BEFORE THE OPENING CEREMONY, people are still hard at work on the bridge. The electrification of the structure requires the installation of one hundred and fifty-two lamps along the deck, and sixteen more powerful ones on the towers that will each be crowned with a red beacon, they're still unrolling miles of cables. The freeway approaches are just barely finished, the poured concrete is still wet on the bridge's access ramps. They're scrubbing the metal, keeping a close eye on the birds; swing stages sway along the piers to clean up the least stain. Here and there along the structure, hanger cables are sprinkled with flags that smack in the wind, and in front of the Coca gate, a giant stage is put up, circled by bleachers and crowned with a meringue circus tent – tomorrow an orchestra is supposed to set up here and launch the fanfare when the Boa comes to cut the magic ribbon, when he places the tip of his shoe on the splendid roadway and walks across to Edgefront, alone at the head of the people, relaxed, triumphant, offered up to their gazes, arms at his sides and chin parallel to the ground, perhaps even a rose in hand, followed twenty minutes later by two thousand guests who will also cross on foot, hand-picked close friends – among them, Shakira, and we hope that Mo will also have managed to infiltrate the little privileged crowd, he will have put on a white shirt and a pair of grey linen pants that will narrow his hips, he'll feel a wild pleasure in crossing this bridge that belongs to him, without a hard hat, full sun on his face. On the other side of the water the welcome will be triumphant: release of doves, cheerleaders, jugglers, Native traditional dances, a parade of municipal police, and free distribution of T-shirts emblazoned with a magic formula: $c = 0\%$, $m = 69\%$, $y = 100\%$, $k = 6\%$, the definition of the structure's vermilion. Draconian security measures have been taken: Jacob and the Natives – among them Buddy Loo and Duane Fisher – are under surveillance in a motel on Colfax with a giant screen; the younger generation is excluded from the celebrations, Matt plans to watch the ceremony from the viewpoint, Liam will come too, they'll bring Billie, their father has said he doesn't want to see any of it, and anyways he's got the TV.

IT'S THE END of the afternoon and Katherine's going to park her vehicle for the last time in the parking lot for the levelling machines, she taps the base of her seat – how many hours will she have spent in here? – picks up the photo of her kids tucked into the windshield, the bottle of water, the pair of gloves, and then, passing by the facilities, gathers her things from her locker – soap, towel, change of T-shirt – and goes to hand in her hard hat, her badge, and her padlock in the administrative building. Don't dwell on it, make your gestures quick.

Diderot is waiting for her past the work site, wedged into the Impala that's soon heading upstream, towards the river bend, where there are no more villages, just a few cabins and coves. It's not the last time they'll see each other, there isn't a last time, no one is dead yet in this car, and their only idea right now is to find a place for themselves, it's still hot, they choose the wild reeds and the sandy grass, take off their shoes, prick their toes. They have beautiful feet, Katherine with slender ankles and wide heels, gently flared at the edges, Diderot with slim slightly curving toes. They walk along the bank lifting their knees high; their skin is erased in the brown, inhabited water. Far off, the bridge, and before them, very unsettled, the river, worked by strong currents that create a froth on the surface, there's only one landscape left around them, shall we? They get undressed quickly, toss their splashed clothes onto the bank, and with long strides run into the water yelling, pushing away the branches floating in their path, a carton of Campbell's soup, a pink sandal, then catch the current and drift off in a sidestroke.

THE AUTHOR thanks Ewa Z. Bauer, Robert E. David, and Alan Leventhal in San Francisco, and Paul-Albert Leroy in Paris.

JESSICA MOORE is an author and a translator. She is a former Lannan writer-in-residence and winner of a PEN America Translation Award for her translation of *Turkana Boy*, the poetic novel by Jean-François Beauchemin. Jessica's first collection of poems, *Everything, now*, was published with Brick Books in 2012. She is a member of the Literary Translators' Association of Canada and worked as the secretary in their Montreal office while completing her master's in translation studies. She is also a songwriter – her debut album, *Beautiful in Red*, was released in 2013. She embarks on frequent adventures and uses her hometown of Toronto as an anchor.

PHOTO: Micah Donovan

This translation project began with an unabashed love of the book – a vibrant, generous novel by one of the most celebrated authors in contemporary France. This love, however, was not initially mine: *Naissance d'un pont* was introduced to me at a party one night in 2010, the year it was published to accolades in France. I have many things to thank David Gressot for, but above all for the introduction and for his exuberance about this author's style – it proved infectious.

And the translation proved to be a terrific challenge. Maylis de Kerangal is a brilliant and difficult author, one so masterfully in control of her craft that she is comfortable taking a number of risks with language and syntax, including the omission of articles, prepositions, and punctuation, and the invention of words or new uses for them. Her stunning vocabulary gives even native French speakers frequent cause to turn to the dictionary. She draws upon antiquated terminology and contemporary slang – sometimes within the same sentence. Beyond deciphering the splendid labyrinths of her writing (an adventure for any reader), my greatest challenge in translating this novel was to avoid flattening her singular use of language.

One of the most refreshing aspects of de Kerangal's writing is that she frequently invents new relationships between words that are not accustomed to being placed side by side. Walkie-talkies are *crocheted* (*crochetaient*) to ears, a couple is *inside love* (*dans l'amour*), Diderot breathes *widely* (*largement*), eyes *screech* (*crissent*) over someone. Because we tend unconsciously towards the familiar (perhaps in all things), and also because dictionaries often give multiple options, I had to be vigilant in order not to normalize word pairings in translation. If there was a choice between an unusual word and a more commonplace one, it was nearly always truer to the original to keep the first; and even when it might stand out as odd or surprising, this is what I chose to do, because the jolt of the unexpected is what makes her writing so compelling. I also had to resist explaining things that were left richly unexplained in French. At times the work was like panning for gold – "keeping watch for the marvellous sparkle" of meaning as I dug through dense lines, and then sifted through the English approximations that swirled around until I found a similar glint.

My aim was also to keep the echo of the French by maintaining as many cultural references as possible. References to landmarks, monuments, and figures from pop culture mostly were kept as is. There were times, though, when a reference would have been obscure if left as it appeared in the original. In the first site meeting, for example, when describing the two types of soil, harder on the surface but soft underneath, Diderot speaks about *le coup de la frangipane* (literally, "the marzipan trick"). This refers to the Galette des Rois – a cake with a flaky crust and soft marzipan filling, traditionally served during the Christmas season and near Lent or Carnival. Any French person would understand this reference, but to most of Anglophone North America, "the marzipan trick" would be a mystery. I chose in this case to call it "the trick of the cream filling" – which I suppose could call to mind either éclairs or cream-filled doughnuts, the latter being more of an across-the-board cultural reference in the English-speaking world.

I am deeply grateful to David, who was so generously available throughout the process for queries and proofreading; I can't count the number of times he answered the questions, "Is this strange? How strange is it?" This translation owes a tremendous amount to him.

Thank you also to Hugh Hazelton and Daisy Connon for advice from the English side of things, to the Collège international des traducteurs and the Centre national du livre for making it possible for me to spend time in France working on the translation; warm thanks to my fellow translators at the residency in Arles – in particular, my neighbour, Charlotte Woillez, for her wisdom in last-minute sessions, and especially Patrick Honnoré, whose patience and insight were unmatched. Essentially, it took a village to help me find my way to this *Birth of a Bridge*, and I was so fortunate to have a rich and multilingual village around me.

Thank you to the wonderful team at Talonbooks, particularly my editor Ann-Marie Metten, for all their thoughtfulness and hard work bringing this English version into being; and thanks to Maylis de Kerangal herself, for her effusiveness and encouragement in response to my questions.

Everything about this author's writing pushes the reader (and translator) to widen her thoughts, to stretch her use of language; nothing is banal or by rote. And within the bounds of this fantastical, haywire work of fiction, this sort of epic tale of globalization, as de Kerangal says – objects and cities are personified, it snows in California, and jackals and bronze-eyed lynx descend at dawn. A fiercely original book.